ED WHIPPED HIS HEAD AROUND AT THE OMINOUS TONE IN Kitty's voice. She was staring at the facade of the warehouse, glowing bright orange from the force of the flames inside. Ed followed her gaze and his body went rigid.

Letters glowed on the exterior of the wall, growing brighter as the heat from within intensified. Ed could just make out the words as the flames began to eat away the wall.

I'm back.

GET DIRTY

GRETCHEN McNEIL

BALZER & BRAY
An Imprint of HarperCollinsPublishers

Balzer + Bray is an imprint of HarperCollins Publishers.

Get Dirty

www.epicreads.com

Library of Congress Cataloging-in-Publication Data
McNeil, Gretchen.
    Get dirty / Gretchen McNeil. — First edition.
            pages   cm
    Sequel to: Get even.
    Summary: After forming a secret society that takes revenge on school bullies, mean girls, and tyrannical teachers, four very different teenaged girls must discover the killer who is coming after them and the ones they love.
    ISBN 978-0-06-226087-1 (pbk.)
    [1. Revenge—Fiction.   2. Secret societies—Fiction. 3. Murder—Fiction.   4. Mystery and detective stories.]   I. Title.
PZ7.M4787952Ge   2015   2014038718
[Fic]—dc23   CIP
                                                                          AC

Typography by Torborg Davern
15 16 17 18 19   PC/RRDH   10 9 8 7 6 5 4 3 2 1

First Edition

For Laurel Hoctor Jones,
the best critique partner a writer could have

Let come what comes; only I'll be revenged
—SHAKESPEARE, *HAMLET*, ACT 4

ONE

ED STOOD IN THE DOORWAY OF THE FIFTH-FLOOR HOSPITAL room and stared at Margot.

She looked like she was sleeping. Other than the IV tube taped in place on her left arm, she wasn't hooked up to any machines that artificially enhanced her vital functions. Just a heart rate monitor, its slow and steady blips a constant reminder of Margot's comatose state.

He closed his eyes and pictured her smile. He'd only seen it a few times: once in the assembly when the members of Don't Get Mad humiliated Coach Creed in front of the entire school, once in the computer lab when she and Bree brought him into the DGM fold, and once in the hallway at Bishop DuMaine when she was talking to Logan Blaine.

Ed's chest tightened. It wasn't Logan's fault Margot had fallen for him. Hell, if Ed were into dudes, Logan would probably be the kind he'd swoon over too—tall, athletic, blond, charming.

Ed's hand drifted to the pocket of his jacket, his fingers brushing the rumpled piece of paper he kept with him at all times. Tall and blond? No, that wasn't his type at all.

He placed a metal chair next to Margot's bed, careful not to make any noise. Why? He had no idea. It wasn't like she was actually sleeping. He could have led the entire Bishop DuMaine marching band in a figure eight through her room and wouldn't have gotten so much as a twitch in response.

Way to be positive, Edward.

He took a deep breath, then exhaled slowly through parted lips. The room smelled of freshly cut flowers mixed with cleaning astringent, the same scent that seemed to permeate every hospital he'd ever visited. Massive bouquets covered the floor near the window, a zoo of stuffed animals piled up around them. The collection had definitely grown since yesterday's visit, and as Ed took a mental inventory, his brain automatically calculated the net cost of all the crap: a sad-eyed puppy holding a Get Well sign (*$14.99*), a T. rex with its arm in a sling (*kitschy, so it probably cost more*), no fewer than three pink teddy bears grasping plastic hearts that said "We miss you" (*clearly on sale*). And a solitary two-dollar Mylar balloon tethered to the floor with a plastic figurine. It rotated in the breeze of the hospital's ventilation system, flashing Ed his own reflection every few seconds.

He wondered which, if any, of the gifts had come from Logan. Maybe the T. rex? Quirky, kinda sentimental, pricey without being ridiculous: that seemed Logan's speed. Or maybe it was from the other members of DGM? Ed clenched his jaw. They'd better have sent something. Kitty, Olivia, and Bree were as much to blame for Margot's coma as the person who'd clocked her over the head.

Ed gingerly placed his hand on top of Margot's. He was going to figure out why this had happened, even if it killed him.

A woman's voice drifted down the hallway, accompanied by the soft squeak of rubber soles on tile floor. "Her room is at the end of the hall."

Ed jumped to his feet. Vicky, the night nurse whose shift, Ed knew damn well, ended ten minutes ago. What the hell was she still doing there?

"Are you sure you won't get in trouble for letting me visit her?" someone asked.

Ed's stomach dropped. He recognized that voice.

Logan.

Vicky clicked her tongue. "The way you look at her? Honey, every girl in a coma should have someone with that much love watching out for them."

Ed tensed as the footsteps approached the door. There was no time to slip out of the room and down the back stairs the way he'd come. This was going to be awkward.

"You have about ten minutes," Vicky continued, "before—"

She stopped short at the sight of Ed standing beside Margot's bed. The bright smile on her face morphed into a suspicious glare. "Who are you? What are you doing here?"

"Er . . ."

"Hey!" Logan said. "I know you." He tilted his head to one side as if it worked better at an angle. "Don't I?"

Really? Margot picked that?

"How did you get in?" Vicky demanded. "The ICU is a secure wing."

The laundry room ain't exactly secure, lady. But he didn't want to give away his secret. Instead, he glanced rapidly back and forth between Vicky and Margot's unconscious figure. "Wait a minute!" Ed gasped. He dropped his jaw in mock surprise. "This isn't Aunt Helen's room. I must be on the wrong floor."

Vicky dropped her chin, eyebrows raised. "The wrong floor?"

"Yeah, sorry." Time for an exit strategy. "You know what? I think I accidentally took two Ritalin this morning instead of one Ritalin and one Wellbutrin so I'm a little"—he whistled and pointed at his temple while he edged closer to the door—"cuckoo." He twitched violently, jerking his shoulder while his head shot back and forth with sharp, erratic movements.

"Yeah!" Logan bobbed his head. "We go to school together."

Not exactly the brain trust, Logan.

"Are you okay, kid?" Vicky asked.

"Yeah, yeah. Sure!" Ed laughed loudly. "I'm totally fine. Just need to, you know, get home and pump my stomach and"— he glanced at his watch—"oh my, will you look at the time!" He pushed past Vicky and the still-confused Logan and walked backward down the hall, flashing two finger guns at them as he retreated. "I am considerably out of here."

Ed hurried to his car. The sun had risen above the distant mountains and was beginning to burn off the layer of fog that had descended over Menlo Park, but he had no time to enjoy the warmth. Instead, he slipped into the driver's seat, pulled the door closed behind him, and hit the automatic lock.

He probably should have waited for Logan, should have

talked to him about Margot. They both cared about her, and Logan hadn't given Ed any reason not to trust him, but still, Ed hesitated. He wasn't ready. He was still trying to piece together what happened Thursday night, and until he did so, he was going to play everything close to the vest.

There's still a killer on the loose, after all.

TWO

OLIVIA'S BREATH SPIRALED FROM HER MOUTH IN WISPY LITTLE poofs as she rounded the corner to DuMaine Drive Tuesday morning. The bells of the nearby church broke the early morning silence. Was it seven o'clock already? Oops, late again. Kitty would be pulling her hair out.

But instead of doubling her pace, Olivia continued unhurried toward campus. She didn't panic, didn't scurry down the street like prey running from a predator. For the first time in weeks, she felt safe.

It had been four days since Bree turned herself in, just as Christopher Beeman had demanded. And true to his word, he'd backed off. No envelopes, no mysterious messages, and most importantly, no murders. He seemed content with Bree behind bars and Margot in the hospital, and that complacency would be his undoing.

Because now it was their turn. DGM was going to catch a killer.

She felt as if they were finally taking control of the situation

6

as she trotted up the front steps and yanked open the door.

"Olivia!" someone cried the instant she entered the building. Standing in the middle of the corridor was Tyler Brodsky.

He tossed his dark brown hair out of his eyes and beamed at her. He had three rolls of packing tape shoved up his arm like bulky bracelets, and a sheet draped over his shoulder. Behind him, an eight-foot ladder spanned the width of the hall with Kyle Tanner on top, attaching one end of a banner to the ceiling.

Kyle and Tyler wore the same long-sleeved Henley shirts— Tyler in slate gray, Kyle in navy—over the same faded, slim-cut jeans, and Olivia couldn't help but wonder if they called each other every morning to pick out matching outfits. If it wasn't for Kyle's dark skin and closely shaved head, they'd be indistinguishable.

"What are you doing here so early?" Tyler asked.

Kyle glanced over his shoulder. "Come to help?"

"Um . . . ," she sputtered. She and Kitty had specifically decided to meet at that ungodly hour because no one would be at school, and now she'd run into two members of the 'Maine Men, which was the last thing she wanted.

Tyler and Kyle stared at her, expecting an answer. *Better play along.* "Sure?"

"Awesome." Tyler shifted the banner off his shoulder. "Hold this. I'm gonna grab another ladder."

Olivia took the vinyl fabric from his hand as Tyler trotted off down the hall. What were they doing at school this early? Only one way to find out.

"So," she began, smiling up at Kyle. "What's going on?"

"Didn't you hear?" Kyle said. "Father Uberti's big announcement after the school board meeting yesterday. He's declared today V-D Day."

Olivia blinked. "V-what day?"

Kyle cocked his head to one side. "V-D Day. You know, like in World War Two. It's Victory over DGM Day!"

Olivia held out her arm, stretching the banner to its full length. "Celebrate V-D!" she read aloud. "Victory is ours!"

Kyle started down the ladder. "Isn't it awesome? Rex's idea."

Of course it was.

"We're hanging them all over campus," Kyle continued. He dragged the ladder to the other side of the hallway, then took the banner from Olivia's hand. "Rex is in the leadership room, prepping the flyers. I think he's . . ." Kyle cleared his throat. "Alone."

Ew. "I'll go see if he needs help," Olivia said quickly, jumping at any excuse for an escape. Not that she would be caught dead alone in a room with Rex Cavanaugh, especially not since he and Amber broke up. That was practically an invitation to get molested. But at least it gave her a reason to bail.

Olivia strolled casually down the hallway toward the leadership room, but as soon as she was out of Kyle's sight, she broke into a run. If Rex and his 'Maine Men were decorating the entire school, it would only be a matter of time before they reached the hall outside the computer lab where Kitty was waiting. They needed to get in and out of there as quickly as possible. She dashed past her locker and double-timed her way up the stairs like a marine in basic training.

As she reached the top, she froze midstep, her senses on alert. She'd heard something, she was positive. Footsteps close behind her.

Olivia swung around and gazed down the staircase. No one was there.

Motionless, she slowly counted to ten. Still, no one appeared in the hallway below. She was being ridiculous, the old paranoia affecting her judgment. No one was following her, and no one knew what they were up to. With a dismissive wave, Olivia turned and hurried to the computer lab.

Kitty paced back and forth across the slick tile floor. It wasn't a real shocker that Olivia was late, but they were about to take a giant step in the hunt for Christopher Beeman, and the wait was killing her.

She glanced down at a glowing monitor. On the screen, a window was open to an anonymous email account. She'd already plugged in the thumb drive and uploaded the entire DGM dossier on Christopher Beeman: the emails between Christopher and the now-deceased Ronny DeStefano, the link between Christopher and the also-now-deceased Coach Creed. With one click of the mouse, she would send the file hurtling through cyberspace to Sergeant Callahan at the Menlo Park Police Department.

The killer had given them a reprieve after Bree turned herself in, and they needed to use this freedom to end Christopher's reign of terror once and for all. Sergeant Callahan would have to realize Christopher was the killer and would mobilize the entire police force to find him. Bree would be exonerated, and

Christopher's killing spree would soon be over.

She hoped.

In the distance, Kitty heard the rapid clickety-clack of impractical footwear hurrying down the hallway, followed by a faint knock on the door: once, a pause, then three quick raps. Kitty whisked open the door and a breathless, pink-faced Olivia rushed inside.

"Sorry!" she panted. "I got caught downstairs by Kyle and Tyler." Olivia braced herself against the wall. "Have you seen what's going on?"

"Father Uberti contacted the leadership class about it yesterday afternoon after the school board meeting. Said he wanted to celebrate victory, now that Bree's been arrested." Kitty sighed. "Super classy considering two people are dead."

"Classy is F.U.'s middle name," Olivia said.

Kitty took a deep breath and sat down at the computer screen. "It's all good to go."

Olivia leaned over her shoulder and read the prepared email message out loud. "Attached is some information you might find enlightening in regard to the Bishop DuMaine killings. Christopher Beeman, formerly of Archway Military Academy in Arizona, has connections to the victims, and motives to kill both Ronny DeStefano and Coach Richard Creed. Sincerely, A Friend." Olivia straightened up. "That's perfect. This is totally going to work."

"Ready?" Kitty asked.

Olivia bit her lower lip, scraping most of the iridescent gloss off in the process, then gave a quick, decisive nod. "Ready."

Kitty clicked the mouse and a window with the words "Your email has been sent" filled the screen. She leaned back in her chair and let out a long sigh. "There it goes. Christopher Beeman will soon be behind bars."

"You sure about that?" said a familiar voice.

Olivia's elation turned to anger as she spun around and found Ed the Head's grinning face in the doorway. "Where have you been?"

"The moon and back, baby," he said, pumping his eyebrows.

Kitty took a step closer to him. "I've called you approximately seven thousand times since Thursday night. Nothing but voice mail. You want to explain that?"

Ed the Head shrugged. "I flushed it. The component pieces of the burner phone formerly belonging to Ed the Head are now floating somewhere in the San Francisco Bay."

"Why did you flush your phone?" Olivia asked.

"Well, last I checked, I was texting with Margot just a few hours before she was attacked. Every cop in town is probably trying to find that phone."

Kitty narrowed her eyes. "That sounds like an admission of guilt."

Ed calmly pulled out a chair and sat down. "Ladies, chill. If I attacked Margot, do you think I'd be here right now talking to you?"

Olivia exchanged a glance with Kitty. He had a point.

"Why *are* you here?" Kitty asked.

Ed the Head slipped a piece of paper from the front pocket of his bag. "I wanted to show you this."

Kitty snatched the paper from his hand, glancing at it briefly. "It's a speeding ticket."

"Highway 101 North," Olivia read from the carbon copy. "Exit three sixty-seven, Morgan Hill."

Ed the Head nodded. "Check the date and time."

Olivia's eyes zipped to the top of the form. "October seventh, nine thirty p.m."

"Exactly," Ed said. "And Margot was attacked at approximately nine fifty according to the police report. There's no way I could've made it forty miles in fifteen minutes. I didn't do it."

"Then why did you wait three days to tell us?" Kitty asked.

Ed dropped the glib facade, his face suddenly hard. "Because you were the only ones who knew I was supposed to meet Margot that night."

Olivia stiffened. "What are you trying to say?"

"It might have crossed my mind that you were setting me up to take the fall."

"You think we tried to kill Margot?" Olivia asked, horrified. "She's our friend, you little weasel. If you think for a second—"

"Was she really your friend?" Ed jutted out his chin. "I seem to recall some pretty horrific photos of Margot from back in junior high." He pointed at her accusingly. "Photos you took."

Olivia's hands began to shake as the shame of what she'd done to Margot washed over her anew. "Oh yeah?" she said, lashing out. "Well, how do we know you're not Christopher Beeman?" She wasn't entirely sure it made sense, but someone had to be Christopher, and they were running out of options.

Instead of denying it, Ed the Head burst out laughing.

"Why is that funny?" Kitty asked.

"If I'm Christopher Beeman," Ed gasped, "I've got bigger problems than a murder rap."

A creeping sensation spread down Olivia's spine, as if she'd just backed into a spiderweb. Something about Ed's tone put her on edge. "What do you mean?"

"That's what I discovered in Arizona," he said. "Christopher Beeman is dead."

THREE

THE DAY ROOM AT THE SANTA CLARA COUNTY GIRLS' JUVENILE Detention Center was by far the most depressing place Bree had ever been.

Intended as some kind of free space, the day room was a windowless, color-blocked cell furnished from a cut-rate office supply catalog where inmates were allowed to watch TV, play board games, read, or tackle homework as their privilege level allowed.

The bland atmosphere mirrored the inmates' moods. Everyone looked worn down and half-dead, like a room full of lobotomy patients. They slogged from table to door to bookcase, eyes aimlessly searching for something new and interesting to break the monotony, and as Bree stared at TV commercials during the overly chipper local morning news, she wondered how long it would be before she felt as beaten down as the rest of the girls in her housing pod.

She could already feel the hopelessness seeping in. It had been a long four days since her arrest after claiming responsibility for the DGM pranks, during which time she'd endured seemingly endless police interrogations about the murders of Ronny DeStefano and Coach Creed. Bree had stonewalled mercilessly, taking great pleasure at Sergeant Callahan's growing irritation as she refused to answer any of his questions. Then the daily therapy sessions with Dr. Walters, who seemed intent on connecting Bree's "attention-seeking" behavior to her relationship with her parents. Again, she gave the doctor very little satisfaction. Even in jail, Bree couldn't help rebelling against authority.

Meanwhile, it had been radio silence from everyone she cared about. Bree had no idea what had happened to Margot, and no clue as to whether or not Christopher had left the rest of DGM alone after Bree turned herself in.

Not that she'd expected to hear from Olivia or Kitty. They had work to do. If the killer had been true to his word, then he would have backed off once Bree confessed. She needed Olivia and Kitty to use this truce to find Christopher and get her the hell out of there. They were her only chance at freedom.

Because, as Bree well knew, dear old dad wasn't going to come to her rescue this time. He'd made that abundantly clear last week when he saved her from expulsion after she punched Rex Cavanaugh in the face. *Next time, you're on your own.*

And then there was her mom. Bree blinked and stared at the wall, slabs of concrete painted butter yellow and Pepto pink. Had anyone told her? Would she even care?

Bree swallowed and fought back the emotion welling up inside. Despite her bravado, Bree was scared. She felt utterly alone, abandoned by her friends, her family, even John.

I know you didn't kill them.

No, not John. He would never abandon her. Would he?

Bree clenched her teeth so hard she felt the tendons pop around her jaw. She was a convict now, being held on suspicion of murder. Would he feel the same way about her? Would he forget about her if she spent the next twenty years behind bars? Was she destined to become as forgotten as the rest of these inmates?

"Bree Deringer?"

Bree jumped in her chair at the sound of her name. Dr. Walters stood in the doorway. "Come with me, please."

Every set of eyes in the room turned to Bree. Some looked combative, as if they resented the new girl being singled out. Others watched her wistfully, wishing they too had been summoned away for reasons unknown just to break the routine.

Dr. Walters was all smiles as she led Bree to her office. "Lovely day, isn't it?" she said, making small talk.

Apparently, the esteemed doctor had missed the fact that she'd just retrieved Bree from a windowless room. "Um, yeah."

Dr. Walters closed her office door behind her. "Well, it's about to get even better for you."

Bree had no idea what she was talking about, but took a seat while Dr. Walters shuffled through some papers on her desk.

"Here's the schedule for the group therapy outpatient sessions," Dr. Walters said, handing Bree a printout. "It's the same setup as here—everything we discuss is completely confidential and all the girls are former inmates of the Santa Clara County Girls' Juvenile Detention Center."

Bree took the schedule from Dr. Walters's outstretched hand, her brain still focused on the word "outpatient."

"Excuse me," Bree said, hardly allowing herself to believe it might be true. "Are we being transported somewhere for group therapy?"

Dr. Walters tilted her head to the side. "No, Bree. You're being released today."

"What?"

"You'll be fitted with an anklet at the processing desk, and then remanded to parental custody under house arrest." Dr. Walters beamed. "Isn't that exciting?"

Oh, shit. Her dad was going to rip her a new one when he hauled her out of juvie. Maybe he already had a cell reserved for her at that East Coast convent school he kept threatening her with? Bree swallowed, her tongue suddenly two sizes too large for her mouth. "When is my dad coming to get me?"

"He's not," Dr. Walters said. "We're releasing you to your mother."

FOUR

KITTY STARED AT ED, DUMBFOUNDED. "WHAT DO YOU MEAN, Christopher Beeman is dead?"

Olivia shook her head. "That's impossible."

Ed knew they wouldn't believe him. "You think I'd make up something like that?" He pulled a folder from his backpack and handed it to them. "Check it."

With Olivia perched by her arm, Kitty perused the official copy of Christopher Beeman's death certificate, and Ed watched as a harsh realization dawned on them—for the last few weeks they'd been chasing a ghost.

"How did we not know this?" Kitty asked.

"Like everything else about the mysterious Mr. Beeman," Ed said, "the internet was totally purged. Someone wanted to erase him."

Olivia glanced at him sidelong. "Then how did you find out?"

Ed straightened his shoulders, offended. "I'm a professional."

"What does that mean?" Olivia asked.

Ed shrugged. "It means I bribed the janitor at Archway to tell me what he knew about Christopher Beeman."

"Death by strangulation, ruled a suicide." Kitty studied the death certificate as if she couldn't quite believe what she was reading. "This happened last year around the same time that article about Christopher going AWOL was published in the local paper."

"How did it . . ." Olivia swallowed, her face pale. "I mean, how was the body . . ."

"He hung himself from the overhead pipes in the boiler room below the gym at Archway," Ed said matter-of-factly. He tried not to imagine how miserable Christopher's death must have been—cold, dark, and alone.

Olivia gasped and rushed over to one of the computers. "Oh my God! We have to unsend that email."

"Email?" Ed asked.

Kitty ran her fingers through her hair. "We sent an anonymous email to Sergeant Callahan with all our evidence against Christopher Beeman."

Ed whistled low. "Yeah, they're going to delete that in about ten seconds."

"I don't understand," Olivia said. She took the death report from Kitty's hand and looked through it again. "All the clues, the missing yearbook photos, the deaths—everything pointed to Christopher Beeman."

"Someone wanted you to believe you were dealing with

Christopher," Ed said simply. "Pretty epic snow job, if you ask me."

"What are we going to do?" Olivia asked.

"Stay calm," Kitty said, sounding anything but. "The killer doesn't know we found out about this."

Olivia bit her lip. "Okay . . ."

"So while he lays low, thinking this is all over, we go back and look at our suspects again," Kitty explained.

"Yeah," Ed snorted. "Beat that dead horse."

Kitty narrowed her eyes. "You have a better idea?"

"Actually, yes." Ed threaded his fingers together and rested them on his knee. "Aren't you guys missing the most obvious suspects of all?"

Olivia tilted her pretty head. "I don't get it."

Ed smiled at her. "I know."

"Spit it out, Ed," Kitty snapped.

These girls had no imagination. "Did you ever think that maybe your DGM exploits are coming back to haunt you?"

"You think one of our DGM targets is behind this," Kitty said, catching on. Better late than never.

"They do kinda have a reason to hate you," Ed said. "Like a lot."

"But why would one of them kill Ronny?" Kitty asked. "Or Coach Creed?"

"At least Christopher had a reason," Olivia said.

Ed snapped his fingers in front of Olivia's face. "Wake up! Unless he's a vengeful spirit hunting down his tormentors, he didn't kill anyone."

Olivia's brow clouded. "I guess."

You guess? "But what if someone was trying to frame you by going after other DGM targets?" Ed leaned back. "Creed and the Ronster were the most recent."

Kitty sighed. "It's worth looking into." She pointed at the nearest computer. "Ed, I need your Google-fu."

Ed swung around and poised his fingers over the keyboard. "Ready."

"Let's start with DGM's first target," Kitty said. "Wendy Marshall."

Ed got a hit right away. "Senior at St. Francis High School. Updated her Twitter feed this morning."

"That's practically down the street," Olivia said.

Kitty pulled a sheet of paper from the printer and scribbled down Wendy's name. "Now look for Christina Huang."

Again, Ed got a result within seconds. "Looks like her parents shipped her back east to Choate."

"Still alive?" Olivia asked.

Ed shrugged. "If you can call Choate Rosemary Hall alive."

"Okay," Kitty said. "But she lives, like, four thousand miles away. Probably not our killer."

"Try Xavier Hathaway," Olivia suggested.

"That douche who used to stick my head in a toilet and flush it freshman year?" Ed asked.

Olivia nodded. "They didn't call him the Swirlie King for nothing."

Xavier didn't have a Facebook page, so it took Ed longer to

find a reference. The result, however, was unexpectedly gratifying. "Looks like he works for the Hayward Department of Sanitation." He looked up, smiling broadly. "That is the best thing I've ever heard."

"And he might be a killer," Kitty added. She clearly didn't appreciate the irony of Xavier's craptastic job.

"Coach Creed and Ronny are dead, so that leaves three more," Olivia said, counting them off on her fingers. "The Gertler twins, Melissa Barndorfer, and Tammi Barnes."

Ed cocked an eyebrow. "That's four."

"Just look them up!" Kitty cried.

"Fine." Ed quickly sought online references to DGM targets three through six. "The Gertlers work at a surf shop in Mountain View, and according to Melissa's Facebook page, she's in Prague with some Eurotrash boyfriend."

"And Tammi?" Olivia asked.

"Working on it." Ed typed furiously, cycling through all of his stalkery internet go-tos. One by one, they all came up blank. He slumped back in his chair. "I can't find any current info on her."

"Nothing?" Kitty asked.

"That's what I said."

"Okay." Kitty glanced at her watch. "We'll look into it later." She held up her list of suspects. "Wendy, Xavier, Maxwell and Maven Gertler, and Tammi Barnes. Plus person or persons unknown, connected to Christopher Beeman. All of them are possible suspects."

Olivia threw her arms wide in despair. "We're never going to figure this out. Bree's going to rot in jail. She'll shave off all her hair, take over a prison gang, and start calling herself Bitchslap."

Ed smirked. "That sounds like a great porno."

"Look," Kitty said, grabbing Olivia by the shoulders. "We can't panic and we can't give up. We have to keep fighting for Margot and Bree."

"How?"

"We start with this list. Initiate contact, see what we can learn," Kitty said.

Olivia sniffled. "Okay."

"And don't forget Amber and Rex," Kitty added. "We still don't know what they were doing in Ronny's room the night he died."

Olivia nodded, her lips pressed together as if she was trying to steel herself against an unpleasant task. "I'll try."

"And I," Ed the Head said with a flourish of his arm, "will look into Christopher's family and friends." He wasn't going to trust either of them with that task.

Kitty looked at him suspiciously. "We don't need your help, Ed."

This time, his laugh was completely genuine. "You need it now more than ever."

Olivia placed her hand on Kitty's arm. "Maybe we should let him? Margot . . ." Olivia paused, her lip quivering. "Margot trusts Ed. And she doesn't trust anyone."

"Fine." Kitty pulled him to his feet. "But there's something you have to do first."

"Blood pact?" he asked, feigning excitement. "Initiation ritual? Do I get a DGM pin or a secret decoder ring?"

Kitty took a deep breath, then she thrust her hand forward.

"*I, Kitty Wei, do solemnly swear, no secrets—ever—shall leave this square.*"

He watched intently as Olivia grasped Kitty's wrist.

"*I, Olivia Hayes, do solemnly swear, no secrets—ever—shall leave this square.*"

Together, they turned to him. "I dig, I dig," he said. "Secret oath. I'm in."

He grabbed Olivia's wrist and then moved his arm closer to Kitty so she could link to him.

"*I, Ed the Head—*"

"You don't have a last name?" Kitty asked.

Ed sighed. "Fine." He cleared his throat dramatically. "*I, Edward Headley, do solemnly swear—*"

Olivia giggled. "Headley? Are you serious?"

"Do you want me to finish or not?" Ed asked.

"Sorry," Olivia smirked.

"*I, Edward Headley, do solemnly swear, no secrets—ever—shall leave this square. Er, triangle. Whatever.*"

"Good enough."

"Yay." Ed cheered with fake enthusiasm. "Now shouldn't we get out of here before those 'Maine Men goons defile this corridor with their V-D crap?"

Kitty didn't answer, but her eyes hardened as she looked at

him. "We'll meet at the warehouse tonight to debrief, under-stood?"

Olivia nodded, while Ed just winked.

"I'll take that as a yes," she said. "Now, let's get our hands dirty."

FIVE

THE BLACK STRAP OF THE ANKLE MONITOR FIT SNUGLY AROUND the base of Bree's shin, just above the joint, and the attached GPS tracker looked like an old flip phone had been duct taped to her leg.

"The band is a conductive circuit," the guard explained as he tightened the strap. "If you tamper with it in any way, the authorities will be alerted."

"Can I get it wet and feed it after midnight?" Bree joked.

The guard glanced up, unamused. "The tracker is water-proof."

"Oh." Clearly not a fan of *Gremlins*. Or senses of humor.

"The GPS unit is calibrated for your parents' house," he con-tinued. "If you move beyond the one-hundred-meter radius of the perimeter, the authorities will be alerted."

Great. She'd be a prisoner in her own home. Still better than being stuck in juvie for another day.

Once the tracker was securely in place, the guard led Bree into the holding area, where a tall, expensively dressed woman was deep in conversation with another officer.

Bree didn't recognize her mom at first. The sun-streaked hair and deep tan threw her off. And the conservative vest and pantsuit made it look as if her mom were a legal consultant on a twenty-four-hour news network rather than a dilettante home-maker who'd run away to the French Riviera.

But her personality hadn't changed one bit. The sparkling voice, the easy manners—Bree's mom possessed the singular tal-ent of making everyone feel instantly comfortable, from CEOs to panhandlers. The trick, Bree had observed, was flirtation. Male or female, gay, straight, or other, anyone was fair game for her mom's shameless flirting. And it almost always got her what she wanted.

"She'll have to wear the anklet all the time?" her mom asked, eyes wide, voice plaintive.

"Yes, ma'am," said the young officer.

"I can't even take her out to dinner?" her mom pressed. "Or to the movies?"

The officer shook his head. "I'm afraid not."

She sighed in resignation, then turned and looked directly at her daughter.

Bree expected some kind of recognition, but after a few sec-onds, her mom glanced down at her wristwatch. "Any idea when my daughter will be ready?"

The guard eyed Bree. "Um . . ."

"Hey, Mom," Bree said, hoping her voice sounded as unen-thusiastic as she felt.

Her mom started, and slowly returned her gaze to Bree. She

stared, confused, for a full ten seconds, before her face lit up.

"Darling!" Bree's mother flew across the room and embraced her daughter, encircling her with the aromatic mix of Jean Patou and gin. "I've been so worried."

So worried that it took you three full days to fly back from Europe?

"Let me look at you." Her mom pulled away and gripped Bree's head on either side of her face. "When did you cut off your hair? Is that a prison thing?"

Bree narrowed her eyes. "Six months ago."

"Oh." Her mom pursed her lips. "Well, no wonder I didn't recognize you."

Right, not the fact that you haven't been home since Christmas.

"Mrs. Deringer," the processing attendant said. "There are just a few forms you need to sign, accepting custody of your daughter."

With a dramatic sigh, as if signing her name a half-dozen times was some kind of supreme sacrifice, Bree's mom finished the paperwork, and then she and Bree were escorted from the building.

Neither of them said a word as they followed the guard across the courtyard. Bree wasn't going to make things easy on her mom by opening the conversation, and Mrs. Deringer seemed content with the silence.

An enormous black Cadillac Escalade with tinted windows was parked just outside the fence. It looked like the kind of car used by drug cartels. Or the CIA. As soon as the entry gate began to roll, the driver's side door burst open and an equally enormous blond man emerged.

He looked like a Norse god: bronzed skin, flowing hair, and muscles practically ripping through the taut fabric of his black jacket. The skinny tie that encircled his neck resembled a piece of dental floss trying to contain a hot air balloon, and as he walked around the car, Bree was pretty sure she could feel the earth tremble with each mighty step.

Without a word, he whisked open the rear passenger door and offered a hand to Bree's mom, which she accepted with a dainty coquettishness that made Bree's stomach churn.

"Thank you, Olaf."

Olaf?

He nodded, and without offering Bree the same courtesy, he closed the door in her face.

"Yeah," Bree muttered, stomping around to the other side of the car. "Thanks, Olaf."

As soon as Olaf eased the SUV away from the curb, her mom's demeanor changed.

"Do you want to explain to me," she began, "how you thought it was a good idea to confess to a murder?"

"Two murders," Bree corrected, smiling sweetly as she pulled the seat belt across her body. "And I didn't confess to them."

Her mom rolled her eyes. "Whatever." She pressed a button on the door and a minibar slid out from between the passenger seats. Crystal decanters of fluid, clear and dark brown, tinkled and sloshed with the movement of the car, but Bree's mom poured a cocktail from a shaker into a martini glass without spillage. "Wretched place," she said, dropping two olives into the glass. "I'll have to burn this outfit when we get home."

Bree jabbed the tongue of the seat belt into the buckle. It refused to click into place, merely sliding out with each attempt. "Sorry to be so much trouble," Bree said coldly, as she searched for an alternate buckle. "You're welcome to go back to Nice or Cannes or wherever the hell you've been living."

"Villefranche-sur-Mer," her mother said wistfully. "Didn't you read the postcards I sent?"

Not before dumping them in the trash. "Go back," Bree said through clenched teeth. She tossed the seat belt away, annoyed by her futile attempts to get it secured. "I don't need you."

Bree's mom laughed. "Of course you don't *need* me. I raised you so that you wouldn't need anyone."

The word "raised" might have been a stretch, considering how little her mother had been around, especially since Henry Jr. went off to college.

"But at the moment," her mom continued, "someone has to be here to keep an eye on you. Apparently, parental custody means that either your father or I have to supervise your house arrest. And since the senator has oh-so-important policy to not be making in Sacramento, the job fell to me."

"Really feeling the love, Mom."

Her mom arched an expertly crafted brow. "Oh, like you're so excited to spend the next few weeks holed up in the house with Olaf and me?"

Bree blinked. "Olaf?"

"Of course!" her mom cried, as if surprised by her daughter's lack of vision. "I can't be without my Olaf. Who'll drive the car?

Keep the press at bay? Administer my daily rub—"

Before her mom could finish the word, the Escalade swung violently to the left. The back of the car whipped around, slamming Bree into the window. Olaf revved the engine; the tires screeched in protest, filling the backseat with the acrid smell of burning rubber, and the SUV spun in the other direction.

Bree screamed, gripping the door handle for dear life as her body, unrestrained by the defective belt, was torn from her seat by the force of the maneuver. As the SUV fishtailed, she saw the cab of a bright yellow moving truck blow by, so close she could see the driver—baseball cap, dark aviators, and all.

The truck careened on; horns blared from a half-dozen directions, and the SUV bounced fiercely as Olaf drove directly over the island in the middle of the roadway. Bree's head smacked the ceiling, her mom let out a muffled yelp, then suddenly the engine noise returned to normal and the instant of chaos was over.

Beside her, Bree's mom gasped. "Oh my God."

Bree massaged the sore spot on the top of her head. "It's okay," she panted, trying to catch her breath. "I'm not hurt."

"Look at that!" Her mom held her martini glass out for Bree to see. "I didn't spill a drop." Then she lifted the glass to her lips and drained what remained of the cocktail.

I'm so glad you have your priorities straight. "What the hell happened?"

"Truck run red light," Olaf said, his vowels open and round, hinting at Scandinavian roots.

"Shouldn't we go back?" Bree asked. "Call the police? File a report? That guy could be dangerous."

That guy could be a killer.

Bree knew she was being paranoid, but after what Christopher Beeman had put her and the rest of the girls through over the last month, she felt justified in her suspicions. She glanced down at the faulty buckle. Was it just a coincidence that her seat belt didn't work and a truck almost ran them off the road? It would be the perfect way to kill someone and make it look like an accident.

She crouched down in her seat and examined the buckle. Even in the moving car, she could clearly see scratches around the base of the red release button, as if someone had tried to pry it off with a screwdriver.

Bree's blood ran cold. The seat belt had been tampered with.

"No one hurt." He sounded completely unfazed by the near-death experience. "Olaf employ evasive maneuvers."

"Olaf was in the French Foreign Legion," her mother said proudly as she lifted the cocktail shaker from the center console.

Bree eyed the behemoth in the driver's seat and dropped her voice. "Aren't they, like, mercenaries?"

Her mom wiggled her shoulders and slowly raised the martini glass to her lips. "I'd pay him to fight in my army any day."

For the second time in as many hours, Bree fought the urge to puke in her lap.

SIX

CHRISTOPHER BEEMAN IS DEAD.

Olivia couldn't quite wrap her head around the concept, and as she navigated the hallways, she felt a familiar sense of uneasiness growing in the back of her mind.

She shook her head, forcing away the paranoia. The killer had stepped back into the shadows, which meant this was the perfect time to discover his—or her—identity.

And she could start by figuring out how Amber and Rex were connected to Ronny DeStefano.

With a reluctant exhalation, she turned her feet toward the leadership room.

Rex was alone, as Kyle and Tyler had suggested, leaning against a desk as he texted furiously on his phone.

"Knock, knock," Olivia purred, trying to sound seductive.

Rex's head snapped up, his features sharp and aggressive, but at the sight of Olivia, they quickly melted into something more akin to the leer of a dirty old man. "Well, well, well. Looks like my prayers have been answered."

Olivia forced a smile. "Kyle and Tyler said you might need some help."

Rex ambled toward her, backing her up against the wall. "I can always use a helping hand from you, Liv. If you know what I mean."

Great. Zero to rapey in two point five seconds. That had to be a new record, even for Rex. She wedged her hands between them and pushed Rex to arm's length. "What about Amber?"

"We broke up."

Not that she didn't know already, but it was the opening she needed. "You're kidding!" Olivia said, gasping in fake shock. "But you guys were so perfect together."

Rex shrugged, then pressed himself against her outstretched arms. "I've always been holding out for something better."

Olivia's elbows buckled and Rex's body came crashing against hers. She turned her face away just in time to avoid a lip-lock, and instead, Rex planted a slobbering kiss on her neck.

"You taste so good," he said.

Olivia fought the urge to spit in his face. "I'm really surprised," she said, trying to stay on track while she wrestled against Rex's wandering hands. "Amber bragged that you'd never break up with her. Some kind of secret she knew about you."

"What?" Rex pushed himself off her. "What did she say?" His voice was sharp.

"I don't know," Olivia said truthfully. "Something about Ronny DeStef—"

Without warning, Rex gripped her by the shoulders and slammed Olivia against the wall, knocking the breath out of her. "What the fuck did that bitch tell you?"

Nostrils flared, fingers digging into her flesh, Rex's face grew redder by the moment. Pure rage, ignited in an instant, the kind of temper capable of murder.

She tried to wrench free of Rex's grasp, desperate to get away from him. "I . . ."

"Mr. Cavanaugh," Father Uberti said, his voice drifting in from the hall. "I wanted to talk to you about—" He stopped dead just inside the classroom. "Am I interrupting anything?"

Olivia had never been so happy to see old F.U. in her entire life. "No, not at all, Father Uberti," she squeaked. Rex lessened his grip and Olivia shimmied down the wall toward the door.

"She, like, fainted or something," Rex lied, avoiding Father Uberti's eyes.

"I see." Father Uberti nodded, completely satisfied.

"I should be getting to French class." She whisked her bag off the floor and ran out of the room.

Olivia's hands were shaking as she raced away from the leadership classroom. She'd always known that Rex was a top-notch asshole, but suddenly he seemed positively dangerous. There'd been a murderous gleam in his eye as he slammed her against the wall, and it wasn't a stretch to imagine him picking up a baseball bat and bashing Ronny's head in.

She was going to have to be more careful in the future. She wouldn't be able to bring up Ronny again so directly. Rex would be on guard. But as she opened her locker, a plan formed in her mind.

There was more than one way to skin a Rex.

Ed inched open the door to the men's room and watched as first Olivia, then Kitty vacated the computer lab. As soon as they were out of sight, Ed slipped into the hall and doubled back.

Christopher Beeman. Ed doubted that either DGM's fearless leader, Kitty, or the computer-challenged Olivia would have the wherewithal to ferret out the killer's connection to Christopher and his family. And he wasn't sure he trusted either of them with such an important task. He reminded himself that they were at least partially responsible for Margot's state.

So if there was anything left on the internet, Ed wanted to find it first.

He began with a cursory Google search by name, then gradually added pertinent information about his target. The internet purge of Christopher's presence had been a thorough job, except for the AWOL article, the only reference that had been allowed to remain intact.

Ed slouched back in his chair, staring at the article. Why? The answer was obvious: to make Christopher look like a killer on the loose. But Christopher wasn't on the loose. He was dead and buried and . . .

The late bell blared, but Ed ignored it. School was his last priority right now. *Buried.* Christopher had gone to St. Alban's with Bree Deringer, which may have meant his family was Catholic. And if so, there must have been some kind of funeral mass last year, a family gathering, a Rosary, a vigil. Even if "Christopher Beeman" had been purged from the World Wide Web, there might still be a reference to his memorial, or his family.

Why didn't you think of this before?

Ed quickly searched for Christopher's local parish. After all, prayers for the dead were a Catholic specialty. He pored through the church bulletins, starting the day Christopher's body had been found in the boiler room at Archway. He didn't have far to look. The special intention for the eleven o'clock mass that Sunday was "For Brant and Wanda, and the memory of their beloved Christopher."

Ed's pulse quickened. The killer had missed this online reference to Christopher's parents: his first mistake.

New search criteria: "Brant and Wanda."

The hits were instantaneous. Brant and Wanda were social butterflies in the greater Menlo Park area. Wanda was a bigwig in the Junior League, and she and her husband were mentioned on the guest lists at a dozen charity events, a handful of high-profile cocktail parties, and . . .

Ed froze as he read through a twenty-year-old notice in a local paper about a graduation. Not just any graduation: the police academy. His eyes raced over the short blurb, reading it once, twice, then a third time in rapid succession.

The Beemans knew someone in the police department. A relative? A family friend? Someone with a personal connection to Christopher Beeman, and perhaps the desire to find justice in his death? It would explain so much about the utter failure of Menlo P.D. to find any leads on the murderer.

His right hand strayed to the pocket of his jacket, fingering the piece of paper that he always kept with him. All his hope and excitement from a moment before had vanished.

Had anyone seen this yet?

Slowly, he returned to the keyboard. With a few deft keystrokes, he hacked first into the newspaper's database, then into the post itself, and methodically deleted Brant and Wanda's names from the article.

Bree stood on the doorstep, staring up at the columned facade of the Deringer mansion. The uneasiness she'd felt after the moving truck almost pummeled her mom's car into scrap metal was instantly replaced by dread.

Her mom stepped up beside her. "Prison," she said. "For both of us."

At least I'm here for doing something selfless, Bree thought to herself. It was a concept her mother wouldn't understand.

"Ah, well," her mom said, with a cheerful sigh. "Better make the most of it. Olaf? I'll take a massage in my room and then I'll nap until dinner."

Bree looked at her sidelong. "It's, like, eight thirty in the morning."

"Which means it's happy hour in France." And without any attempt to explain her nonsensical time-zone math, Bree's mom flounced inside.

Olaf lumbered behind his mistress, carrying a plastic bin labeled "Deringer, Bree." Her belongings. Everything she had with her when she was arrested would be in that bin. Including her cell phone.

She followed Olaf into the house, eyeing the former Legionnaire from afar. She wasn't sure whether her phone would be off-limits or not, but it was better not to remind anyone. She slipped off her shoes in the entryway and watched as he deposited the box in her father's study, then climbed the stairs to her mother's room.

Shaking off the disgusting image of her mom and Thor going to town above her head, she tiptoed into her dad's study, careful not to touch the door in case the housecleaning crew had neglected to oil the hinges. She wasn't taking any chances. She needed that phone.

It was in the front pocket of her army surplus bag, just where she'd left it. And thankfully, she'd had the presence of mind to power it down after she sent that last text to Olivia and Kitty. With any luck, there'd be a little bit of juice left, just enough to send a couple of texts to John. He'd be in first period by now, but would hopefully check his messages at lunch and then be able to come over after school. Or better, maybe he'd ditch gym class! Her stomach fluttered as she pressed and held the power button.

Success was immediate. The screen came alive and the telltale electronic ding of a smartphone startup melody broke the silence of the house. She hugged the phone to her chest, hoping no one heard, and waited impatiently while the phone detected a signal and connected to the network.

The phone beeped, warning that her battery was danger-ously low. With trembling fingers, she hurriedly texted John.

Out of juvie. Under house arrest.
How is Margot? Is she okay?
Phone's dying, but really want to see you.

"No phones!"

Bree spun around, dropping her cell onto the plush carpet as her heart leaped to her throat. Olaf stood in the doorway, feet shoulder-width apart, hands planted on his hips. He looked like a drill instructor, except for the fact that he was almost completely nude. His hairless chest glistened with a layer of either perspira-tion or baby oil, she couldn't quite tell which, and his thighs bulged from a tiny pair of gold booty shorts.

No amount of mind bleach would ever wipe this image from her brain.

"What the hell are you wearing?" Bree blurted out. She couldn't help herself. He looked like Dr. Frank-N-Furter's man toy in *The Rocky Horror Picture Show*.

"Olaf's massage uniform." He picked her phone up off the floor and powered it down. "Senator Deringer say no phone. No computer. No nothing."

"You can't just take my phone!" Bree cried. "I'm sixteen. You might as well cut off my hands."

"Olaf has orders," he said simply, and disappeared upstairs.

SEVEN

COACH MILES BLEW HER WHISTLE THE SECOND KITTY LED THE team into the gym after warm-ups. "Huddle up, ladies! I have an announcement."

"More line drills?" Mika quipped under her breath as they jogged over to Coach.

Kitty snorted. "Only if we're lucky."

"Got word last night," Coach Miles began in her usual gruff manner, "that the Northern California High School Athletics League will be sponsoring a tournament this weekend, right here at Bishop DuMaine, with scouts from all the major NCAA programs."

College scouts? What an opportunity! Bishop DuMaine had one of the premiere girls' volleyball programs in the country, and Kitty guessed that all the big universities would be there. She held out her fist to Mika, who returned the bump. They both knew this was the chance of a lifetime.

"So that means some of our usual foes," Coach Miles continued. "Mitty, St. Francis, and Gunn."

Kitty caught her breath. Barbara Ann Vreeland went to Gunn. Ever since Kitty had accidentally gotten her expelled from Bishop DuMaine freshman year, she'd been hoping for an opportunity to make things up to her. Barbara Ann had been one of the best high school players in the country before she quit the sport, and if Kitty could just convince her to join the Gunn team, she was positive her old teammate would make an amazing impression.

"So we're doing two-a-days," Coach continued. "Until the tournament. We're the reigning state champions, and I want each and every one of you to have a college offer before Sunday dinner, understood?"

"Sir, yes sir!" the team barked in well-trained unison.

"Good." Coach tooted twice on her whistle. "Water break while I get the new practice schedules from my office, then scrimmage. Ten minutes."

The girls filed out of the gym to the water fountain, Kitty trailing behind. She was finally going to have a chance to make things up to Barbara Ann. But would she listen to Kitty? The last time they'd seen each other, the night of Ronny's candlelight vigil, Barbara Ann had looked as if she'd wanted to rip Kitty's face off. It was doubtful that she'd listen rationally to anything Kitty had to say.

But she might listen to Mika.

"Mika," Kitty said, as they waited in line. "You're still friends with Barbara Ann, right?"

Mika shrugged. "I mean, we don't hang out. But I see her at the Coffee Clash."

"Do you think," Kitty said slowly, "that she'd consider joining the varsity team at Gunn?"

"I doubt it," Mika said, shaking her head sadly. "Sounds like she's done with volleyball."

Kitty scrunched up her face, not willing to give up so easily. "What are you doing after school today?"

"Why?" Mika snapped.

Kitty was taken aback. "Sorry, I just thought maybe we could go to the Coffee Clash and talk to Barbara Ann about—"

"Can't," Mika said. She moved up to the vacant water fountain. "Got a thing."

A thing? "Okay, how about tomorrow night?"

"Can't," Mika said. "Sorry." She took a long sip of water, then turned away from Kitty. "I need to change my knee pads," she said. "For the scrimmage. Later." And she bounded back into the gym.

Okay, fine. If Mika wouldn't help her, she'd find another way. Kitty spun on her heel and headed to Coach Miles's office. Maybe if Coach called over to Gunn, she could get Barbara Ann on the team in time for the tournament? It was worth a shot.

But as she rounded the corner, she stopped dead. Standing at the other end of the hall, heads close together in conversation, were Mika and Donté.

She opened her mouth to say hello, but the words died on her lips. There was something odd about their postures. Donté's body was tense, and Mika's shoulders were hunched as she cast a furtive glance behind her. As she turned, Kitty saw Donté reach out and graze his fingers against Mika's palm.

"Hey!" Kitty cried, marching toward them.

Mika and Donté jumped apart as if they'd just received an electric shock.

"Kitty!" Mika squeaked.

Kitty eyed them both. Mika looked scared, her face pinched and drawn, while Donté was visibly uncomfortable. "I thought you were changing your knee pads?" she asked innocently.

"I—I am," Mika stuttered, her eyes roaming the hallway. They rested on the floor, then the ceiling, then a spot on the wall over Kitty's left shoulder.

"I guess I'm interrupting something," Kitty said, turning on her heel. She felt dizzy and off-balance, as if her world had exploded in an instant. Her best friend and her boyfriend? It was a girl's worst nightmare come true.

"Baby!" Donté dashed after her, catching her by the arm. "Don't be like that. You weren't interrupting anything." He pulled her into his body and wrapped his arms around her, then lowered his lips to her ear. "I promise."

Her knees turned to jelly, but a nagging little voice in her head prevented her from melting into Donté's arms. *They're lying to you. They're hiding something.*

Mika cleared her throat. "I should go. We'll, um, chat later." She turned and disappeared down the hallway.

Donté waited until Mika was gone before he glanced down at Kitty. "Are you okay?"

Kitty shrugged. "Sure."

Donté pulled away and took her face in his hands. "Kitty, what's wrong?"

I just caught you holding hands with my best friend? "What's wrong with me?" Kitty asked with a tight laugh. "What's wrong with *you?*"

Donté jolted, dropping his hands from her face. "What do you mean?"

"I'm not an idiot," Kitty said, her voice shaking. "There's something going on. With us. Something you're not telling me." She glanced down the hallway where Mika had just disappeared. "If you're going to break up with me, I'd rather you just do it now."

Donté's eyes grew wide. "Break up with you? Are you crazy?"

"Um . . ." Kitty paused. She'd steeled herself against the inevitable "I've met someone else" excuse, but instead, he looked horrified.

Donté reached his hand out to her. "Kitty Wei, I do not want to break up with you. What made you think that?"

Kitty tentatively slipped her hand into his, but stared at the floor. "I don't know. I thought maybe you . . ." Realized I'm kind of a spaz? Knew you could do better?

"Kitty," he said, wrinkling his lower lip. "I'm so sorry. I swear, there's nothing between Mika and me. I know it looked weird, but it has nothing to do with you. Or us. Nothing at all."

Kitty glanced up at him. She knew there was something he wasn't telling her. "Donté, what's going on?"

A wave of pain washed over his face. "I . . ." His voice faltered and his eyes flicked away from her face. Regardless of his insistence that his issues had nothing to do with her, he was definitely hiding something. Not just a school or family issue he didn't want to talk about, but an actual secret. She could see the shame in his eyes, see the inner struggle as he tried to decide whether or not he could share it with her.

"I need to get back to practice," he said at last.

Kitty tightened her grip on his hand. "Donté, you can trust me."

"Of course I can trust you." Donté took a step closer and bent down, his lips inches from her ear. "But right now, I need you to trust me."

Kitty's pulse was still racing long after Donté ducked into the boys' locker room. Her heart ached with a dull pain that reminded Kitty of getting punched in the stomach, and she couldn't quite shake the feeling that she was somehow losing her boyfriend.

With a heavy sigh, Kitty peeled her eyes away from the locker room door, and trudged down the hallway to Coach Miles's office.

The door to the office was closed, but Kitty could clearly hear the sounds of someone typing at the computer. Not wanting to interrupt her cantankerous coach, Kitty peeked through the window to see if she looked busy.

Instead, she found Theo Baranski typing furiously on Coach Miles's computer.

Without knocking, Kitty flung the door open and watched with some satisfaction as Theo jumped out of the chair.

"Kitty!" he cried, his face red. "What are you doing here?"

I should be asking you the same thing. "I came to talk to Coach."

"Oh," Theo said, fumbling around for the mouse. "Right. Sure." Before he could completely close out the screen on Coach's computer, Kitty saw that he'd been accessing the school email system. Which was innocent enough. So why did he look so scared?

"I—I was just checking my email," he said at last, stating the obvious.

"Uh-huh."

He reached down to the CPU, then popped out of the chair and scurried past Kitty into the hallway, shoving something into his pocket with trembling hands. "I've got to go."

What the hell was going on with everyone?

EIGHT

THE GOOD THING, AND PERHAPS THE ONLY GOOD THING, about Rex Cavanaugh was that he was predictable. Olivia was well aware that she wasn't as smart as Margot, or as sharp as Kitty, or even as ballsy as Bree. But like any great actress, she was observant.

Which is why Olivia knew that Rex would be leaving his iPhone bundled up in his Bishop DuMaine jacket, next to the chain-link fence around the tennis courts, during sixth-period gym.

He did it every day, as if he was so important he might miss a call if he left his phone in his locker for fifty minutes, and his massive ego might afford her the opportunity to nab his phone for a quick look-see.

Olivia sighed as she crouched behind a tree next to the tennis courts. If only Bree were here. She was so much better at the criminal stuff. Olivia's role was always decoy and informant, but doing the actual theft? She wasn't sure she had the nerve.

Rex's sidekicks emerged from the locker room first. Kyle and Tyler scanned the yard like Secret Service agents prepping the area for the president's arrival, then stepped aside and allowed Rex to lead them across the blacktop to the same corner court they used every day.

"Two against one," he barked at Kyle and Tyler as he stepped onto the court. "I'm gonna kick your asses, ladies."

Then the move she'd been waiting for. Rex peeled off his jacket, carefully wrapped it around his cell phone, and placed it in the corner of the green hard court, nestled beside the chain-link fence.

So predictable.

Now, the tricky part. With his back to her, Rex wasn't likely to spy her sneaking out from the trees, unless she was unlucky enough to have a stray ball roll right up on top of her as she was reaching her hand through the fence. The catch was Kyle and Tyler, who had a clear view of her. The trees only came within a few feet of the fence, and as soon as she broke from behind them, she'd be fully visible. She just had to wait, and hope that Rex's overly aggressive play would send a ball flying across the nearby courts. With all eyes following Rex's errant shot, she might just have enough time to snag the phone.

"Dude," Rex said, as he casually tossed a ball to Kyle. "Your serve."

Kyle caught the ball in midair. "I suck at serving."

"I know," Rex said with a grin.

Pursing his lips, Kyle bounced the ball several times, then tossed it over his head and took a massive swing.

The ball bounced in front of him. Nothing but air.

"A swing and a miss!" Rex crowed.

Kyle chased down the ball and snatched it off the green court. He repeated his setup, swung again, and missed.

"Fuck!" Kyle growled.

Rex cupped the side of his mouth. "Strike two!"

Olivia could see the scowl on Kyle's face as he kicked the ball against the fence. "Stupid ball."

"Come on, dude," Tyler said. "You can do this."

His lips pressed together, Kyle tossed the ball, arched his back, and whapped it as hard as he could.

To Olivia's amazement, it soared over the net.

Rex pounced on Kyle's serve immediately with a swing that utilized all of his strength. The yellow ball zipped through the air, over the net, over the back of the court, over the net of the court behind them, and finally dribbled to a stop three courts away.

"Home run!" Kyle cried, and burst into laughter. "Point to me."

Rex glowered at him. "Go get the fucking ball, will you?" Then he pointed his racket at Tyler, who was trying to contain his not-so-manly giggling. "Don't look at me, dickhead. I'll punch that smile off your face."

Rex marched up to the net, arms folded across his chest, while Kyle and Tyler jogged across the courts to retrieve their ball. Suddenly, Olivia had her chance. As silently as she could, she slipped out from behind the tree, dashed to the fence, and wiggled her hand between the links. It only took her seconds to locate Rex's phone in the folds of his jacket. She carefully extricated it and hurried back to the safety of the trees, panting.

Bree would be so proud of me.

Rex's phone had an access code, but there was no need for one of Margot's high-tech hacking devices. She'd seen him type it in a dozen times: 6969. So classy. His home screen popped up instantly.

She started with the texts. Conversations with Kyle, Tyler, and a half-dozen other members of the 'Maine Men posse. She skipped through those. Amber, of course. She'd check that last. She continued to scroll, looking for Ronny's name or, more likely, a phone number without a contact entry.

Nothing unusual jumped out at her, so she scrolled back up to Amber and opened all five hundred messages in the thread.

Moving backward in time through the final days of Rex and Amber's relationship, Olivia felt almost bad for her frenemy. Rex was truly a douche, and despite the fact that Amber had dumped *him*, Amber was desperate to get him back; she must have really loved him.

About fifty texts in, something caught Olivia's eye. Rex had just called Amber a frigid bitch, which was followed by a rapid series of responses.

Oh yeah? How about I share your dirty little secret, huh?

I'm sure Kyle, Tyler, and the rest of the guys would just LOVE to know about Christopher.

Maybe you should go back to him? I'm sure you'd make a lovely couple.

Finally! So that's what Ronny knew about Rex. Olivia recalled the emails Margot found between Christopher and Ronny. Hadn't Christopher mentioned that he'd had a sexual encounter with someone at St. Alban's? Could that possibly have been Rex?

His response showed just how terrified he was that Amber might follow through on her threats.

You fucking bitch.
If you breathe a word about that I'll make you wish you'd never been born.
Don't forget, I know where you were the night Ronny died.
You want me to point the cops toward your dad's missing Rolex?

Olivia felt her fingertips tingling as she read the texts. The pieces were finally coming together.

She looked around the wooded area, wishing there was someone nearby with whom she could share her discovery. Usually it was Margot or Kitty or even Bree figuring out the mystery, but now Olivia was rocking her Nancy Drew-ness to the nth degree and feeling pretty badass about it. She needed to find Kitty and tell her—

In the distance, the bell blared.

Dammit! She'd totally lost track of time. See? Bree wouldn't have done that.

Olivia canceled out of Rex's messaging app and peeked from behind the tree. Too late. Rex jogged over to his bundle, tucked his jacket under his arm, and trotted off across the court.

This was her chance. Swift and silent, she dashed to the fence and carefully laid Rex's phone on the blacktop, as if it had just fallen out when he picked up his jacket. She was back in the safety of the trees not a moment too soon. Rex wasn't even off the tennis courts before he shoved his hand into the bundle, looking for his phone. He paused, unfurled his jacket, and shook it, then swung around toward the corner he'd just vacated.

He ran back to his phone at a full sprint, as if concerned that some unseen thief might nab it before he got there, and plucked it off the ground. He shoved the phone into his pocket and started back to the locker room when he paused. Rex slowly turned and stared into the wooded area. Olivia crouched even lower, her heart thundering in her chest, and waited what felt like forever before she heard the squeak of his sneakers as he retreated.

NINE

BREE LAY ON HER BED, STARING UP AT THE CEILING. WITH HER phone confiscated by Olaf and the password for the wireless changed, she was basically cut off from the world.

It had been six hours since her release and she still had no idea how Margot was, no clue as to what had become of Christopher Beeman. Were her friends safe? Or was he still after them? She'd been half-expecting to discover another manila envelope on her bed when she got home, taunting her, and was almost disappointed when all she found was her bedspread and pillows. At least it would have been some acknowledgment that she still existed.

Bree sighed and rolled onto her stomach, cradling her head in the crook of her arm. She just needed a touchstone. Someone who could be her eyes and ears on the outside. If John had gotten her texts, maybe he would—

Ding-dong.

Bree vaulted out of bed. Someone was at the door. She glanced at her alarm clock and saw that it was almost three o'clock. School let out exactly twenty minutes ago.

She sprinted down the stairs, hydroplaning on the Persian runner in the hallway, then stopped short. The colossal bulk of Olaf blocked the wide-open front door.

"What do you want?" Olaf asked.

"I'm here to see Bree."

"John!" she cried, racing up behind Olaf. Her heart almost burst from her chest at the sound of his voice.

"No visitors," Olaf said. And before either of them could protest, he slammed the door in John's face and threw the bolt.

"What the fuck?" Bree yelled. She made a dash for the door, but Olaf's massive arm was around her waist before she could reach the handle. He tossed her over his shoulder like a bag of potting soil.

"No visitors," he repeated as he traipsed down the hallway.

Bree tried to wiggle out of his grasp, but it was no use. Olaf's arm was like a vise, pinning her to his shoulder. He mounted the stairs two at a time and deposited Bree on her bed with a heavy bounce.

"Olaf following orders," he said as he left and slammed the door behind him.

"Olaf following orders," Bree mocked in a deep, hollow voice. "Dick."

"Olaf hear that," came a muffled voice from the other side of the door.

Ugh. Bree went limp on the bed. Was she going to be trapped in the house for God only knows how long with Olaf the Gorilla as her prison guard? This was so not going to work.

Tap. Tap tap.

Bree turned toward her bedroom window in time to see several small pebbles bounce off the outside of the glass. *Tap. Tap.*

John! Bree threw open the window. Below, on the gravel path next to her house, was her best friend.

"Hey!" he said as soon as she poked out her head. "I got your text. Tried to call but it went straight to voice mail. Are you okay? Are you out for good? And who the hell was that douche at the front door?"

Bree held her finger to her lips—apparently, Olaf's superpower was excellent hearing—and pointed toward the servants' entrance at the back of the house. With any luck, Olaf hadn't thought of that yet.

John gave her a thumbs-up and headed around to the backyard. Now all Bree had to do was get there too.

She tiptoed across her room and cracked the bedroom door a fraction of an inch, just enough to see that the hallway wasn't blocked by two hundred pounds of muscle. She listened intently for the sound of his mouth breathing; then, emboldened by the lack of noise, she swung the door open enough to stick her head into the hallway.

A quick sweep from left to right showed her that the coast was clear.

Bree was down the stairs in a heartbeat, through the laundry room to the back entrance. She yanked the door open and saw John's beaming face.

"I wasn't sure if I should—" he started, but Bree tackled

him before he could finish, wrapping her arms tightly around his neck.

John stumbled from the force of impact, carrying her with him into the backyard. Almost instantly, an alarm blared. "Warning!" an electronic voice cried from the security pad next to the door. "Perimeter breach. Rear exit. Warning! Perimeter breach. Rear exit." Rinse, repeat.

"What the hell is that?" John said, still holding Bree's weight in his arms.

She slid down his body, until her toes touched the hard concrete. Pulling up the leg of her pajama pants, she saw a red light blinking on her anklet.

"Son of a bitch," she said, pointing at it. "They've hooked up the GPS on my anklet to the home security system." So much for one hundred meters. Someone wanted to make sure she couldn't leave the house at all.

"Damn," John said. She felt his arm slip around her waist and pull her close. "I'm sorry."

"Warning! Perimeter breach."

"Oh, shut up!" Bree cried in frustration. As if on cue, the alarm switched off and Olaf appeared in the doorway.

"No visitors," he said, a broken record. "Olaf—"

"Yeah, yeah," Bree interrupted. "Olaf following orders. I get it."

John leaned down and whispered in her ear. "Is this guy for real?"

"He comes with the parole." Bree sighed as she gazed up at

John. "I don't know when I'll be able to see you again."

"You'll see me again."

"Promise?"

John's hazel eyes sparkled with mischief, as he sung a line from one of Bree's favorite songs. "And if I had to walk the world, I'd make you fall for me. I promise you, I promise you I will."

"Now!" Olaf barked.

Bree turned to go inside, then suddenly realized she had the messenger she'd been hoping for. She thought of her near-death experience on the way home from juvie, of the seat belt buckle that had clearly been tampered with. If Christopher had been behind it, she needed to warn the girls, and John was her best chance. She flew back to him, arms wrapped tightly around his neck. "I need you to deliver a message," she whispered.

"Huh?" John asked.

"Olaf carry you now." She felt Olaf's meaty hands on her shoulders, but held tight to John for one more second.

"Tell Olivia Hayes that he's not done with us."

Then Bree released John, and watched him stare at her in confusion while Olaf dragged her into the house.

TEN

ED CHECKED THE ADDRESS ON HIS PHONE FOR THE BAZIL-
lionth time, then looked around the desolate alley. It was like
something out of a postapocalyptic sci-fi movie. A single light
cast eerie shadows across the trash-strewn, semi-abandoned
industrial neighborhood, a mix of boarded-up warehouses and
gated repo lots that, according to Ed's cinematic expertise, meant
it was a breeding ground for zombies, vampires, or homicidal
motorcycle gangs.

Really? This was where the notorious DGM made their
secret headquarters? He had a difficult time imagining Olivia
picking her way down the broken pavement in heels.

He hurried to the next building, squinting to read the
address. *This is it.* A large storehouse marked "Custom Furniture
and Imports." He shoved his phone back into his pocket and
lifted his hand to knock on the door when he paused.

In the distance, he distinctly heard the sound of footsteps.

It was just a light patter, like shoes crunching across the
gravel of broken pavement, but as he stood frozen at the door,

eyes straining against the darkness, everything seemed deathly still.

Great. All this DGM crap was starting to make him paranoid.

He turned quickly back to the door and knocked.

"Who is it?" Kitty asked from the other side.

Ed rolled his eyes. "Jack the Ripper. Who do you think it is?"

There was a pause, then the sound of scraping metal as Kitty threw a bolt and the heavy door inched open. "Could you be any louder?" she asked as Ed slipped inside. The words were sharp but Ed noticed that both her voice and her body were relaxed. "You probably woke up the whole neighborhood."

Ed snorted. "Who, the rats? Or the homeless guy shantied up in the alley?"

Kitty heaved the door closed and threw the bolt. "You're hilarious."

"I try."

Ed followed Kitty as she snaked around dining room tables and bureaus, armoires and princess beds, all in various stages of construction. In the back of the warehouse, an unfinished table was positioned under a bank of fluorescent lights in a small clearing amid the furniture. Several mismatched antique chairs had been arranged in a semicircle, one of which contained Olivia, who was examining her face in a compact.

Olivia looked up, smiling brightly. "At least I wasn't the last one here."

"For once," Kitty said under her breath.

"I'm not *always* late," Olivia said, snapping the compact shut.

Kitty half-smiled. "Oh really? Name one time before this that you weren't the last one here."

"Um . . ." Olivia jutted out her chin. "Okay, fine. But I blame public transportation."

"What is this," Ed asked, "teatime? Can we get this show on the road? I have things to see and people to do."

Kitty's eyebrow shot up. "Don't you mean things to do and people to see?"

Ed settled into a chair. "No. No, I do not."

"Okay," Kitty said slowly, missing the joke. She leaned against the table, gripping the edge with her fingers. "Who's first?"

Olivia raised her hand. "Oooh, me! Me!"

Kitty laughed. "Miss Hayes?"

Olivia stood up, like a teacher's pet, and clasped her hands in front of her. "Today I learned—"

Click.

"Shh!" Ed held up his hand, his senses immediately on alert. This time, he was positive he'd heard something. A snap, like two pieces of wood lightly knocked together, followed by what he thought once again might be footsteps.

"What is it?" Olivia whispered.

Ed waited, searching for any sign of movement in the darkened recesses of the warehouse, then shook his head. Was he going crazy? "I thought I . . ." His voice trailed off and he sniffed at the air. "Do you smell smoke?"

Before Kitty or Olivia could respond, the back corner of the warehouse erupted in flames.

It looked like it happened in slow motion: one minute it was completely dark except for the lights above them, the next, the south wall was on fire. The warehouse was like a tinderbox—the unfinished wooden furniture crackled as the blaze jumped from cabinet to armoire to dresser. Tongues of orange and yellow flames raced along the floor as if they were following a track, igniting everything in their path.

Kitty leaped into action. "Grab your stuff!" she yelled. She whipped her duffel bag off the floor and hauled a stunned Olivia to her feet, practically tossing her into Ed's arms. "Head for the door."

"What's happening?" Olivia cried, clutching her purse to her chest.

Ed pulled his backpack over his shoulders. "I think the warehouse is on fire."

"Move!" Kitty barked.

Ed grabbed Olivia by the hand and dragged her toward the metal door through which he'd entered just minutes before. The interior was already heavy with smoke, and he could feel the heat of the fire in every breath. He glanced over his shoulder at the south end of the warehouse, now completely engulfed in flames. How had the fire moved that quickly? And how did it start? Furniture doesn't spontaneously combust.

Just as they reached the door, the sprinkler system kicked in, dousing the interior with water. But it was like trying to use a garden hose against a forest fire—the water sizzled to steam as the inferno blazed forth.

The metal door was already hot to the touch. Ed pulled the sleeves of his jacket over his hands and leaned all of his weight against the sliding metal bar that locked the door from the inside. Beside him, Olivia was doubled over, coughing uncontrollably as more and more oxygen was consumed by the flames. He felt his chest seize up, his nose and throat seared from the heat of the air that was becoming more impossible to breathe with each passing second. Ed strained against the metal bar as he gasped for air, but his knees buckled and his body sank to the floor.

Suddenly, a rush of cool air swept over him; Ed opened his mouth and let it fill his lungs. He felt a strong arm around his waist, dragging him to his feet. He stumbled forward, his sneakers crunching against the gravelly surface of the alley. He could still feel the heat of the fire against his skin, but it was growing less intense by the second. Ten steps, twenty. The arm let him go and he collapsed on the ground.

"Thank you, officer," Ed panted. Thank God the fire department got there so fast.

Kitty coughed, and slapped him on the back. "That was me saving your ass, idiot."

Ed pushed himself to his feet. "Oh."

In the distance, they heard the scream of a siren.

"We could have died in there," Olivia whimpered. Tears were flowing down her cheeks, creating shiny trails through the soot and ash that stained her face.

"We could have been killed," Kitty said. Her voice was tight.

"That's what I said." Olivia wiped her nose.

"No," Kitty said softly. "It's very, very different."

Ed whipped his head around at the ominous tone in Kitty's voice. She was staring at the facade of the warehouse, glowing bright orange from the force of the flames inside. Ed followed her gaze and his body went rigid.

Letters glowed on the exterior of the wall, growing brighter as the heat from within intensified. Ed could just make out the words as the flames began to eat away the wall.

I'm back.

ELEVEN

BREE SLOUCHED ON THE SOFA IN THE MEDIA ROOM, ABSENTLY clicking through stations. Why was morning television so terrible? Her choices seemed to be news, sports news, talk shows, soap operas, or guessing whose Showcase Showdown estimate came closest without going over. She switched the television off and flopped onto her stomach. House arrest was even more boring than juvie.

The doorbell rang, its harsh electronic peal so jarring that Bree practically fell off the sofa. She pushed herself up on her elbows and glanced at the grandfather clock. Nine o'clock in the morning? Who could possibly be coming to see her mom at that hour?

Bree waited several seconds to see if Olaf the Gorilla would open the door, but apparently it was too early for him as well. The doorbell rang again, and Bree reluctantly rolled off the sofa and shuffled down the hall.

She opened the door, but instead of the Avon lady or a Jesus pamphlet, she was greeted by Sergeant Callahan.

"Good morning," he said with a nod.

"What are you doing here?"

"It's good to see you too, Bree."

"No visitors!" Olaf's booming voice filled the foyer. Bree turned and saw the blond god leaning over the banister, wrapped in one of her mom's silk kimonos. "Olaf has orders."

"Good morning," Sergeant Callahan said, shouldering his way past Bree into the house. "Is Mrs. Deringer available?"

"Mrs. Deringer not up yet," Olaf said. He gripped the belt of his undersized kimono, as if trying to make sure it didn't fall off. Yeah, that was the last thing Bree needed to see.

"Can you let her know that Sergeant Callahan is here to interview Bree?"

"Again?" Bree said.

Sergeant Callahan ignored her. "And that I'll need her to be present."

Olaf grunted, which Bree assumed was some kind of affirmation, and lumbered down the hall.

Bree stood with her hand on the open door, a clear signal that she planned to be as uncooperative as possible.

"You can close the door, Bree," he said with a tight smile. "I'm not going anywhere."

Bree shrugged and pushed the front door with the tip of her index finger. It swung silently, then clicked into place.

"Is there someplace we can talk?" he asked, amazingly calm.

Again, without a word, Bree sauntered down the hall, unhurried and uninterested, and turned into her dad's study. She dropped into an oversize leather chair and swung both legs over the tufted arm, easing back into a reclining position while she twirled a strand of her hair.

"You realize this isn't helping you, right? Your continued silence?"

Actually, it's the only thing that's helping me.

"I'm hoping your mother will be able to talk some sense into you."

You don't know my mother.

"Before this entire situation gets out of hand. There are a great many people pressuring the DA's office to charge you as an adult."

Bree continued to twirl her hair.

"And I can't help you if you won't talk to me."

Exasperation. She could hear it in his voice. Could she possibly push him over the edge? It was worth a try. She turned and looked directly at Sergeant Callahan. "If you had any real evidence," she said, flashing him a big, shit-eating grin, "you'd have charged me by now."

Sergeant Callahan shot to his feet. "Goddammit!"

Bree turned back to the wall. She'd finally gotten a rise out of him, but it was a hollow victory. She was in a dangerous position, and she knew it. If they didn't find the real killer, even without any evidence against her, the DA's office might push through to a trial.

He paced the room. "Is everything a joke to you? This is serious, Bree. Two people are dead. There's a girl in a coma that may or may not be related. Arson in the warehouse district that may or may not be related . . ."

Bree sat straight up. The girl in a coma was Margot, she was sure, the first real news she'd had of her friend. But it was the second statement that made her stomach drop. "The warehouse district?" It couldn't be Kitty's uncle's place, could it?

Sergeant Callahan eyed her sharply. "Yeah," he said, his voice back to its polished smoothness.

"Was . . ." Bree swallowed. "Was anyone there at the time?"

"No," he said, slowly shaking his head. "It was empty."

Bree's mind raced as Sergeant Callahan continued to watch her. It could just be a coincidence, right? There were a lot of warehouses in that area, most of which were abandoned. Probably just some squatters trying to keep warm.

Or maybe it was Christopher.

Were Kitty and Olivia okay? Sergeant Callahan said there was no one in the warehouse, but that only meant no one he found. Maybe Kitty and Olivia had been there for a meeting and managed to get out before the fire department arrived. Dammit, she needed more information. Was this meant as a warning or had Christopher tried to kill her friends?

Bree eyed the policeman. Maybe she should tell him the truth? He was right: two people were dead and Margot was, apparently, in a coma. If the warehouse fire and the sabotaged seat belt were related, maybe it was better to tell the police before someone else got hurt.

"You know," Sergeant Callahan said, leaning closer to her as if he was about to share with her the third secret of Fátima, "if you tell me what you know, it'll go better for you. We can cut you a deal, make sure you get off with just a slap on the wrist.

You weren't *really* to blame, were you, Bree? Someone else had to be involved. . . ."

Bree stiffened. She was an idiot for thinking he was on their side. Sergeant Callahan wasn't going to listen to her about Christopher. He was just looking for the quick fix, for Bree to snitch on her friends to save herself.

Over my dead body.

She shrugged and turned away. "I hope you find the guy."

"Darling!" Bree's mom swept into the room before Sergeant Callahan could respond. She was wearing the same kimono Olaf had just sported. Bree cringed, wondering what, if anything, Olaf had on now. Her mom took Sergeant Callahan's hands in hers and kissed him on both cheeks. "It's been ages."

"You look wonderful, Diana." And he meant it too. His eyes traced every line of her mom's body.

Barf.

Her mom winked, then swirled into an armchair, patting the ottoman next to her for Sergeant Callahan. "To what do we owe this pleasure?"

"I wish I was here under more favorable circumstances," he said, lowering himself to the ottoman like a courtier paying homage to the queen. "But it's about your daughter."

"Bree?"

Bree smacked her forehead. As if her mom had another daughter.

"Er, yes," Sergeant Callahan said.

She leaned in to him. "Is she in a great deal of trouble?"

"She might be."

Bree's mom gasped, her hand flying to her throat. "Oh no! My poor sweet baby girl!" Her voice shook, her eyes welled up, and Bree had to turn away to keep from laughing out loud.

"Diana, don't cry," Sergeant Callahan said, his voice tender. "I'm doing everything I can for her. But your daughter is being stubbornly uncooperative."

"Yes," her mom said. "She can be like that."

"Is there anything you can do to convince her to talk? I can't help her if she refuses to tell me anything."

Bree's mom laid her hand on Sergeant Callahan's knee, and dropped her voice. "Are you going to charge her with murder if she doesn't cooperate?"

"Well," Sergeant Callahan said, clearing his throat. "We, uh, don't actually have any evidence linking her to the crimes."

I knew it!

"Wonderful!" Her mom popped out of her chair and clapped her hands. "Then you can remove the anklet and send her back to school."

Sergeant Callahan rose to his feet. "Er, actually, Diana—"

"I'll be back in France in time for the weekend." Her mom dashed into the hallway. "Olaf? Pack the bags. And see if Johan can get us a first-class upgrade on a flight for tomorrow."

And with that, her mom disappeared upstairs.

Sergeant Callahan sighed. "I guess that's all for today."

Bree sprang from the chair and led the police officer to the front door. She couldn't help but feel bad for him, yet another man swept up in the insanity that was Diana Deringer.

Bree held the door open, then pulled up the leg of her

pajamas. "So when can I get this thing off?" He'd admitted they had no reason to hold her, and now she was desperate to get out of the house.

"The anklet?"

No, my foot. "Um, yeah."

Sergeant Callahan smiled. "Oh, that's not up to us."

Bree didn't like the snide look on his face. "What do you mean?"

"The Menlo Park Police Department isn't holding you under house arrest. That's by order of your father."

Then he pulled the handle, and closed the door in Bree's face.

TWELVE

OLIVIA STRODE OUT ONTO THE QUAD, SQUINTING INTO THE bright sunshine. The weather was warm, but she felt cold and clammy, and the skin on her neck puckered with goose pimples.

The fear was back.

She wanted to hide from it, to lock herself away from the killer who stalked DGM, but deep down, she knew that even if she ran forever, she'd never be safe from him.

Any sense of reprieve, any ideas that the killer had backed off since Bree turned herself in, had vanished in one awful moment. Two simple words glowing on the side of Kitty's uncle's warehouse as it burned to the ground. *I'm back.*

All of her panic and fear had been reignited in that instant. The killer wasn't going to leave them alone, wasn't content with Bree's confession. He wanted more. He wanted to destroy them.

They'd fled from the scene of the fire just before the engines arrived. She had no idea what the fire investigators would find, but she hoped rather than believed that there would be some clue to the killer's identity. He'd meticulously covered his tracks so far, and there was no reason to think he'd slip up now.

They only had one course of action: find him before he struck again.

Olivia took a deep breath, steeling herself for the epic song and dance she was about to perform, and plastered a fake smile on her face as she approached the lunch table where Amber and Jezebel sat. She desperately needed Amber to trust her, and to let her back into the bosomfold of her intimate secrets, if she was going to figure out what had happened to the missing Rolex.

She took a seat across from Jezebel, who was devouring a burrito the size of a log. Beside her, Amber nibbled on a piece of what looked like cardboard. The contrast between the two of them was mesmerizing.

"So where's Peanut?" Olivia asked.

"Purging, I hope," Amber said, breaking off a teeny bit of what may or may not have been a rice cracker and placing it daintily in her mouth. "I swear that girl has put on five pounds in the last week."

"You didn't tell her that, did you?" Olivia asked, horrified. Nothing would send Peanut down the path to full-blown anorexia faster than Amber telling her she looked fat.

"Of course I did," Amber said with a toss of her hair. "That's what friends do."

Jezebel devoured the last morsel of bean-and-cheese burrito and nodded. "Friends know when to tell friends they have a problem."

"We have a certain reputation to maintain," Amber continued. She held her head high, like a queen at a coronation. "People look up to us, and we need to act like we deserve it."

From the table behind them, a group of guys burst out laughing. Olivia turned to find Rex and his 'Maine Men posse mimicking Amber's regal stance.

"You're better off without Rex," Olivia said, as she watched Amber's mask of indifference falter.

Jezebel ferretted a Clif Bar out of her bag. "He was getting you into some shady shit."

Shady shit? That sounded promising. "Really?" Olivia asked with wide-eyed innocence. "Like what?"

"Nothing," Amber snapped.

Jezebel's eyebrows shot up. "But what about the night—"

Amber elbowed Jezebel in the ribs. "I said, nothing."

"Ow." Jezebel rubbed her abdomen. "Fine. Nothing."

Dammit. She was so close.

The conversation dropped and Olivia was just about to open with the non sequitur, "Doesn't your dad own a Rolex?" when something on the other side of the quad caught her eye. John Baggott, standing near the science building, waving his arms over his head, trying to get her attention.

When he realized she'd seen him, John gestured for her to follow. Why would John want to talk to her?

Olivia paused, considering her options. John had been a suspect in the murders, and even Bree had questioned his innocence at one point. The killer had just announced that he was back: maybe it really *was* John? Maybe he was trying to lure her away from her friends in order to make her the next victim?

Then again, if anyone might have news of how Bree was doing, it would be John.

"Ladies' room," Olivia said, pushing herself up from the table. "Back in a sec." It was worth the chance that John might know something about Bree.

He was waiting in the science building near an alcove in front of what Olivia thought was the physics lab.

He's not going to kill you, Olivia said to herself as she approached the alcove. Still, she stood in the middle of the hallway, a good ten feet from John.

"You wanted to see me?" she said, copping her best bitchy attitude.

John leaned against the door jamb of the physics lab and smirked. "Wow, nice *Mean Girls* impression. Are you trying to make fetch happen, too?"

Olivia was too good an actress to break character. "What do you want?"

"Okay, fine. All business." He pushed himself off the wall and held up his hands in surrender. "I come in peace. With a message from Bree."

Olivia felt the excitement bubbling up inside her, and tried desperately not to let it show on her face. She needed to warn Bree that the killer was back. If he'd gone after them in the warehouse, who knew what else he was capable of?

But could she trust John? Was it worth the risk?

"I can't think of any reason," she said, trying to sound glib, "why Bree Deringer would want to talk to me."

"Come off it, Olivia," John said. "I know you're a member of DGM."

Olivia froze. How could he know she was a member? Only the killer knew that.

John seemed to read her mind. "I saw the way you reacted when Bree turned herself in, plus I found the photo of the four of you from freshman year. So just give up the act. This shit is serious."

First Ed the Head, now John Baggott. Part of her was freaked out that so many people were now privy to their carefully guarded secret. Still, Bree trusted John. Maybe she needed to as well.

"What is it?" she asked. "What's Bree's message?"

"She told me to tell you, 'He's not done with us.'"

Olivia's eyes grew wide. How did Bree know? Had he gone after her, too? "Is that all she said?"

John nodded. "She was being hauled away by a Swedish bodybuilder named Olaf."

Olivia tilted her head to the side. "Juvie has Swedish body-builders?" Maybe her impression had been all wrong.

John laughed. "No. She was released yesterday. She's under house arrest."

"Oh my God!" Olivia cried. This was so amazing! House arrest probably didn't mean she was entirely free from suspicion, but at least she wasn't in jail anymore. Olivia threw her arms around John's neck. "This is the best news ever!"

"What are you doing?" a voice boomed.

Olivia let her arms fall from around John's neck and turned to find Amber teetering down the hall on her platform sandals, fists balled up at her sides.

John glanced at Olivia. "Um, nothing?"

Amber pulled up short, huffing and puffing from the exertion, and tried to look uninterested, as if she hadn't followed Olivia but just happened upon her and John while out for a stroll in the science building. "Hi, John. How are you?"

"Fiiine," John said slowly, drawing out the vowel.

Amber stood smiling at him, eyebrows raised in anticipation, as if she was waiting for him to say something else.

"And, um, how are you?"

She giggled. "I'm good! Even gooder now that I've seen you." She paused, aware that what had just come out of her mouth hadn't made sense. "I mean, better now. I mean . . ." She shimmied up to him and grasped his hand. "I mean, hi."

Wow. Amber had gone completely Cutesy McFlirtypants over John. The last time Olivia had seen Amber this desperate to snag a boy had been the freshman year homecoming dance, where she'd latched on to Rex and wouldn't let go until they'd swapped spit and officially been labeled an item. It wasn't the most attractive way to land a boyfriend, but she definitely scored points for persistence.

"Sorry, Amber." John finally managed to pry her fingers off his wrist. "I need to go."

She moved closer to John, backing him up into the alcove. "Where?"

John swallowed. "Anywhere but here?"

John and Amber as boyfriend and girlfriend. What a strange . . .

Olivia froze. John and Amber. This was an opportunity

Olivia would never have. Maybe if John just pretended to be interested, he could succeed where Olivia had failed, and find out exactly what happened between Amber and Ronny the night he was murdered? It was worth a shot.

"You two are so cute together," Olivia said.

"Aren't we?" Amber asked, glancing over her shoulder at Olivia.

Behind her, John mouthed, "What the fuck?"

"Totally," Olivia said.

Amber beamed at John, while Olivia shot him a hard, pointed look. "Trust me," she mouthed. "For Bree."

A wave of confusion passed over John's face, followed by a look of concentration as he glanced back and forth between Amber and Olivia. He sighed, then smiled down at Amber. "Can I walk you to drama class?"

THIRTEEN

OLIVIA FOLLOWED AMBER AND JOHN INTO THE THEATER, SMILing to herself as Amber chatted away about a variety of topics Olivia had never heard her discuss in the history of their friendship, including her love of musicians, her deep empathetic understanding of the artist's soul, and how she'd always believed she needed to be with someone who understood that part of her. John couldn't get a word in edgewise, which was probably a good thing, judging by the dazed look on his face. Amber didn't seem to notice. She was delighted by her escort, and her mood was positively giddy by the time they grabbed seats near Jezebel and Peanut.

"Quiet down," Mr. Cunningham said, the moment the bell faded into the echoes of the theater. "Unfortunately, I have some bad news. You all worked extremely hard to get *Twelfth Precinct* up and running in time for opening night, and I know we all hoped we'd be able to resume performances this week, so it is with great sadness that I must report the cancellation of the rest of the run."

"What!" Amber cried, her good mood evaporated. "You can't do that. My parents paid for this production."

"My hands are tied, Miss Stevens," Mr. Cunningham said, palms raised in surrender. "This decision was handed down from the archdiocese in light of what happened to poor Miss Mejia on opening night, and there is nothing I can do."

If this had been last year, even last semester, Olivia would have been devastated at having an entire production canceled after opening night. It was an actress's worst nightmare, the old Broadway joke about shows closing at intermission because the early reviews were so bad.

But now, with everything that had happened, Olivia was almost relieved.

"But do not despair," Mr. Cunningham continued with a smile. "I also have some good news! We have a guest professor auditing our class for the next two weeks." He gestured to the wings and Fitzgerald Conroy strode purposefully onto the stage.

Amber gasped. "No!"

"Yes!" Fitzgerald said, matching her tone to perfection. He wore a dark turtleneck under a piped black blazer, with his wavy white hair poofed up into a modern pompadour. "Ladies and gentlemen, I am at your disposal. I find myself with an unexpected gap in my schedule which I decided to spend here in California, enjoying the hospitality of my dear friend Reginald, who has indulged my curiosity by allowing me to come and observe his classes in person."

Mr. Cunningham beamed. "It is no trouble at all, Fitzgerald. I assure you."

"I thought I'd take the opportunity to get to know Reginald's *Twelfth Precinct* more intimately by working with the original cast," Fitzgerald continued. "Since we'll be mounting the production at Aspen this summer."

"Oh my God!" Olivia cried. "Congratulations!" She knew how desperately Mr. Cunningham had wanted this production to catch Fitzgerald Conroy's eye.

Mr. Cunningham dipped his head. "Thank you, Miss Hayes."

"Kiss-ass," Amber said under her breath.

Olivia almost countered with "Takes one to know one," but she managed to bite her tongue.

"I'm merely here to observe," Fitzgerald said. "I don't want to step on any toes."

"Step on any toes?" Mr. Cunningham said. "Nonsense. I wouldn't dream of depriving my class of your knowledge and experience. *Mi class es tu class.*"

Fitzgerald threw back his head and laughed heartily. "Excellent!" He clapped his hands and brought everyone to attention. "Let's get right to it, then." He pointed to Olivia. "Miss Hayes, will you join me onstage for a little exercise?"

Amber grunted in disgust and Olivia sensed an opportunity. "I'm not feeling very well today," she said. "Maybe Amber could take my place?"

"Very well," Fitzgerald said. "Amber?"

Amber rose regally to her feet, casting a glance at Olivia, her face a mix of skepticism and confusion, as if she thought that Olivia might be trying to trap her by giving up her one-on-one time with the famous director. Unable to figure it out, she scurried up to the stage and began a posture exercise with Fitzgerald.

Olivia watched but was only half paying attention. Being back in that space was still strange. It was like her second home, the place she felt most alive in the world, but after what happened to Margot, the theater felt dark and unfriendly, and it gave Olivia a jittery feeling in her stomach that she couldn't quite shake.

She leaned back in her chair and stared at the stage. Fitzgerald was poking and prodding Amber's body, pointing out the lazy, unengaged way with which she held herself. And Amber was clearly starting to get irritated by the constant criticism. Olivia smiled to herself. It was the same look Amber had on her face during the curtain call opening night, when Mr. Cunningham insisted that Olivia, not Amber, take the coveted final bow.

That's when Amber had stormed off the stage. Which might have given her just enough time to attack Margot.

Would it have, though? Barely. It made more sense that Margot was attacked during the finale, when the noise of the band would have obscured any offstage commotion.

Fitzgerald called the class up to the stage, but Olivia lingered in her seat, staring intently at the wings as she tried to picture who was where during the final dance number: the band, the crew, and the actors.

"I can't stop thinking about it either," someone said close behind her.

Olivia jumped, and swung around to find Logan. She'd been so lost in thought she'd never even heard him take the seat behind her.

"Margot?" she asked.

Logan winced as if in pain, and Olivia was instantly sorry she'd been so blunt with her question.

"Have you seen her at all?" she asked gently, hoping not to sound too anxious for information about her friend.

Logan blinked rapidly. "Family only in the ICU," he said.

"Oh."

"But I meant opening night," he continued quickly. "I can't stop thinking about what happened."

"Me neither."

Logan stared at the stage, his eyes unseeing. "Do you remember what the cops said? About how we should report anything suspicious we might've seen?"

Olivia tensed. Was it possible Logan had seen something? "Yeah," she prompted.

"I . . ." He paused, then shook his head. "It's nothing."

"What did you see?"

Logan's eyes flitted across her face, then back to the stage. "I don't know. It's kinda fuzzy. I told that police guy, but I don't think he cared. Still . . ." He paused again, searching for the words, then suddenly turned to her, animated and speaking quickly. "You know how when you can't get something out of your mind and you say to yourself, 'Dude, maybe you're crazy?' but somehow you just know you're not but still maybe?"

Olivia had no idea what he was talking about but nodded encouragingly.

"It's like that. I saw something. From the stage. And I can't shake the feeling that, I don't know, it's important."

Olivia swallowed, her throat constricted. This could be it. The break they'd been waiting for. "What did you see, Logan?"

Logan took a deep breath. "I know this is hella stupid, but there are these two dudes—brothers—who work at the place where I get my board waxed, and I'd been telling them about the play because they used to go to Bishop DuMaine. I invited them to see the show, and they laughed and said there was no way in hell they'd ever be caught dead on this campus."

Olivia's hands were tingling. Brothers who worked at a surf shop and used to go to Bishop DuMaine? It couldn't be. "Maxwell and Maven Gertler?"

Logan's eyes grew wide. "You know them?"

Olivia shook her head. "Not really."

Logan looked disappointed. "Oh. Well, anyway, I guess there was some trouble when they were at school here, and they got kicked out. Or arrested. I forget which."

Trouble was an understatement. DGM had busted the Gertlers for selling topless photos of their classmates to a Russian porn site. After DGM outed their anonymous username, they'd spent six months in a rehabilitation camp in lieu of juvie, and their parents had settled out of court when they were sued by the victims' parents. It had been the ugliest DGM fallout.

Until Ronny turned up dead.

"I kind of remember that," Olivia lied.

"Yeah, well, after laughing in my face, they were the last people I expected to see in the theater opening night."

Olivia blinked. Could former DGM targets have really been at the show that night? "Are you sure?"

"Totally. I saw them hurrying down the aisle during the finale."

"And Sergeant Callahan didn't take you seriously?" Olivia couldn't believe what she was hearing. Wouldn't he want to follow up every possible lead in this case?

"Not really," Logan said. "Guy's kind of a prick. He said I probably couldn't see clearly from the stage with all those lights in my eyes."

"But you can see the first eight rows perfectly," Olivia said. She knew that theater better than anyone, its sight lines and its blind spots. If the Gertlers had been in the first few rows, or leaving the theater after exiting through the stage door, Logan could easily have spotted them.

If only there was some way to see what was happening on stage during the finale. Like a photo or a video . . .

Olivia caught her breath.

"What's wrong?" Logan asked.

"The video," she said, her voice trembling. "The opening-night recording. Mr. Cunningham has every single opening performance videotaped so we can watch them later." Why hadn't she thought of that before? If she could get her hands on the recording, she might be able to see who had attacked Margot.

"Come on." Olivia ran up the aisle to the back row, where Mr. Cunningham sat in the first seat by himself, flipping through pages on his ever-present clipboard. "Mr. Cunningham!"

"Miss Hayes. Mr. Blaine. Is everything all right?"

"Fine," she said, her voice breathless with excitement. "We were just wondering about the recording of opening night."

"The video recording?" he asked, his British accent sounding more prim and proper than ever.

Olivia nodded eagerly. "I'd love to see, er, how the finale turned out with all that choreography."

Mr. Cunningham sighed, his eyes rolling back in his head in ecstasy. "Ah, yes. It was a glorious sight. One which we absolutely must watch in class."

"When?" Logan asked.

"Alas," Mr. Cunningham sighed, "I know not. The police have confiscated the camera, and though they've promised to give it back to me in due course, as of yet, I've had no word."

Dammit. She had to get her hands on that recording.

"Mr. Cunningham," she began, laying on her sweetest voice and widening her eyes. "Do you think you could call Sergeant Callahan and ask when it might—"

"Miss Hayes! There you are."

Olivia turned and saw Fitzgerald descending the steps stage right. Behind him, the entire class was walking around—chests raised, arms in a ballet first position—trying not to bump into one another. Dammit. She hadn't been paying attention and now Fitzgerald was going to think she was a diva.

"I'm so sorry, Mr. Conroy," Olivia said, hurrying toward him. "I was asking Mr. Cunningham about the video of opening night and I didn't hear your instructions."

Fitzgerald waved his hand dismissively. "No matter. This isn't really an exercise you need."

Olivia smiled at the compliment, proud that he'd noticed her command of the stage.

"Mr. Blaine, however . . ." Fitzgerald jutted his thumb toward the stage.

"Right," Logan said. "Sorry." He cast a backward glance at Olivia as he scurried up the steps.

"I was hoping I could speak with you after school today," Fitzgerald continued, as soon as Logan was out of earshot. "To discuss the details of your internship this summer?"

Olivia froze, all thoughts of the Gertlers momentarily forgotten. Fitzgerald had mentioned the internship on opening night. He came up onstage during the final bows and kissed her hand, then said, "You'd make an excellent addition to our company at Aspen." But she hadn't had any sort of formal offer. This was it. The beginning of her professional career. Working with a director of Fitzgerald Conroy's caliber would put her on the map in theatrical circles, not to mention the lifetime's worth of stage experience she'd learn from him. For the first time in days, she forgot about the killer she was hunting, and thought only of herself.

"Of course," Olivia said.

"Meet here in the theater?"

Olivia nodded eagerly.

Fitzgerald winked at her as he turned back to the stage. "I shall see you then."

FOURTEEN

BREE WAITED A FEW HOURS BEFORE SHE APPROACHED HER mom. She'd been rehearsing the speech in her head since Sergeant Callahan left: *It's Dad's fault we're both trapped here; it's Dad's rules that are keeping us cut off from everyone. Wouldn't it be an epic "fuck you" to Daddy if you let me have my phone back?*

She needed to get in touch with DGM. It was a matter of life and death.

Bree's mom was in the library, manhandling a cocktail shaker in an earsplitting cacophony of ice and metal like she was the lead maracas player at the Copacabana. She watched silently as her mom cracked open the shaker and poured a long stream of clear liquid into a martini glass. She took a quick sip, wrinkled her nose, and then added two olives from a crystal bowl on the tray. The second sip proved more satisfactory, and her mom closed her eyes, inhaling deeply as the liquor began to take effect.

After a few seconds, she seemed to notice that Bree had entered the room. "Oh," she said. "You frightened me."

"Sorry."

She stared at her daughter for a moment, as if unsure how to proceed, then took a seat in a wing-backed leather chair near the bay window and crossed her legs, ready for an audience.

"So," her mom said, balancing the martini glass on her knee. "Are you, um, having fun?"

Fun? Bree was a prisoner in her own house, guarded by a semiliterate muscleman who referred to himself in the third person. It was like San Quentin with a more comfortable bed and better food.

"Sure," she said instead, trying to sound upbeat. She needed her mom in a good mood.

"I know being stuck in the house with Olaf and me isn't your idea of a summer in the Hamptons . . . ," her mom began, punctuated by a dainty sip of her cocktail.

Bree had never experienced a summer in the Hamptons, but she took her mom's word for it.

"But this is only temporary," her mom continued. "Soon we'll both be back where we belong."

"Back where we belong?" Bree blurted out. *What are you doing? Don't antagonize her.* But she couldn't help it. "Don't you belong here? With your family?"

Her mom looked genuinely taken aback. "I have family in France, too."

"Really?" Bree planted her hands on her hips. "Are you a bigamist now? Do I have more siblings I don't know about?"

Her mom waved her hand dismissively. "Don't be ridiculous. I mean—"

But Bree didn't wait to listen. "Fuck you, Mom. You hear

me? Fuck you. Go back to your beach and your massages and your cabana boys. I don't want you and I don't need you."

She didn't care about her phone or DGM or Christopher Beeman. As she stormed out of the room, hot tears began to pour down her face, and all she felt was anger.

Olivia headed to Mr. Cunningham's office after class. She couldn't wait to get her hands on the opening-night video of *Twelfth Precinct*, and hoped she could convince her drama teacher to ask the police for a copy of it. They'd been lulled into a sense of safety while the killer had been planning something even more sinister. Maybe the next attack would be on her home. Or Margot in the hospital. She couldn't waste a single moment. That video might hold the key to the entire mystery.

She rounded the corner, and collided with someone coming out of his office.

"Peanut!" Olivia cried.

Peanut jumped and let out a sound somewhere between a squeak and a gasp, then seemed to choke on her own saliva and doubled over into a coughing fit.

Olivia slipped her arm through Peanut's. "Are you okay?"

"Fine," Peanut sputtered, as she straightened up, face still flushed pink from coughing.

"I wanted to talk to Mr. Cunningham," Olivia said.

"He's not here," she said quickly.

"Then what were you doing in his office?"

"Nothing!" Peanut squeaked.

Olivia arched an eyebrow. "You sure about that?"

Peanut took a deep breath, then the words tumbled out of her mouth, one on top of another. "Sorry. I, um, guess I'm not feeling very well. My mom has me on a cleanse and the lack of calories is making me a little cray. She thinks the stress of what's been happening at school has knocked my third and eighth chakras out of whack, so I need to purge the toxins from my blood."

Olivia had always been skeptical of Mrs. Dumbrowski's alternative medical practices, which seemed only slightly more scientific than bloodletting and leeches. "Does that work?"

"Dunno, but if I lose some weight in the process, it's a bonus." She shook her arm free of Olivia's grasp. "So I have to go. See you tomorrow!"

Olivia stared after Peanut as she practically raced down the hallway. Well, that was more like the Peanut she knew and loved—spacey and confused.

With a quick laugh, she turned toward the theater, hoping Mr. Cunningham would be there. Instead, she saw John storming down the hall toward her.

"You want to explain to me," he said through clenched teeth, "why you threw me at Amber?"

Olivia smirked, remembering the look on John's face as Amber led him to drama class. "She's single, you're single. What's to explain?"

John's face hardened. "I am *not* single."

Olivia remembered Bree, sacrificing herself for their safety, and felt instantly guilty. "How is she?"

"Don't know," John said. "I only saw her for like twenty

seconds before a gorilla named Olaf dragged her back inside the house."

"The Deringers have a gorilla?" She knew they were rich, but that seemed excessive.

John blinked. "No."

"Oh." What was he talking about? Had John been hitting the pipe with Shane White and his burner friends?

"Look," John said. "Can you just tell me what the hell is going on? I'm pretty sure Amber thinks we're dating now. She even forced me to give her my cell number."

Olivia sighed. Clearly, he wasn't just going to play along without asking questions like she'd hoped. "Fine. But you have to do something first."

He looked at her sidelong. "You're not going to hit on me too, are you?"

Ew. "No." Then with a quick exhale, Olivia thrust her hand forward. "Grab my wrist and repeat after me."

"Am I going to have to give up my firstborn?"

She so didn't have time for this. "Just do it!"

Without another word, John grasped Olivia's right hand with his left, and then she did the same, creating a two-person version of the DGM square.

"*I, Olivia Hayes, do solemnly swear, no secrets—ever—shall leave this square.*" She squeezed his wrist. "Your turn."

John grinned wickedly. "Do you guys seriously do this?"

"It looks cooler when there are four of us," Olivia said, narrowing her eyes.

"I believe you," he said. "Just having a hard time picturing Bree holding hands."

The fifth-period warning bell rang. "Hurry up!"

"Sorry." John cleared his throat. "*I, John Baggott, do solemnly swear . . .*" He paused. "Um, what was next?"

"*No secrets—ever—shall leave this square.*"

"*No secrets—ever—shall leave this square,*" he repeated. "Happy?"

"Thrilled." She dropped his hand and took a step closer. "Amber and Rex were with Ronny the night he died."

"*What?*"

Olivia pressed her finger to her lips. "Shh!"

"Right." John shook his head, as if dumbfounded by the news. "Why haven't you gone to the police?"

"Um . . ." That was a longer story than Olivia was prepared to explain. "We don't have any proof," she said instead, "that Amber and Rex were involved in his death. We don't even know for sure what they were doing with him that night. Just a guess."

John inhaled deeply. "Which is where I come in."

"Exactly." Thank God John was on the ball. The less she had to explain, the better. "I'm pretty sure they were trying to bribe Ronny with one of Amber's dad's fancy Rolexes. If we can find out where the watch is now, we might have the evidence we need to prove Bree's innocence."

"So you think if I make goo-goo eyes at Amber, she'll spill her guts to me?"

It sounded so much lamer when he said it. "I'm hoping."

"I'll do it. But only because this is going to help Bree." He began to walk away, then paused and turned back. "Speaking of, any message you want to send to her? They've confiscated her cell phone and I'm guessing she doesn't have internet at the moment."

Olivia caught her breath. "You're going to see her?"

"That's the plan."

"How are you going to get past the gorilla?"

John patted his backpack. "You leave that to me."

As Olivia grabbed a piece of paper she wondered what, exactly, John had in his bag. Bananas? Tranquilizers?

She folded it in thirds, and handed it to him. "Don't read it."

"I won't." John raised an eyebrow. "Will you be expecting a response?" he asked formally.

Olivia sighed. "I certainly hope so."

FIFTEEN

BREE WASN'T SURE HOW LONG SHE'D BEEN CRYING. HER chest had continued to heave for what felt like forever as the uncontrollable sobs overwhelmed her.

If her mom didn't want a daughter, then Bree didn't want a mom.

Only she did. Desperately.

In the back of her mind, Bree had always blamed her dad for her mom's prolonged absence. It wasn't exactly a secret that he was a cold, determined man, and Bree could count on one hand the number of times he'd actually hugged her with any real affection. It made sense that her mom would want to leave, to get as far away from him as possible.

But what didn't make sense, what Bree couldn't ignore anymore, was that she'd leave her youngest child behind to fend for herself.

Tap. Tap tap tap.

Bree hastily wiped the tears from her cheeks and rushed across her room.

"John!" She threw open the window, never so happy to see anyone in her life. "What are you doing here?"

"I'm Luke Skywalker," John said. "And I'm here to rescue you."

"Huh?"

John smiled. "I think Leia's line is actually 'You're who?' but I'll take that in a pinch."

Bree's tears began to flow afresh. She couldn't help it. All the pain and sadness of the last few days, and here was her best friend who, with one quote from *Star Wars*, reminded her that someone cared.

John's smirk vanished. "Are you okay?"

"Yeah," Bree sniffled. "I'm just happy to see you."

"Aha!" John said. He dropped his backpack into the gravel and unzipped it. "Well, if the mere sight of me brings you to tears, maybe I'd better not show you this." With a flamboyant magician's flourish, John yanked what appeared to be a tangled mass of rope out of his bag.

"What is that?"

"Stand back," John said. "And I'll show you."

Bree stepped away from the window. She heard John grunt, and then there was a thud, as if something soft had hit the side of the house.

"Dammit," John said, his voice muffled.

Another grunt, and another thud. This time, Bree could hear him swearing under his breath.

"Would it help if I got out and pushed?" Bree said, smiling at her own *Star Wars* quote.

John's voice drifted up through the window with the expected response. "It might."

A third grunt, and this time the end of a rope soared through the window. Bree grabbed it before it slipped back down.

"Pull it up!" John instructed.

Hand over hand, Bree drew the rope up the side of her house. It was heavier than she thought it would be, and she had to brace herself against the wall to haul it in. After ten feet, two metal hooks appeared over the windowsill, and suddenly Bree realized what John had brought.

She secured the hooks on the sill and stuck her head out the window. Below her, a rope ladder descended to the gravel path.

"Nice thinking," she said, impressed.

John looped his backpack over his shoulders and grasped the bottom rungs. "Okay, wish me luck."

A minute later, John's pale arm popped over the windowsill, and with a deep groan, he hauled himself onto Bree's bedroom floor.

Bree stood dumbstruck as John scrambled to his feet and brushed dirt from his jeans and black button-down shirt. He smiled at her sheepishly, and all the awkwardness of a thousand unsaid emotions descended upon them. Bree wasn't sure if she wanted to joke with John as they usually did, or throw her arms around his neck and kiss him.

"I . . . I can't believe you're here," she said at last.

John approached her slowly, calmly, as if she were a skittish kitten, and reached out his hand to cup her face. He brushed away a lingering tear with his thumb, which was rough and calloused from years of playing bass. She closed her eyes and inhaled deeply, noting the spicy mix of aftershave and perspiration from scaling the outside of her house.

Then she felt the heat of his breath close to her face and her heart stopped. She remembered the first time he'd almost kissed her. She hadn't realized how much she'd wanted him to, but now, after all they'd been through, after the *L* word had been spoken, she wanted to feel his lips against her own more than ever.

Bree raised her chin, angling her face toward him. "Please," she whispered, unaware the word had escaped her mouth until she heard it.

She felt his fingers creep around to the back of her head, and then his lips were pressed against hers. She kissed him back hungrily, her hands firmly planted on his chest, and then she felt his arm around her back, pulling her closer to him.

John moaned and gripped the back of her dress with both hands, twisting the fabric into bunches. Before Bree even knew what she was doing, she had unbuttoned John's shirt, peeled it off him, and was kissing the muscular lines of his chest.

"Bree," John said, his voice thick and throaty.

She heard it through a haze, her mind far away. "Yeah?"

He placed his hands on either side of her face and looked directly into her eyes. "Are you okay with this? I mean, you've been through a lot and I don't want you to think I came here just to . . ." His voice trailed off and she watched a flush of pink wash over him.

Could he be any more adorable? "John, I love you."

"I love you, too."

Her heart pounded in her chest. "Then there's your answer."

SIXTEEN

FITZGERALD WAS SITTING IN THE FRONT ROW OF THE HOUSE reading an issue of *American Theatre* magazine when Olivia arrived after school.

"Miss Hayes!" he exclaimed as she approached, tossing the magazine aside and leaping to his feet. "I'll be delighted to have you at Aspen this summer."

Olivia tried to keep her mounting excitement under control. "Thank you, Mr. Conroy."

"It will be a grueling six weeks," he said, tilting his head toward her, "full of laughter and tears and misery and elation. And you won't get any special treatment as a high school student."

Olivia smiled. "I don't expect any."

"And it will be lonely," he said.

"Lonely?"

"Away from your friends." Fitzgerald glanced at the floor. "And your mother."

"Lonely" wasn't the word Olivia would have chosen. More

like "vacation." She opened her mouth to reassure him that she'd be fine, when he interrupted her.

"How are things at home, if I may ask?"

"Fine." How are things at home? That sounded like something a guidance counselor would ask.

"And your mother? How is she?"

"She's fine too."

"Such an odd coincidence. I once directed your mother onstage, and now I'll direct you." He laughed nervously, then glanced at his watch. "Shall I drive you home?"

"Um, I thought we were going to discuss my internship?"

Fitzgerald waved his hand dismissively. "Of course, of course. In the car, my dear." Then he linked his arm through hers and hustled her out to the parking lot.

They pulled onto DuMaine Drive in silence, Olivia's address programmed into the GPS in Fitzgerald's rental. After two blocks, Fitzgerald cleared his throat and glanced at Olivia sidelong. "Do you think your mother will be home?"

Olivia tensed. Was he going to demand some kind of sexual payback for offering her the internship at Aspen? He knew she was only sixteen, right?

She clutched her tote bag to her chest and slowly, silently, reached her hand into its depths until her fingers closed around her house keys. When they got to her building, she'd dash out of the car and sprint up the stairs to her apartment. She could be inside with the door locked before he even knew what was happening.

"She's *always* there when I get home from school," Olivia

bluffed. There was probably a fifty-fifty chance her mom hadn't left for work yet.

She eyed Fitzgerald, expecting his face to fall, but instead, his features lit up. "I'd love to see her again." His eyes sparkled, and for an instant, Fitzgerald looked positively boyish. She'd seen that look on his face once before, in her dressing room before the opening curtain for *Twelfth Precinct*, when he ran into his former protégé June Hayes.

A smile spread across Olivia's face as they pulled up in front of her building. It wasn't *her* Fitzgerald wanted to spend time with. It was her mother.

"You should come up and say hello," she said, noticing her mom's car still in the carport. Cinderella-type fantasies of her mom rescued from poverty by the hottest director on Broadway played out before her eyes. "My mom talks about you all the time. The *Twelfth Night* you did together is still her favorite production ever."

Fitzgerald smiled broadly. "Is it?"

"Totally." *Come on, take the bait.* "And she was just saying yesterday that she hoped she'd see you again soon," she lied.

He pulled the parking brake and cut the engine. "In that case, I'd love to say hello."

Olivia hurried up the stairs ahead of Fitzgerald. She prayed her mom was actually up and ready for work as opposed to hibernating in the daybed after calling in "sick" for her shift. As she burst through the door, she heaved a sigh of relief. The sheets on the daybed were neat and tidy, her mom's purse and leather jacket laid across the bedspread, all ready for work.

Game on.

"Mom?" she cried. "Mom, someone's here to see you."

"What?" her mom called from the bathroom.

Olivia turned back to Fitzgerald, who tentatively entered the living room.

"She'll be right out," she said with a nervous laugh.

Fitzgerald nodded. His eyes swept the small interior of their apartment, resting on the peeling paint near the kitchen ceiling, the stained carpet, and the cramped quarters of the living room where Olivia's mom slept. There was no judgment on his face, only curiosity.

Then curiosity turned to surprise, and Olivia noticed that his gaze lingered on the coffee table. There, amid a haphazard pile of magazines and remote controls, stood an assortment of prescription pill bottles.

Olivia was shocked. She knew her mom was on antidepressants, and had been prescribed anti-anxiety meds to take as needed for the occasional panic attack, but there had to be at least a half-dozen different bottles on the table—three times the normal collection—all neatly labeled from the pharmacy.

"We're, um, not used to company," Olivia said, fumbling for a way to draw Fitzgerald's attention away from the pharmaceutical display.

"Quite all right, my dear." He smiled warmly. "It's an artist's life."

"Is someone with you?" her mom yelled. The bathroom door opened and her mom walked into the living room, fastening the belt on her skintight black jeans. "If it's Anthony, tell him I'll have the rest of the rent by—"

"Hello, June."

Olivia's mom froze at the sound of Fitzgerald's voice, and Olivia was astonished to see the color drain out of her lovely face.

"Fitz," she said, her voice barely above a whisper.

"How are you?"

"I'm well." She swallowed slowly. "And you?"

Fitzgerald smiled. "Also well."

They stood in silence, gazing at each other. Olivia barely knew Fitzgerald Conroy, but she recognized the look in his eyes—he had a crush on her mom.

Olivia half-expected them to fly into each other's arms and confess their decades-long love for each other. Then he'd carry Olivia's mom out of the apartment and into his luxury rental car like Richard Gere at the end of almost every Richard Gere movie.

So she was shocked when her mom snatched her purse and jacket from the daybed, and hurried past Fitzgerald to the door.

"Yes," her mom said, clearly flustered. "Well, I'm off to work and I'm sure you have other places to be. So nice of you to stop by." She held the door open for him, steadfastly refusing to look Fitzgerald in the eyes.

"Oh!" he said, looking as if she'd just slapped him across the face. "Yes, of course. So sorry to intrude." He was out the door and down the stairs before Olivia could protest.

"What was that all about?" Olivia said, as soon as her mom closed the door.

Instead of apologizing, her mom whirled on her. "Don't you *ever* bring that man to this house again. Do you hear me?"

"Why?"

"Do you hear me?" her mom repeated through clenched teeth.

There was something wild in her mom's eyes; it wasn't anger or fear, but a mix of the two that seemed to ignite from nothing.

"Are you okay?" Olivia asked.

"Of course I am," her mom snapped. "Why wouldn't I be?"

"It's just . . ." Olivia glanced at the pill bottles on the table. "Are those new prescriptions from Dr. Kearns?"

Her mom shrugged. "How am I supposed to know? She phones them in, I pick them up." She took a step closer to her daughter and gripped Olivia by the arm. "You didn't answer me. Promise me you'll never bring Fitzgerald Conroy to this house again."

Olivia winced as her mom's fingers dug into her flesh. "Fine. But why not?"

Instead of offering an explanation, her mom spun around and stormed out of the apartment, slamming the door behind her.

SEVENTEEN

STILL SWEATY FROM VOLLEYBALL PRACTICE, KITTY HURRIED UP the steps to the private gym. She taught volleyball lessons there every summer, and in addition to a small stipend, she received an annual pass to use the facilities. Which was unnecessary most of the time, considering that Bishop DuMaine had state-of-the-art weight and cardio equipment on campus, but today it was going to come in particularly handy. Last summer, Kitty had noticed an old classmate working out every evening around five o'clock. It was someone Kitty knew only too well: DGM target number one, Wendy Marshall.

If truth be told, Kitty had a soft spot for Wendy. Her label-shaming, queen-bee fiefdom at Bishop DuMaine had inspired Kitty to form DGM freshman year, and though the plan against Wendy wasn't one of their finest, it still gave Kitty a special thrill when she thought about it. The first time is always the sweetest.

It had been a simple mission, and kind of stupid when she thought about it, but DGM hadn't fine-tuned their roles yet, and hacking into the camera feed from Wendy's online LARPing group was the best they could do. But the image of Wendy dressed as a steampunk cowgirl for online sessions with her group was amazing. Again, Kitty admired the way Wendy dove into her role with 100 percent commitment, and under different circumstances, she felt as if she and Wendy could have been friends. After all, Kitty had done her fair share of dressing up in Hogwarts robes, running around straddling a broom as she pretended to be the Ravenclaw Seeker. But after terrorizing the female population of Bishop DuMaine for nondesigner clothing labels and questionable fashion choices, Kitty was seriously pissed off by Wendy's hypocrisy.

The printouts of Wendy in a homemade costume, posing in character, ended her tenure as queen bee once and for all.

Kitty flashed her membership card and climbed the stairs to the cardio room. One sweep told her she was in luck: Wendy Marshall was going to town on an elliptical.

Watching the petite brunette work out like she was training for a marathon, Kitty found it difficult to believe her capable of murder, arson, or the half-dozen other crimes associated with their suspect. Then again, maybe that was the key to her success—underestimation.

Wendy eyed Kitty as she climbed onto an adjacent machine, but didn't break stride. Kitty stood there for a moment—shoes planted in the footplates, fingers gripping handles—and stared at the console. She'd never actually worked out on a cardio machine other than a treadmill, which seemed so much more straightforward than this medieval torture device. Set speed, start running. But what were all these buttons? Freestyle, CardioBurn, FatBurn.

"Push the green one," Wendy said, panting.

"Oh." Kitty found the green button marked "QuickStart" and the console lit up. "Thanks."

"No problem."

Okay, conversation had been broached. Now what the hell was Kitty supposed to say?

"Aren't you Wendy Marshall?" she blurted out, as if she was a famous celebrity instead of a disgraced former mean girl.

Wendy slowed her pace. "Yeah . . . ," she said skeptically.

"You went to Bishop DuMaine, right?" *Wow, was that the best you could come up with, Kitty?*

Wendy abruptly stopped her elliptical. "I did," she said sharply. "And before you crack a joke, yes, I still LARP with the Frontier League of Peculiar Individuals."

"I wasn't—"

"And I'm proud of it. In fact, I've been selling my Frontier League fanfic for the last year. Over one hundred thousand downloads. Do you know how much money I've made?"

"Um . . ."

"Ninety-nine cents each. You do the math." Wendy whipped her towel off the console and threw it over her shoulder. "So before you and the rest of those assholes at Bishop DuMaine start tossing my name around as the butt of your jokes again, think about that and suck it."

And without another word, Wendy flounced out of the gym.

An electronic bell sounded as soon as Olivia pushed open the door of Aquanautics, the surf and water-sports store where Maxwell and Maven Gertler had found gainful employment after their "rehabilitation."

The shop was small, but jam-packed with merchandise. Racks of shirts, shorts, and hoodies in both men's and women's varieties ran down the center of the room, while a large selection of shoes were displayed on the far wall. On the opposite side of the store, wet suits in sizes from toddler to adult hung from the ceiling like meat in a freezer, and TV monitors were set up throughout, displaying surf competitions at nearby Mavericks. Above her head, every inch of ceiling space was covered with surf and body boards suspended from the rafters, and a range of kayaks was tilted against the checkout desk.

The effect was homey, the store was abnormally warm, and combined with the pungent aroma of coconut and beeswax, and the pumped-in sound track of ocean waves, it gave the impression that the beach was right outside the door.

Olivia eyed the cash register at the back of the store. It was empty, which made her nervous. She would have been much more comfortable if there had been other customers around. What if the Gertlers were the killers? And here she was alone and outnumbered?

Oh, hell no. Olivia had turned and was hurrying back toward the door when she heard someone's voice nearby.

"Can I help you?"

Olivia recognized the deep, gravelly voice of one of the Gertler twins right away.

Okay, fine. She could do this. She turned to the nearest rack of Hawaiian shirts.

"I'm looking for a birthday gift for my boyfriend," she said, making sure she had an unobstructed path to the exit, just in case. "And I'm not sure what to get him."

Maxwell or Maven, whichever one it was, sighed as if helping a customer was the last thing he wanted to do, and ambled over. "Is he a surfer, a skater, or . . ." His voice trailed off. "Olivia?"

She spun toward him, allowing her face to reflect confusion at first, then morph into recognition and surprise. "Maxwell?"

Maxwell beamed at her. "You're like the only one who can tell us apart." He reached out and gave her a hug, squeezing her tightly and allowing his hands to roam up and down her back in an almost inappropriate kind of way. "It is so good to see you."

Olivia wiggled free, straightening her dress in the process. "So how are you?"

"Good," Maxwell said, gazing around the store. "You know. It was kinda rough after the arrest and all. But our cousin owns this place and he basically lets us run it. Pretty cool."

"It's awesome," Olivia said, trying to sound suitably impressed.

"But we're still in the game," he said slowly, as if speaking in code.

"The game?" What was he talking about: Murder? Arson? Assault and battery?

"Yep. We've got our own studio now." Maxwell stepped back and steadied his chin between his thumb and forefinger, apprais-ing her body from head to toe. "How old are you?"

Ew? "Sixteen."

A sly smile crept up the right side of Maxwell's face as he

slid closer to her and dropped his voice. "Have you ever thought about modeling?"

Really? He was propositioning her? Desperate to change the subject, Olivia turned her attention back to the shirts. "I wonder if my boyfriend might like—"

Maxwell traced Olivia's bare arm with his finger, and whispered in her ear. "You know, there's a huge market for sexy photos of a girl like you. Europe, Asia. No one would ever know. . . ."

As much as she wanted to knee Maxwell in the crotch and make a run for it, Olivia was there for a reason. She needed to bring the conversation back to the school play.

"Funny I should run into you here," she began, fluttering her eyelashes. "I was just talking to Amber Stevens today, and she said she thought she saw you and your brother at the opening of the school play last week."

Maxwell snorted. "At Bishop DuMaine? I doubt it. We're never setting foot back in that shithole."

"Are you sure?" Olivia continued. "She seemed pretty positive that it was—"

"He said we weren't there!"

Olivia spun around. Maven Gertler stood in the back of the store, arms folded across his chest. Where did he come from?

Involuntarily, Olivia backed toward the door. "Oh, sorry!" she said. "Amber must have been wrong."

"She is," Maxwell said. His congenial attitude of ten seconds ago had completely vanished. Instead his face was sharp and tense, his eyes narrowed. "We wouldn't violate the terms of our parole by going anywhere *near* a school, would we, Mave?"

Maven shook his head. "Absolutely not."

So they weren't allowed near a school? Based on her experiences in the last five minutes she understood why, but that did give them somewhat of an alibi.

"And besides," Maxwell added, "it's kinda hard to see with all those stage lights in your face, isn't it?"

Olivia froze. Stage lights? How did they know that Amber was *in* the play?

Suddenly, she was desperate to get out of there.

"Oh my God!" she cried, looking at her wrist that was conspicuously devoid of a watch. "Look at the time! I'm going to miss my bus."

She was out the door and down the street as fast as her heels could carry her.

EIGHTEEN

BREE LAY ON HER SIDE. JOHN'S ARM WAS DRAPED AROUND her bare stomach, pulling her tightly to him as he spooned behind her. Never in her life had she felt so protected and loved.

She sighed deeply, snuggling back into his arms.

"You okay?" he asked.

Bree laughed. "That's like the millionth time you've asked me in the last hour."

"I know, it's just . . ." He stroked her arm with his fingertips and her skin prickled with excitement. "You've got a lot going on."

Bree burst out laughing. She couldn't help it. It was the understatement of the century.

John rolled his eyes. "Why is this funny?"

"Sorry," she said, through her heaves. "But you have to appreciate the humor." She rolled over onto her back and counted on her fingers. "I'm under house arrest, suspected of murder, I'm in bed with my best friend, and someone might have tried to run me off the road yesterday morning. 'A lot going on' is an understatement."

John tensed. "Someone tried to run you off the road?"

"I'm sure it's nothing," Bree said, instantly regretting she'd let that nugget slip. She didn't want John any more involved than he already was.

"Don't downplay this," he scolded.

"'Don't downplay this,'" Bree mocked.

John glared at her for a moment, then a smile spread across his face and he pounced on her, kissing her full on the mouth. They tumbled over each other across the bedsheets, Bree's legs wrapped tightly around John's torso. Then she flipped him over and straddled him. "I win," she said.

John reached up and slid his hands down either side of her body. "No," he said softly. "I win."

She bent down to kiss him, when a cell phone dinged. "Who's texting you?" she said, arching an eyebrow. "Your other girlfriend?"

"You don't know the half of it." John shifted Bree off him. "Amber Stevens has decided I'm her new conquest."

"I'm sorry. I must have heard you wrong." This was worse than a hundred screaming girls throwing themselves at John onstage. "Did you say Amber Stevens covets your bod?"

"It gets better," he added, groping around on the floor for his jeans. "I'm supposed to play along."

Now it was Bree's turn to be serious. "Excuse me?"

"I know, I know. Olivia asked me to. Something about

Amber being with Ronny the night he died."

Bree gasped. "She told you that?" Olivia wasn't supposed to break the code. Damn, had everyone lost their minds?

John sat straight up, jeans in hand, and thrust his free hand forward. "*I, John Baggott, do solemnly swear, no secrets—ever—shall leave this square.*"

Bree couldn't believe what she was hearing. "They swore you in?"

"Yeah," John said. "Well, Olivia did. Oh!" He smacked himself in the forehead with his palm. "I'm an idiot. I almost forgot. She wanted me to give you a message."

Finally! She'd had zero news from DGM about what was going on. Had the police followed their link and investigated Christopher? Did they have proof that he was the killer?

John pulled a folded-up piece of paper from his pocket and handed it to Bree. She opened it hungrily, expecting some news of the police investigation and Christopher Beeman's imminent arrest, but what she read on the page sucked the breath right out of her.

CB committed suicide last year. Killer burned down the warehouse. Be careful.

Bree felt as if she'd been punched in the chest. Her lungs froze up, and a flash of blackness momentarily blinded her. Christopher Beeman was dead?

The words swam on the page, and Bree had to brace herself against the pillows. Everything around her faded to nothingness at the realization that her old friend had killed himself. And somehow, she knew it was partly her fault.

The guilt was paralyzing, as were the implications for DGM. If Christopher had been dead for a year, then all this time the taunting, the threatening, the framing them for murder—it had been someone else entirely. She shook her head, trying to grasp the concept. Christopher Beeman was innocent.

"Yeah, it's Amber," John said, reading through his text. "She's asking me to dinner tonight. Told her I have band practice." He looked up at Bree, smiling sheepishly. "You know I'm not into her, right?"

"Right," Bree forced herself to say.

"Bree, are you okay?"

She swallowed. "Yeah, just . . . the note from Olivia. It's not what I was hoping to hear."

"Oh." He pulled his jeans on and whisked his shirt off the floor. "I think she's expecting a response."

A response? How about "We are so screwed!" or "What the fuck do we do now?" That was pretty much all her brain could process at the moment.

Instead, Bree crumpled up the note and tossed it into the garbage bin. "Tell her I don't know what to do next." It was the truth, plain and simple. "And I'm praying to God that they do."

Kitty had been apprehensive about offering up her house for the next DGM meeting, especially after what had happened at the warehouse, but she didn't have much of a choice. They had to continue to meet, to share the information, if any, they'd managed to dig up, and to try and piece the puzzle together before it was too late. She figured the best option would be to move all future meetings around, never hitting the same location twice so the killer wouldn't have a chance to set a trap for them.

But the moment Kitty arrived home from the gym, she regretted her decision. Parked in front of her house was a police cruiser.

She panicked as she pulled the car into the drive. Had the police found her fingerprints in the warehouse? Had they traced the fire to her? Had they figured out her involvement with DGM? Should she throw the car in reverse and get out of there before anyone knew she'd gotten home?

In the midst of her fight-or-flight decision, the side door flew open and Sophia and Lydia tumbled out of the house.

"You're home!" Sophia cried, racing up to the car. "There's a cop in our living room."

"Isn't that awesome?" Lydia said, her hands clasped together.

Kitty opened the door and climbed out of the car, trying to act as calm and uninterested as possible. "Why are the police here?"

"The fire at Uncle Jer's warehouse," Lydia said. Her eyes were wide with excitement. "They're questioning Mom about it."

"Why would they question Mom?" Her mom worked part time at her brother-in-law's warehouse, helping out with the accounting, but her mom wasn't even there last night. How could she have any information the police would need?

"Do you think they'll arrest Mom?" Sophia asked with a disturbing amount of glee.

"Of course not," Kitty snapped.

"But then we could be fugitives," she continued. "On the run from the law."

"And we'd have to change our names," Lydia said, instantly entranced with the new role-playing game.

"And cut our hair."

"And move to New Mexico."

Normally, Kitty loved her sisters' flights of imagination, but this fantasy hit a little too close to home. "Go inside," she said, grabbing her duffel bag from the backseat. "And leave Mom alone."

But instead of scampering into the house, the girls dashed past Kitty down the driveway. "We're going to Yolanda's to tell her the news," Lydia called out.

Great.

Part of Kitty wanted to join her sisters, to be anywhere else in the world rather than in her house with a member of Menlo Park's finest. But her best course of action was to play it cool, so she shouldered her bag and strolled leisurely into the house.

"Mom?" she said, her voice calm but with a hint of concern. "I saw Sophia and Lydia out front. Is everything okay?"

"Hello, Kitty," said a familiar voice as she rounded the corner into the living room. Kitty felt her hands go clammy. Sergeant Callahan was standing before the fireplace, notebook in hand. "Nice to see you again."

Nice to see me again? Sergeant Callahan had only spoken with her once before, when the police executed a mass interrogation of students after Ronny DeStefano's murder. He must have interviewed dozens of students that day. Why did he remember her?

"Um, yeah," she mumbled. "You too."

"I'm just asking your mom some routine questions about the fire at your uncle's warehouse last night."

"Oh," Kitty said. She glanced at her mom, who sat perfectly still on the sofa, her back straight as a rod, her hands neatly folded in her lap.

He smiled broadly. "You wouldn't happen to know anything about that, would you?"

His face might have been disarmingly cheerful, but his sharp eyes were locked on to Kitty's. Was he fishing? Or was he actually suspicious of her?

She fought the urge to look away. "No, I don't."

His smile deepened. "I didn't think you would have anything to share with me."

Something in the tone, the forced lightness and the choice of words, put Kitty immediately on alert. "I've got some classmates coming over," she said, turning to her mother. She desperately wanted to get out of that room. "To work on a school project. Is that okay?"

"Of course," her mom said with a faint smile. "Dinner will be at seven. Let me know if they're going to join us."

"I won't keep you long, Mrs. Wei."

Sergeant Callahan remained silent until Kitty entered her room at the end of the hall. Not that she had any intention of staying there. She closed her door loud enough that the police officer would think she was safely out of earshot, then as silently as she could, Kitty slipped through the bathroom that joined her room to her sisters' and crept to the door and listened. It was crucial that she find out what Sergeant Callahan knew.

"And you have no idea who might have had a grudge against your brother-in-law or his business?"

"He designs and imports custom furniture," Kitty's mom said, a hint of derision in her voice. "Not methamphetamines."

"Disgruntled customer?" Sergeant Callahan prodded. "Former employee?"

"Nothing I can think of."

Sergeant Callahan paused, and Kitty could picture him scribbling in his ever-present notebook. "Anything I should know about the company's finances?" he asked at last.

"I don't know what you mean."

"Were you in debt? Was your brother-in-law in danger of losing the business?"

"Absolutely not," Mrs. Wei snapped.

"I'll need to see the company files," he continued. "I'm sure you keep a backup somewhere?"

"Yes." Kitty heard the sofa creak as her mom shifted in her seat. "At the warehouse."

"How convenient."

Kitty gritted her teeth. She didn't like the sarcasm she heard in Sergeant Callahan's voice.

"Are you implying that my brother-in-law set this fire on purpose?" Mrs. Wei asked, cutting to the chase.

"I'm not implying anything," Sergeant Callahan said drily. "But he carried rather hefty insurance on his business, and the arson investigator found traces of a known accelerant at the scene."

"Which means?"

"Which means the fire was no accident." Kitty heard the door open. "Good day, Mrs. Wei."

NINETEEN

"SO NICE OF YOU TO ARRANGE A POLICE RECEPTION FOR US at your house today," Ed said, the moment he was settled into the desk chair in Kitty's bedroom. The last thing he'd expected to see at the Wei residence was Sergeant Callahan leaving the house.

Olivia pulled her legs up on the bed, crossing them. "Is everything okay?"

Kitty nodded. "He was questioning my mom about the warehouse fire. They think my uncle set it on purpose."

"Oh no," Olivia said.

Ed whistled. "Aggravated arson carries a minimum sentence of ten years, plus he'd be in violation of his insurance policy."

Kitty winced. "Not helping."

"Sorry."

"And I think maybe he suspects me," Kitty continued, her eyebrows pinched together.

Olivia gasped. "Of starting the fire? Of being DGM? Of killing Ronny and Coach Creed and—"

"I'm not sure," Kitty said sharply, interrupting the panicked rant. "It seemed like he knows I'm hiding something. Just a feeling, really."

Ed straightened up in his chair. Kitty thought that Sergeant Callahan might be on to her? "If he really thought you were involved," Ed said dismissively, "don't you think he'd just haul you in for questioning?"

"I guess."

Ed forced a laugh. "This is a murder investigation, with some arson thrown in for shits and giggles. I don't think he'd dance around the issue."

"Maybe." Kitty looked less than convinced. "Let's just get started, okay?"

"Okay," Ed said, thankful to be changing the subject. "I have something that might cheer you up. I made a little visit to the Hayward Sanitation Plant this afternoon. Got to see our old pal Xavier at work."

"How was it?" Kitty asked.

"Amazing. He literally monitors shit." Ed sighed. "It might have been the best moment of my young life."

"I mean," Kitty said, "did you learn anything? Could he be behind all this?"

"I didn't get a chance to initiate contact," Ed said. "But I did follow him home. He lives with his mother, which is a point in favor of him being a serial killer."

Kitty turned to Olivia. "Maybe you can follow up? Xavier might be receptive to your, um, approach."

"I guess I can try," Olivia said with a heavy sigh. "I've already been eye-molested by Maxwell Gertler today. How much worse could it be?"

"You visited the Gertlers?" Kitty asked.

Ed watched Olivia closely.

"Yes!" she cried, and sat up straight, her energy revitalized. "I was talking to Logan in drama class, and he thinks he saw the Gertlers in the theater opening night."

"Is he sure it was them?" There was desperation in Kitty's voice.

"I think so," Olivia said. "It's hard to say with the stage lights, but they work at the surf shop where he gets his board waxed and—"

Ed smirked. "Dirty."

"And he was pretty sure it was them," Olivia said, ignoring him. "When I brought it up they denied being there, but they were super shifty about it."

"Great," Kitty said. "That's another possible suspect. But I think we can definitely cross Wendy Marshall off that list."

"You talked to her?" Olivia asked.

"I 'accidentally,'" Kitty said, using air quotes, "ran into her at the gym. Apparently, she's selling LARP fan fiction online now. Something like a hundred thousand downloads."

Ed cocked his head. "Is she single?"

"You're not her type," Kitty countered.

"If she spends a few years in prison for murder," Ed said, flashing a finger pistol, "I might be."

"Prison . . . ," Olivia repeated slowly, as if the word triggered a memory. Then she sucked in a breath. "Oh my God! I forgot to tell you. Bree's out of juvie!"

"What?" Ed and Kitty said together.

"She's under house arrest, but she's out. So that's good, right?"

Kitty sank back against the bed. "That's the best news I've heard all week."

"And how did you come by this information?" Ed asked.

Olivia smiled sheepishly. "Promise you won't be mad."

"Mad?" Kitty said.

"John's helping me figure out what Amber was doing with Ronny the night he was killed."

"Ah, yes," Ed said slowly. "Amber's got her panties in a wad over John Baggott. Bree's going to be thrilled. I should start taking odds on that catfight ASAP."

Olivia slugged Ed in the arm. "This is serious."

"It sure is," Kitty said, narrowing her eyes. "You told John about Amber and Ronny?"

"Wasn't he a suspect like a week ago?" Ed asked.

"Bree trusts him," Olivia said. "Enough to have him make contact with us. I thought that was a good enough reason to swear him into DGM."

Ed laughed. "Awesome. I was getting tired of being the only penis around here."

Kitty narrowed her eyes. "You may not be the only penis, but you'll still be the only dick."

Ed dipped his head in approval. "Touché."

"But I have even better news," Olivia said, clasping her hands together.

"You do?" Kitty asked.

"I snagged Rex's phone yesterday during gym." Olivia spoke quickly. "He and Christopher Beeman had some kind of romantic encounter back in sixth grade."

"Like the one Christopher mentioned in his emails with Ronny?"

"Exactly like that," Olivia said.

"Rex Cavanaugh." Ed snorted. "The biggest assholes are always hiding the biggest secrets."

Kitty chewed on her lip. "So Ronny found out that it was Rex and blackmailed him."

"Yep," Olivia said. "And I'm pretty sure Amber was trying to buy Ronny's silence the night he was killed."

"With what?" Ed asked. "Cash? Stock options?" He pumped his eyebrows. "Sexual favors?"

Olivia wrinkled her nose, clearly disgusted. "With one of her dad's Rolex watches."

"I'm sorry." Ed cupped his hand behind his ear. "Did you say 'one of'?"

"Yep."

Ed leaned forward. "And is *she* single?"

Kitty stood up and began to pace in front of the table. "Ed, if Amber gave you a thousand-dollar watch—"

Ed snorted. "Try ten thousand."

Olivia's eyes grew wide. "That much?"

"That much."

"Damn."

"Okay," Kitty said with a deep breath. "If Amber gave you a

ten-thousand-dollar watch, what would you do with it?"

"Strap it to my wrist and never take it off until my dying breath," Ed said without hesitation.

"Exactly." She chewed on her lip again. "Does anyone remember the crime scene photos Margot showed us?"

"Margot hacked into the Menlo PD crime lab database?" Ed asked. He knew she was good, but not that good.

Olivia nodded, her face suddenly pale. "We saw . . ." She swallowed. "The body."

"I wish Margot was here," Kitty said. "We need to see those photos."

"Pshaw," Ed said. He pushed himself out of his chair and pulled his tablet from his backpack. Margot wasn't the only one with mad hacker skills.

"Do you think you can?" Kitty asked.

Instead of answering, Ed propped his tablet up on Kitty's desk and unrolled a flat wireless keyboard. Then he went to work, the girls gathering around him, peering down at the screen. In a matter of minutes, he had the crime lab's database open, all of their open cases labeled by victim and date. His eyes flitted over the list, pausing for a split second on the folder marked "Mejia."

Dammit. He should have realized it would be in the database. He could only hope neither of them noticed Margot's file. He didn't want Kitty and Olivia to see what might be in there. Ed quickly scrolled down so her file disappeared off the top of the screen, then located the DeStefano case.

"Okay," Kitty said, leaning close to the screen. "We're looking for any photos that show Ronny's wrists."

Ed scanned through thumbnails, cringing at the tiny photos of Ronny's lifeless body. However much Ronny might have deserved to pay for his actions, the harsh reality of his murder scene was not something Ed needed to see. After scrolling through the first page, Ed finally found a photo that seemed to have an arm in it.

As the photo enlarged on the screen, all three of them gasped.

"Holy shit," Ed whispered. It was Ronny's body, facedown on the bed. Well, *facedown* might have been a bit of a stretch, considering the fact that there wasn't much left of his head. It was more of a bloody mass of hair and brain tissue, splattered across the sheets, pillows, and headboard. Ed pulled his eyes away from the kill wound and glanced quickly at one of Ronny's arms, splayed out over the side of the mattress, before he closed the full-screen view.

"N-no Rolex on his right hand," he said, quickly averting his eyes.

Kitty let out a sigh. "Okay. I'm almost afraid to ask, but any photos of his left hand?"

Ed scrolled quickly, not allowing his eyes to linger on any one photo for more than a split second, and finally found what they were looking for. The photo that popped up on the screen showed Ronny's left hand, which had been placed on top of a white card with the letters "DGM" typed across it.

"Damn," he said. "Someone really did try and frame you guys."

"No watch," Olivia said. "So he wasn't wearing it when he was killed."

"Or," Kitty added, "the killer removed it."

Or the cops, Ed thought to himself.

Kitty tapped him on the shoulder. "Any way to see the evidence list from Ronny's room?"

Ed zipped back to the main folder and scanned to the bottom. "Your wish is my command."

The three of them pored over the list together, noting all the items removed from Ronny's room, including the clothing he was wearing at the time. One thing was definitely missing: the Rolex.

"The killer must have taken the watch," Olivia said. "Don't serial killers do that? Take a memento?"

Could it have been pocketed by a police officer before it was admitted into evidence? Absolutely. And if so, had it been taken out of greed, or was someone—say, a relative of the Beeman family—actively attempting to hamper the investigation?

Because he might be the killer.

"We find the watch," Ed said, "we find the killer."

"It definitely seems to point to . . ." Kitty's voice trailed off. She was staring intently at the screen. "What's that?"

"What's what?" Ed followed her eye and found that he'd stupidly left the page open to the list of evidence folders. Shit.

Kitty jabbed her finger at the screen. "That." She was pointing at the file marked "Mejia."

"Nothing we don't already know," Ed said, trying to turn their attention away. "You guys were there, I mean. The thing we need to focus on is—"

"Open it!" Olivia cried. "Maybe there's something we'll recognize. Something the cops might have overlooked."

"I hardly think the upstanding members of the Menlo PD need our help in—"

"Ed!" Olivia and Kitty cried in unison.

"Fine." *Ed, you're an idiot.* He opened the file and leaned back in his chair.

Kitty and Olivia scrolled through the photos while Ed averted his eyes. He could see Margot's unconscious body in his mind; he didn't need to see it in three hundred dpi.

"Stop!" Olivia cried after a few moments. "Go back."

Ed peeked at the screen as Kitty scrolled backward. After a few photos, Olivia pointed at the screen. "There!"

It was a photo of Margot's prompter's script, open to the last scene, which clearly showed that a piece had been torn away from the corner.

"A torn page in her script?" Ed asked, trying to sound unimpressed. "Big deal."

"I've seen Margot go through that script a dozen times," Olivia said. "She was meticulously neat. No way that piece was missing before opening night."

"That doesn't prove anything," Kitty said. She closed the web browser and straightened up. "Except maybe she pulled it away when she was attacked?"

"Maybe," Olivia conceded. "But it does seem weird."

"Ladies," Ed said, rolling up his keyboard. "It's getting late and the Head needs his beauty rest."

"Okay," Kitty said. "Before we go, any updates on Tammi Barnes or Christopher's family?"

"No," Olivia said.

Kitty's eyes shifted to Ed.

"Nothing," he lied.

"Then we keep searching," Kitty said, with a strong nod of her head. "And meet again tomorrow night. Agreed?"

Ed didn't hesitate. "Agreed."

Kitty stood up and grabbed her bag from the floor. "Come on, Olivia. I'll drive you home."

Olivia was oddly subdued as she followed Kitty through the kitchen and out to her car. She'd been so elated yesterday afternoon when she discovered the link between Amber, Rex, and Ronny, but even with that amazing piece of information about the Rolex, they seemed as far away from finding the killer as they had been a few days ago. The hopeless feeling that had swamped her after the Bangers and Mosh concert was threatening to overtake her once more, and it took every ounce of her courage to keep fighting.

Were Kitty and Ed feeling the same sense of deflation and futility that was making Olivia want to give up? They must have been, because no one said a word as they walked to their cars.

Until Kitty opened the front door of her Camry and gasped.

"What?" Olivia said.

"What the hell is this?" Ed cried from the street. He was standing with his car door open, staring down at the driver's seat.

Olivia felt her stomach fall away. She didn't want to look inside the car, knowing what she would find there, but her eyes weren't listening to her brain.

There, on the passenger seat of Kitty's car, was a manila

envelope with her name on it.

"Did you guys get one too?" Ed asked.

"Yep," Kitty answered, her voice flat.

Olivia gazed at the envelope through the window, unwilling to open it or even touch it, as if doing so might make it real. But Kitty had already lifted hers from the seat and had popped the seal. "It's a note," she said.

"Do I want to know what it says?" Olivia asked.

Ed trotted up behind her. "Nope, but you're going to." He shoved a typewritten note in front of her eyes.

I will destroy everything you love.

TWENTY

KITTY WAS EXHAUSTED AS SHE WALKED INTO FIRST-PERIOD leadership Thursday morning. The last of her hopefulness had come crashing down around her at the sight of the manila envelope in her car. The fact that her uncle might be accused of arson combined with the message in the envelope had left Kitty panicked and absolutely unable to sleep.

The killer wasn't just going after them anymore. He was going after everyone they loved.

She dropped into her desk chair, her mind so agitated that she almost didn't feel her phone vibrating in her pocket.

The leadership classroom was about half-full as Kitty yanked out her phone and noticed she had an email. It was from a Bishop DuMaine email address sent through the school system with the subject "MUST READ."

Some new rules and regulations? That was the usual correspondence from the administration. Kitty clicked open the email and scanned the contents.

The body of the email contained a single line of text: a web address for the video-hosting website old F.U. often used to upload content for school-wide consumption, usually Catholic education crap or addresses from the Pope. Without a second thought, she opened the link.

A video started almost immediately, but instead of Father Uberti's smarmy face seated behind his desk, the scene was a birthday party.

Huh?

About two dozen tweens were sprawled across someone's living room—some on sofas and chairs, some lounging on the carpet, all looking hopelessly bored. The room was massive and expensively furnished—the fireplace alone was large enough for a family of four to dine in, and it was crowned with an enormous oil painting of a pastoral hunting scene, mounted in an ornately carved gold frame. Two gigantic vases stood guard on either side of the grate, and from the top of the frame, Kitty could just make out a crystal chandelier peeking into view.

A woman dressed in a questionably appropriate minidress and four-inch heels strutted out in front of the fireplace. Her hair looked as if it had been professionally blown out and Kitty could see the diamonds glittering in her ears.

"Are you all ready for the main event?" the woman cried.

"Yeah," a couple of the tweens said without an ounce of enthusiasm.

"Excellent," she said, clearly oblivious to their reaction. "Where's my perfect little birthday boy?"

From the back of the room, one of the kids slowly pushed himself to his feet. Even though Kitty couldn't see his face, she could sense his lack of interest as he shuffled toward his mom.

"Hurry up, baby!" she cooed. Then laughed. A light, tinkling that reminded Kitty of a silver dinner bell.

The kid finally made it to the front of the room and his mother grabbed him firmly by the shoulders and spun him around to face the camera.

Kitty gasped. She knew that face. It was midpuberty, but the disdainful scowl was already fixed about the eyes and mouth. All she had to do was imagine him older, angrier, and significantly douchier, and Kitty was staring at Rex Cavanaugh.

"And now," Mrs. Cavanaugh said, "for the main event. Flown in from Montreal especially for my little man's thirteenth birthday, the star of Cirque du Soleil's new hit show *Le Pitre Triste*, Marcel Fontanable!"

A look of terror passed over Rex's face as a seven-foot-tall Victorian-era clown jumped into view. He wore a bald cap with tufts of reddish brown hair spiking out from each ear, and his face was a mask of white, with dramatic hot-pink triangles above the brows and cheeks, and black hollows of makeup encircling each eye. His lips were painted blue, as if he'd spent the night in a freezer, and overdrawn to such an extent that they looked like collagen injections gone wrong.

His costume consisted of a tight polka-dot jacket topped with a floppy, high-necked collar and frilly tiered bloomers. Lace-up boots completed the outfit, and as he began to move, Kitty realized that his excessive height was the result of short stilts, camouflaged by the boots.

Marcel pirouetted in front of Rex, kicked his leg above his

head, and ended in a split before the fireplace, arms open wide, as flames erupted from his palms.

The audience cheered with more enthusiasm than they'd displayed so far. Everyone but Rex. Kitty could see his knees shaking, his chin quivering, his face turning beet red.

His mother didn't seem to notice or care. She squealed with delight as Marcel reversed his splits as easily as if he'd been raised up by a crane, tottered around the living room like a drunkard, then produced a cupcake with a sparkler on top and presented it to Rex.

It was as if time stopped. The clown, Mrs. Cavanaugh, and the tweens all stared at Rex, waiting for him to take the cupcake. And with all eyes on him, a dark stain began to appear in the crotch of Rex's chinos. It grew, spreading down the leg of his pants, while Rex just stood there, paralyzed.

The poor clown stood up, out of character, and looked confusedly from Rex to his mother as the tweens began snickering and pointing.

It was like a switch had been thrown. Rex stamped his foot, pounded his fists against his thighs, and screamed, "I hate you!" then sprinted from the room.

The video went dark, but only for a split second. An image faded onto the screen of Kitty's phone that made her hands go ice cold.

Black type on a white background.

DGM.

"What the hell is this?" someone asked.

"No idea," was the reply.

Kitty glanced up, aware that the classroom was rapidly filling with students. Rex, Kyle, and Tyler had taken their seats in the front of the room, and each held their phone in their hands, open to the anonymous email.

"I got it, too," Tyler said, glancing at his buddies.

"Do you think it's DGM?" Kyle asked.

"Nah," Rex said, with a toss of his hair. "That bitch is in jail, remember?"

Then in almost choreographed unison, Rex, Kyle, and Tyler all opened the video link.

Kitty tried to pry her eyes from Rex's face, but couldn't. It was like watching a train wreck in slow motion: you know the carnage will be unbearable, but you can't even blink, let alone look away. Around her, the voices of Mrs. Cavanaugh and the birthday guests blared from a half-dozen phones, in the round.

"Are you all ready for the main event?"

"Yeah."

"Are you all ready for the main event?"

"Yeah."

Everyone in the leadership class had gotten an email. Could it have gone to the entire school?

"WHAT THE FUCK?" Rex roared. He bolted to his feet, his chair clattering to the floor behind him. His face was bright red, the color growing deeper by the second, and his free hand was balled up into a fist as if he was ready to punch out the person responsible for his humiliation. Just like thirteen-year-old

Rex in the video. He spun around, eyes wild with a mix of fear and rage, looking for someone to blame. "Who the fuck did this? Huh? I'll fucking kill him!"

"This can't be real," Tyler said, trying to soothe his furious leader.

"Yeah," Kyle agreed. "It's a fake, right?"

Without answering the question, Rex bent down and flipped his desk with both hands, the force so intense it went flying across the room. Then he stormed out, slamming the door behind him.

"I guess that's his answer."

Kitty turned to find Mika smiling at her desk. She looked as if she was thoroughly enjoying Rex's humiliation, as was, Kitty guessed, about 99 percent of the school.

Kitty shook her head. "That's not possible." Her voice sounded strange, distant and croaky, like it hadn't even come from her mouth.

"Are you okay?" Mika placed her hand on Kitty's arm. Her smiled had vanished. "You look like you're about to be sick."

"I think I—"

"What in the name of God is going on?" Father Uberti swept into the room, robes flying, cincture flapping. He wrenched a phone out of Tyler's hand. "What is everyone watching?"

It was all about to start again: the 'Maine Men witch hunt, the police presence, the interrogations. What were she and Olivia going to do?

Olivia. She had to talk to Olivia right away.

The final bell rang just as Kitty pushed herself to her feet and staggered toward the door. Her legs felt shaky and unsure, but she forced herself to move forward.

"Miss Wei," Father Uberti cried. "Where do you think you're going?"

But Kitty didn't hang around to explain. She broke into a run and sprinted upstairs to the computer lab.

TWENTY-ONE

OLIVIA DIDN'T BOTHER TO KNOCK, DIDN'T EVEN THINK THAT the door to the computer lab might be locked. She burst through at a full sprint, threw her arms around Kitty's neck, and hugged her. "Thank God you're here! What is going on?"

Kitty pulled away; her face was tense and drawn. "I don't know."

"Do you think Ed . . ."

Ed the Head barreled into the room, right on cue. "What the hell did you do?" he panted, totally out of breath.

"Us?" Olivia stared at him, momentarily stunned. "You mean *you* didn't do this?"

Ed jabbed his thumb at his chest. "Me? No way. I'm a businessman, not a crusader. I don't give a shit about justice unless it's profitable."

"Right," Olivia said. "Always out for yourself."

"Let's assume," Kitty said, stepping between them, "that no one in the room is responsible."

A faint knock on the door made Olivia jump. "You guys in there?" John whispered.

"Criminy," Ed said, flopping into a chair. "Are you selling tickets or something?"

Olivia smiled meekly and unlocked the door for John. He stepped into the room, blinking under the harsh fluorescent lights. His gaze wandered from Olivia to Kitty, then landed on Ed. "Him too?"

Ed lengthened his neck regally. "I was here first."

Olivia rolled her eyes. "Yeah, yeah. You're the prettiest."

Kitty eyed John warily. "How did you know where to find us?"

"I've seen Bree sneaking in and out of the second floor of the science building." John shrugged. "This is the only room that no one uses. And when I saw that video, I thought it might be related to what I got last night." John swung his backpack off his shoulder and pulled out a yellow envelope.

"Shit," Kitty said.

"You got one too?" he asked.

"We all did." Ed spread his arms wide. "Welcome to DGM."

"'I will destroy everything you love,'" John said, quoting the anonymous note. "Kinda creepy."

Ed waved him off. "Yeah, yeah. Spooky envelope, ominous message." He held up his index and middle fingers. "The way I see it, we've got two options with this new DGM prank. Either the killer is trying to pin this on you, or you've got a serious case of 'I am Spartacus' on your hands."

John nodded his appreciation. "Nice one."

Olivia tilted her head. "Huh?"

"*Spartacus*," Ed said. "Kirk Douglas? Stanley Kubrick?"

Olivia shook her head.

John laughed. "You're supposed to be the acting expert. How could you not have heard of this film?"

"I know, right?" Ed held his fist up for a bump that John readily returned.

Olivia was starting to regret letting boys in the clubhouse. "Is this a guy thing?"

Ed rested his elbows on his knees. "Spartacus is a slave in ancient Rome and he incites a rebellion. There's this scene where the Roman soldiers are looking for Spartacus, and they're going to start killing people unless they give him up."

John dropped into a chair next to Ed and began gesturing wildly with excitement as he described the scene. "So Kirk Douglas—he's Spartacus—he starts to raise his hand so no one else will suffer on his behalf, right? But another dude is all like, 'I am Spartacus.' And then another one—'I am Spartacus.'"

"I am Spartacus!" Ed cried.

"I AM SPARTACUS!" John yelled even louder.

"Shh!" Kitty hissed. "What's your point?"

"Spartacus meant something to them," Olivia said, suddenly understanding the implication. "They were protecting him."

"And what he stood for," Ed added.

John nodded in agreement. "Someone's trying to protect you by carrying on the DGM name."

Olivia wasn't sure how she felt about a copycat DGM. Flattered, of course. But this prank against Rex Cavanaugh had the potential to destroy whatever chance she and Kitty had of finding the killer.

"Attention, Bishop DuMaine students," Father Uberti said over the loudspeaker. There was a tremor in his voice, hinting at his barely contained rage. "All members of the 'Maine Men student group are hereby released from first period and are to report to the leadership classroom immediately. I repeat, all 'Maine Men and anyone interested in joining are to report to the leadership classroom. Now."

Kitty glanced at her watch. "I have to get back to class."

"But what should we do about Rex?" Olivia asked.

"Point and laugh?" Ed suggested.

"Not helpful, Ed." Kitty hauled her bag over her head and pointed directly at John. "Any luck with Amber and the Rolex?"

John shook his head. "So far I haven't been able to get a word in. That girl hardly pauses for breath, let alone gives me a chance to ask a question."

"Tell me about it," Olivia said.

"Double down on her," Kitty said. "She'll be feeling vulnerable, so maybe she'll be more willing to share the details on that watch."

John saluted. "Aye, aye, Captain."

Kitty had that focused game-time look in her eyes, which usually meant she had a plan. "Where are you going?" Olivia asked.

Kitty smiled. "I'm going to infiltrate the 'Maine Men."

◆ ◆ ◆

Packs of 'Maine Men hurried through the halls and Kitty tucked herself behind a group of upperclassmen, heading to leadership class. She still wasn't exactly sure if this was a good idea or not. She'd spent the better part of her time at Bishop DuMaine fighting against tyranny and oppression, two things symbolized by the 'Maine Men. Could she really become one of them?

She reached the door to the leadership classroom and took a deep breath. *I'm about to find out.*

The room was crammed with people. The leadership students sat at their desks, Mika among them, glancing uncomfortably at the legion of guys ringing the room. It was the usual suspects, not exactly a rush of recruits. She recognized a few newbies—a couple of freshmen, noticeable for the looks of fear on their faces; the point guard from Donté's basketball team; a guy from her algebra class; and weirdly enough, Logan Blaine, who stood with his hands shoved deep in the pockets of his jacket, staring at the floor.

Rex, she noted, had not returned.

Mika saw her the second she stepped into the room. She turned to the door, brows pulled together in concern at Kitty's rapid departure minutes earlier. "You okay?" she mouthed.

Father Uberti didn't miss it either.

"Miss Wei," he said. "How nice of you to rejoin us. Where did you run off to after the late bell?"

Great, old F.U. was already irritated with her. That wasn't going to help her cause. "Ladies' room," she said, blurting out the first thing that came into her mind. Then she remembered that she was going to have to appear sympathetic to his agenda. "I felt sick, you know, after what happened this morning. I thought we were free of this DGM menace once and for all, but now . . ." She let her voice trail off, and shook her head in dismay.

Father Uberti took the bait, hook, line, and sinker. "Yes," he said with a heavy sigh. "We've been dealt a blow today. Which is why I've called you all here."

He turned back to the assembled students, and Kitty slipped into her chair.

Mika leaned forward. "Nice excuse," she whispered. "You had F.U. eating out of your hand."

"Yeah," Kitty replied out of the corner of her mouth. "Totally."

Crap. What was Mika going to think of her if she up and joined the 'Maine Men? She'd been one of the organizers of the student body protest against Father Uberti and his pet goon squad, and had gotten a day's suspension over it. Would Mika resent her forever for what she was about to do? Would she ever be able to explain?

And then there was Donté. He'd left the 'Maine Men because he hated their tactics, hated the way they bullied and repressed anyone who didn't agree with them. Would he understand what she was doing? Or would he despise her for it?

Kitty bit her lip while Father Uberti droned on and on about the menace of DGM, his voice a muted sound track to the turmoil raging within her. Mika and Donté. Was she willing to risk both her best friend and her boyfriend?

She pictured the alternative. Margot, unconscious in the

hospital. Bree, falsely accused of murder. And a killer who was still out there, waiting to strike again. *I will destroy everything you love.* What if his next target was Mika? Or Donté? Would she ever be able to forgive herself if she had the opportunity to find out who he was and she didn't take it?

"Clearly," Father Uberti said, rapping the desk with the cross that dangled from his cincture as if he was whipping the poor, innocent piece of furniture into submission. "Clearly, we haven't been vigilant enough. These criminals have slipped through our fingers, and now they've attacked another student. We need more bodies on the front lines. 'Maine Men, it is time to recruit. Your friends, your family. All able-bodied—"

"I'll join," Kitty said. She barely noticed the words flying out of her mouth as every set of eyes in the room turned to face her. "I want to join the 'Maine Men."

Behind her, she heard Mika gasp.

"Um . . . ," Father Uberti said, taken aback. "But you're not . . . What I mean to say is, you've got the wrong . . ." He cleared his throat. "Miss Wei, I'm not sure that's appropriate."

Oh, for chrissakes, was he seriously balking at her gender? "Because I'm a girl?" she suggested. What was this, 1955?

"Well, yes," Father Uberti said. "It is the 'Maine *Men* after all."

"I think we should let her in," Kyle said, rising to his feet.

Father Uberti stroked his trim Vandyke beard. "Perhaps it would be good for school morale."

"What are you doing?" Mika hissed.

Kitty half-turned and gave Mika a look she hoped would

adequately transmit her feeling of "I don't want to do this but I have to" and smiled weakly. "Trust me," she whispered.

"Huh?"

Father Uberti rapped his cross on the desk three times as if it was a gavel. "All in favor of Kitty Wei becoming the newest member of the 'Maine Men?"

Every member in the room raised his hand.

"All opposed?"

Kitty held her breath. The entire room was silent.

"Very well." Father Uberti reached beneath the desk, pulled out a blue shirt wrapped in plastic, and tossed it to Kitty. "Welcome to the team."

Joining the 'Maine Men was one thing. Actually pulling the heinous blue shirt over her head was something else entirely. It triggered some kind of Pavlovian response: Kitty felt instantly nauseous.

"Now, let's get to business," Father Uberti said, grasping the podium with both hands. Then he cleared his throat and launched into a speech about the horrors of DGM.

It was the same speech she'd heard him give at least twice before. How the school needed to band together to stamp out this evil. How it was the students' responsibility to spy on one another. How anyone with information that led to Bree Deringer's accomplices would be rewarded. Blah blah blah.

Kitty seriously didn't have time for this. These tired tactics hadn't worked before, and they weren't going to work now. She had to get them moving in a new direction if there was any chance of actually finding out who was behind the new DGM: a killer, a copycat, or something else entirely. So Kitty took a deep breath and raised her hand, right in the middle of Father Uberti's speech.

He reared back, unused to interruptions. "Miss Wei, do you have a question?"

"A comment," Kitty said.

"I am all ears." He sounded anything but.

"It's just that we've tried this before and it didn't work. Asking students to snitch, promising rewards. It didn't get us anywhere."

Father Uberti narrowed his eyes. "I assume you have a better idea?"

"Yeah," Kitty said, hoping she wasn't digging her own grave. This plan had the potential for a colossal backfire. "Yeah, I think I do."

Father Uberti stepped aside with a dramatic flourish of his arm. "Then by all means, tell us, Miss Wei. Educate us on what we're doing wrong."

Kitty rose to her feet, swallowing hard. This was the plan, after all. To infiltrate the 'Maine Men and use them to help her find a killer. And if there was a copycat DGM, this was the best way to protect them, wasn't it?

She walked to the front of the room, studiously avoiding Mika's eyes. "We thought this was over," she began, facing the group. "Bree Deringer turned herself in and we hoped this was all going to go away."

Several heads nodded in agreement. *Okay, good start!*

"An anonymous threat has reemerged from the shadows, too cowardly to show its face. And so far no one's been able to shine a light on it."

"Exactly," Kyle said.

"Not the police. Not the 'Maine Men. Not the archdiocese."

Father Uberti shifted his feet. "No need to bring the archdiocese into this."

But Kitty didn't pause. She noticed that her audience was sitting forward in their chairs, their eyes wide, lips parted. Everyone but Mika, whose facial expression was slowly morphing from confusion to anger.

But the 'Maine Men were invested in her words, waiting for the payoff. She just had to bring it home.

"I believe," she said, leaning toward them in a conspiratorial pose, "that Bree Deringer was the sole perpetrator of DGM."

The room gasped.

"I hardly think that's possible," Father Uberti said nervously. He edged closer to her, as if trying to repossess the spotlight. "In light of what's happened today."

"I believe," Kitty continued, "we're dealing with copycats—students who don't have the same experience as the original DGM. And do you know what that means?"

"It means they're sloppy!" Kyle cried out.

Kitty stared at him, blinking. He was smarter than she had given him credit for. "We need to look for their mistakes," she said. "Because I guarantee they made some. Where did they find this video? Where did they upload it? How did they get a Bishop DuMaine email address? There's got to be some evidence of who's behind DGM. We just have to find it."

"And then," Tyler added, "we can catch them." Ever the scholar.

"So," Kitty said, planting her hands on the desk and leaning forward. "Go find me a copycat, will you?"

The room broke into cheers. 'Maine Men members new and old leaped to their feet, high-fiving and chest bumping one another in a disturbing display of machismo. Kitty was partly terrified by what she'd managed to accomplish. She'd steered the 'Maine Men in a specific direction, one she hoped would lead to a murderer.

Now she just had to hope none of these misguided idiots became his next victim.

TWENTY-TWO

OLIVIA HADN'T SEEN AMBER ALL DAY. SHE ASSUMED AMBER had left, either to check on Rex or, more likely, to go home to avoid the gossip. But as Olivia walked out onto the quad for lunch, she saw her old friend perched on top of their usual table, one leg crossed over the other with the hem of her barely school-sanctioned pencil skirt inching dangerously up her thighs, holding court in front of a group of curious onlookers.

Olivia smiled to herself. She should have known that Amber wouldn't miss a chance to play the victim in front of the entire school.

"I knew," she said, then thrust her hands before her, palms down. "I could feel it the moment I walked onto campus this morning. Every inch of my body screamed out to me that something awful was going to happen."

"Hey," Olivia said, sliding onto the bench next to Peanut. "How's the show?"

"Tired material," Jezebel said, unwrapping a hoagie. "I feel like I've heard it before."

Amber shot her a glance but didn't drop character. "When I opened my email and saw that link I knew it would change my life forever."

Jezebel rolled her eyes and Olivia had to pin her lips together to keep from smiling.

Amber uncrossed her legs and let them swing casually off the side of the table. "My father is going to have it examined by video experts," she said. "I'm sure it was doctored."

"Have you talked to Rex?" Kyle asked. He and Tyler stood together, arms folded in a matching stance.

"Is he okay?" Tyler asked.

"Did he ask for me?"

"Or me?"

Amber shook her head. "I haven't talked to him. But it's not because we broke up," she added quickly, as if to emphasize that she was still the most important person in Rex's life. "I'm sure he's been in conference with the police all day." Her eyes lit up, a new idea popping into her brain. "Or at the courthouse. You know, one of his father's best friends is the assistant district attorney. I wouldn't be surprised if Mr. Cavanaugh has the National Guard called in to find DGM. Or the army. Or the FBI."

"Or the *A-Team*," Peanut said under her breath.

Olivia snorted.

"Because . . ." Amber's voice trailed off. Her chest heaved and she stifled a fake sob. "Because if they can attack Rex Cavanaugh, who will be next? He's the most popular guy in school. Who else could they go after? It would have to be the most popular *person* in school," she said, laying deliberate emphasis on the gender-neutral noun.

Jezebel yawned, big and loud, then answered Amber's question like a good sidekick. "Like you."

Amber's hand flew to her mouth as she sucked in about a gallon of oxygen. "Me?"

Tyler's arm shot around Amber's shoulder, and Olivia half-wished Rex was at school to see his toady hit on his ex-girlfriend. "Don't worry, Amber. We won't let them hurt you."

"Yeah," Kyle said. He eyed Amber's shoulders as if looking for room to add his own muscly arm, then grabbed her hand instead. "We won't let them hurt you."

Beside her on the bench, Olivia felt Peanut stiffen as Kyle stroked Amber's hand lovingly. Ugh. Poor Peanut.

"Do you think they would?" Amber asked, looking from one suitor to the other. "I mean, would they dare?"

It was getting to be more than Olivia could stomach. She looked around, desperate for an escape. Anything she could use as an excuse to get away from Amber's spectacle. Instead, she saw John wander out of the cafeteria, his nose buried in a comic book.

Perfect timing.

She waved, trying to catch his eye, and when he looked up at her, she flicked her head toward Amber.

John paused and stared at her. "Now?" he mouthed.

Olivia opened her eyes wide and nodded. "Now."

John wrinkled his nose and sighed, big and dramatic. A child being asked to do a chore he doesn't want to do. But it only lasted a moment before he set his shoulders, thrust his hips forward, and sauntered over to their table like a rock star taking the stage.

"John!" Amber squealed the moment she saw him. She quickly disentangled herself from Tyler and Kyle. "Did you hear what happened? Did you see it?"

"Yeah." John eyed Tyler and Kyle. "Really, um, messed up. To go after him like that." He didn't sound like he even remotely believed the words that were coming out of his mouth.

Amber didn't notice. She waved her hand, dismissing her audience. Tyler and Kyle slinked away, hands buried deep in the pockets of their matching jeans. "Rex is terrified of clowns," she said, once they were out of earshot. "I'm not surprised he pissed himself."

Peanut tilted her head to the side. "I thought you just said you were absolutely positive the video was doctored?"

Amber ignored her. "But I'm just so shaken." She shuddered, wiggling her head and shoulders as if she'd been shocked by a cattle prod. "I mean, I could be next."

John stared at her blankly, formulating a response. Olivia knew the words on the tip of his tongue were something like "Yeah, and you'd deserve it" and she could see him struggle to suppress that instinct, and come up with something more in character.

"You?" he said at last. "A target of DGM? But you're Amber Stevens!"

Amber giggled. "I am!" she said, as if being Amber Stevens was somehow a title of honor bestowed by a higher power instead of the name she was given at birth.

"You practically run this school." John smiled, pleased with himself. "Everyone looks up to you."

"They do, don't they," Amber said. It wasn't a question.

John bit his lip like a flirty schoolgirl and looked up at the sky. "I know I always have."

If Bree could see this display, she'd be laughing her ass off. Or punching someone. Or both.

Amber squeezed John's arm. "You are so adorable." She turned back to Jezebel, Peanut, and Olivia. "Haven't I always said that John was totally adorable?"

"No," Peanut said innocently.

Amber scowled. "Yes, I have, Peanut." She looked pointedly at Olivia. "Haven't I?"

"Um . . . sure?" She couldn't keep the raised inflection out of her voice. But thankfully Amber didn't notice. The bell rang, signaling the end of lunch.

Amber launched herself off the table. "Time for drama!"

Olivia smiled. She was right on so many levels.

"Walk me?" Amber latched onto John's arm like a debutante waiting to be escorted into the ball.

John sighed. "Sure." He trudged off, Amber leeched to his side, with all the enthusiasm of a soldier on a suicide mission.

"Thank God," Peanut said. She grabbed the remnants of her lunch and shoved them in her bag, and Olivia noticed for the first time that she'd barely eaten anything.

"You okay?" she asked, quickly following her friend.

Peanut looked at her sidelong, instantly suspicious. "Yeah."

Why so on edge? "You didn't eat any lunch." Olivia forced a laugh. "Still on the cleanse?"

"Cleanse?" Peanut replied, obviously confused.

Olivia made a mental note never to do one of Mrs. Dumbrowski's master cleanses. It had turned Peanut's brain to mush.

Mr. Cunningham bounded out from the wings the moment the bell rang. "Settle down, everyone. Settle!"

Olivia looked up and noticed that he'd wheeled the big-screen television onto the stage.

"Exciting news today!" he said, as the din lowered. He held up his hand. In it was a DVD. "I've got the video from opening night!"

Olivia went rigid in her seat. Finally! The police had presumably gone over the video several times, looking for any evidence in regard to Margot's attack. But they didn't know what to look for.

"I picked it up from the police department yesterday after class," Mr. Cunningham said, "but I haven't watched it yet. I wanted to share that joy with all of you. Now I know we're all excited, but let us remember the tragic events that took place that evening." He gestured to Logan. "And be respectful of those still suffering because of it."

"Thanks, dude," Logan said. His face was stoic.

"So with that in mind, I give you . . ." Mr. Cunningham waved his hand with a dramatic flourish and backed off the stage. *"Twelfth Precinct."*

Mr. Cunningham disappeared into the wings and the house lights dimmed, leaving the theater illuminated only by the blue glow of the television. The screen went static, then the video began. Olivia could see the theater, curtains open to reveal the sets representing seventies New York, and hear the audience twittering, waiting for the show to begin. She held her breath as the house lights dimmed and the screen went black. *This was it.*

Music blared from the speakers, but it wasn't the rock track played by Bangers and Mosh. It was a funky calliope song from a hooty pipe organ, like you'd hear on an old-time merry-go-round.

"Hey!" Shane called out. "That's not our band. Did you replace us for the DVD release?"

Before Mr. Cunningham could answer, a photo popped onto the screen. It was a close-up of a wooden sign, hand-painted in yellow with the words "Camp Shred." After a couple of seconds, another photo took its place. This was a wider shot, showing the Camp Shred sign in the middle of the woods at what appeared to be a summer camp.

Olivia's hands went cold. Had someone accidentally taped over the only piece of evidence DGM had?

A subtitle zoomed into frame.

Camp Shred, Jones Gulch, CA—June, 2005

"Oh my God!" Amber gasped.

The photos accelerated, one every few seconds. They showed groups of kids, age ten or eleven, participating in a variety of camp activities—canoeing, swimming, hiking, arts and crafts. All of them were on the chubby side, a few were borderline obese.

And one girl was prominent in every photo, her wavy light-brown hair eerily familiar.

The slideshow paused on a close-up of the girl's face, the image of her chubby, smiling cheeks lingering on the screen.

It wasn't until Amber shot to her feet that Olivia realized who she was looking at.

"How dare you!" Amber screamed to no one in particular. Then before Olivia could stop her, she ran up the aisle and out of the classroom.

She didn't even see the final image on the screen.

Courtesy of DGM.

TWENTY-THREE

ED COULDN'T BELIEVE WHAT HE WAS SEEING ON HIS PHONE AS he streamed out of English literature.

It was amazing, really. Not the fact that the new DGM had pulled off two pranks in one day, but the fact that Ed didn't know Amber Stevens had been to fat camp.

He took it as a personal affront by these DGM copycats. At Margot's request, he'd been digging into Amber's past for the last six months and hadn't found so much as a hint of Amber's Camp Shred history. Sure, it had probably been in fifth grade, before her family moved to Menlo Park. And of course Amber, who'd cemented her queen bitch reputation by making fun of other people's weight, would have gone to tremendous lengths to ensure no one ever knew about her hypocritical past. But Ed prided himself on being smarter—and sneakier—than almost anyone else at school, and the fact that the new DGM had succeeded where he had failed stung like hell.

He sighed as he shoved his phone back into his pocket. If

only Margot was here to see it. Ed was pretty sure this montage would elicit a smile.

The hallways at Bishop DuMaine were a seething mass of confusion. Father Uberti had dismissed school for the day just twenty minutes into fourth period. He wanted everyone to vacate the campus immediately, pending the police investigation of the newest DGM transgressions. Around him, students were running every which way, gossiping, laughing. Cell phones and tablets that weren't lit up with the Amber montage were playing the video of Rex and the clown. Teachers scurried through the halls, trying to get students to break up their powwows and go home. Ed noted the whistles of gym coaches and the screams of police sirens in the distance.

Everyone thought DGM was dead since Bree Deringer had turned herself in. Idiots.

Now only one question remained: who would get framed for these latest DGM crimes against Bishop DuMaine humanity?

And more importantly, how did Ed make sure it wasn't him?

He wove through the hallways, the only student not transfixed by his cell phone screen, and searched for someone who could help with the answer to this question. It didn't take him long to spot the tall figure of Kitty Wei striding purposefully down the hall, her long ponytail swishing violently from side to side.

"Hola, Miss Student Body Vice President," Ed said, sliding up behind her. "A word, if you will?"

Kitty didn't even look at him. "No time. I have to meet Kyle and Tyler. They're taking me to see Rex."

"In case it's slipped your notice," Ed said quietly, straining to keep up with her long stride, "we're all about to be sacrificial lambs. Old F.U. is going to tear the school apart to find out who was behind these pranks, and do you really think the newbie perps have the fail-safes in place like you hardened criminals? It's only a matter of time before they're caught, and you'd better pray they don't know shit about you."

Kitty stopped dead in her tracks and Ed plowed into her solid frame, momentarily knocking his breath away. Before he could regain his composure, Kitty gripped his arm so fiercely he thought his arteries might pop and dragged him out of the nearest door into the deserted courtyard by the boys' locker room.

"What the hell is wrong with you?" she growled through clenched teeth. He'd never seen Kitty this pissed off before. Apparently, he'd hit a nerve. "Are you trying to get us arrested?"

Ed smiled while he rubbed the numbness out of his upper arm. "I'm watching out for number one, that's all."

"Of course you are." Kitty stuck her finger in Ed's face. "And how do we know you won't protect yourself by turning us in?"

"You don't." Ed smiled broadly. "You just have to trust me."

"Make no mistake about this," Kitty said, glaring down at him. "I don't."

Just then, the side door to the school burst open and Logan lumbered into the courtyard. Instinctively, both Ed and Kitty jumped apart and acted like they hadn't been involved in a heated confrontation just moments before.

"Hey," Logan said, glancing back and forth between them.

Ed immediately donned an affable, friendly demeanor. "Logan, my man." He held his hand up for a high five. "Don't leave me hanging, bro."

Logan stared at Ed's raised hand but didn't reciprocate. "How's your aunt Helen?"

Ed felt his face grow hot.

Kitty arched an eyebrow. "Aunt Helen?"

"Don't ask." Ed eyed Logan, wondering if he was serious or pulling his leg. "She's fine," he said slowly.

"Oh," Logan said with a smile. "Good. Hey, can I talk to Kitty? In private?"

"Anything you can say to Miss Wei," Ed said, channeling a hotshot sports agent, "you can say to me. I have exclusive rights to all professional interviews and—"

"Ed!" Kitty barked. Her sense of humor was definitely lacking. "Get out of here."

"Fine." He desperately wanted to hear what Logan had to say to Kitty, but what could he do short of positively refusing to leave? That would piss Kitty off even further, which was the last thing he wanted to do. He'd just have to take his chances eavesdropping. With a dramatic sigh, Ed slowly dragged his backpack toward the door to the boys' locker room. "I am considerably— and reluctantly—out of here."

Kitty wanted to punch Ed in the face as he sauntered out of the courtyard. How did they ever think it was a good idea to initiate him into DGM?

"Sorry," Logan said. His usually breezy smile felt forced. "I didn't mean to interrupt."

"Trust me," Kitty said. "You weren't interrupting."

"Oh, good." Logan shifted his weight back and forth between his feet as if he were standing on hot coals. "I don't even know if you're the right person to talk to, but I heard your speech this morning. In leadership. And, well, I thought that you might listen to me."

He looked nervous and uncomfortable, like a guy who was keeping a secret. Was it possible Logan knew something about DGM or the killer? "Sure," she said, smiling. "What's up?"

"It's about Olivia Hayes. Do you know her?"

Kitty fought hard to keep from showing any emotion at the mention of Olivia's name. She took a moment to remind herself of their outward relationship.

You know who she is because she's the most popular girl in school and you're dating her ex-boyfriend. Nothing more.

"Everybody knows Olivia Hayes."

Logan laughed nervously. "Right. Sorry. Well, I'm worried she might be involved somehow in all this."

Kitty stiffened. "What do you mean?"

"Like . . ." Logan ran his fingers through his longish blond hair. His eyebrows were pinched together and his nose wrinkled up, as if he was grappling with a difficult concept. "A couple of days ago, we were talking about the night Margot . . ." His voice trailed off and Kitty saw a look of pain wash over his face.

"Opening night of the play?" she suggested, careful not to give anything away.

Logan swallowed. "Yeah. Well, I told Olivia about how I'd seen something weird that night. While I was onstage. Two dudes in the audience who, like, totally shouldn't have been there."

The Gertler twins.

"Did you tell the police?"

Logan nodded. "Yeah, but I don't think that sergeant dude took me very seriously." He shook his head. "Anyway, I told Olivia, right? And then last night I stopped by the surf shop where these dudes work, just to look at some new Uggs, and it was empty."

Kitty looked at him sidelong. "What do you mean, 'empty'?"

"Like, the door was unlocked, the lights were on, but nobody was home." Logan passed a hand through his hair again. "I checked with the lady who runs the shop next door and she hadn't seen anything. She called the owner, who was pissed, I think. I left my number in case anyone heard anything, then this morning I got a voice mail from that sergeant guy, asking if I could come down and answer some questions about their disappearance."

"They're missing?" Kitty blurted out.

Logan shrugged. "I guess so. And, like, right after I told Olivia. Don't you think that's kinda weird?"

It was kind of weird. More so than Logan could possibly have realized.

"Then after that video this morning," Logan continued, "I thought I'd check out the 'Maine Men meeting. You know, like, if this is all connected to what happened to Margot, I want to help."

"Of course."

"And when I heard your speech I thought . . ." He heaved a sigh. "I thought maybe you'd listen to me."

Ugh. How could she ease Logan's mind about Olivia without giving away DGM's secret? "I'm sure it's just a coincidence."

"I guess." Logan hiked his bag up on his shoulder and turned toward the door. "Anyway, thanks for listening."

"You're welcome?" Kitty said as he disappeared from the courtyard.

Kitty slowly dialed her locker combination. The Gertler twins were missing? What did that mean? They were the killers? They weren't the killers? Her head was spinning as she lifted the 'Maine Men shirt out of her locker and stared at it. As much as she loathed the idea of wearing the thing, she had to admit it put her in a position to help DGM, to help Margot and Bree, and to keep everyone she cared about safe.

That seemed mostly worth it.

"So it's true."

Kitty swung around, the blue shirt still gripped in her hands, and found herself face-to-face with Donté. His features were tense, his eyes unusually dark, and Kitty could see anger reflected in his entire body.

"You joined the 'Maine Men?"

Dammit. Had Mika told him? "I can explain," she began.

"What, you just liked the shirt? It's a good color on you?"

Kitty had never seen Donté so angry. He was always good-natured and easygoing. She'd never known a harsh word to pass his lips, not even in regard to his ex-girlfriends, or smack-talking basketball players on a rival team. But now he looked at Kitty like she'd just kicked a puppy, and she didn't like it.

"I know how you feel about the 'Maine Men," she said, trying to suppress the emotional flutter in her voice and afraid she'd burst into tears at any moment.

"They're assholes," Donté said.

"But there's a reason I'm doing this."

"Which is?"

Which is *I can't tell you.* She couldn't exactly explain to Donté that she was the person responsible for forming DGM and for carrying out all of their previous exploits. She'd worked so hard to keep her friends and family away from it. If she shared that secret with Donté and Father Uberti found out, he might get kicked out of school and lose any chance at a basketball scholarship. She'd literally be responsible for ruining his life. And so she'd lied to him, kept him in the dark. Even now, when faced with his indignation over the 'Maine Men, she couldn't bring herself to endanger his future.

"I can't explain it right now," she said, dropping her voice. "You're going to have to trust me."

"Trust you?"

"Yeah," Kitty said, taken aback. "Just like I'm supposed to trust you. Isn't that what you asked me to do?"

"That's different," he snapped.

"How?"

"You don't understand."

Kitty didn't appreciate the double standard. "So I'm supposed to blindly trust you when you say that there's nothing wrong with our relationship, but when I ask you to trust me with this 'Maine Men thing, you get all bent?"

Donté jabbed his finger at the packaged shirt. "They stand for everything I hate about this school."

"Me too!" Kitty blurted out.

"Then why did you join them?"

Kitty clamped her jaw shut. She'd already asked him once to trust her. That should have been enough. It had been when he asked the same of her.

"I have to go," she said, and turned back to her locker.

"Yeah," he said. "You do."

Out of the corner of her eye, Kitty watched as Donté stormed down the hallway, and she fought back the tears as she wondered if those were the last words they'd ever speak to each other.

TWENTY-FOUR

KITTY SQUEEZED HER ARMS TO THE SIDES OF HER BODY AND hunched her shoulders, trying to make herself as thin as possible as she sat sandwiched between Kyle and Tyler in the front of Kyle's pickup truck. "Are you sure the Cavanaughs won't mind if I barge into their house?"

"Nah," Kyle said. He took a corner so fast, Kitty smooshed into Tyler. "They're usually not home so it doesn't really matter."

"I texted Rex that we were bringing you," Tyler added. "So it's cool."

Kitty couldn't imagine that Rex would be thrilled about a girl joining up with the 'Maine Men, and certainly not about her being inducted into his inner circle as Kyle and Tyler had so readily done. "Did he ask why?"

"Nope," Tyler said.

"Oh."

"But I told him that you had an awesome idea about this new DGM," Kyle added. "Which he had to hear." He glanced at her and smiled. "Rex is gonna be so pumped."

Kitty had mixed feelings about this field trip to Rex's house. She'd protested when Kyle and Tyler insisted on bringing her along to visit their de facto leader. They wanted to show her off, share her plan with Rex, and though the visit gave her the opportunity to perv around for the Rolex Amber had supposedly given Ronny DeStefano, the idea of being in his house was almost as nauseating as donning the 'Maine Men shirt in the first place. And that, paired with Kyle's questionable driving skills, was giving her a raging case of motion sickness.

The brakes screeched and Kitty's head whiplashed as the truck lurched to a stop in front of a two-story colonnaded McMansion.

Tyler and Kyle opened their doors in choreographed symmetry and jumped to the sidewalk while Kitty eased herself across the bench seat, head still spinning from the drive, and heaved a sigh of relief as her feet hit the solid mass of concrete. Her legs felt wobbly as she followed Kyle and Tyler up the front walk.

Kyle leaned on the doorbell. From inside the house, Kitty heard Beethoven's "Ode to Joy" ring out in electronic bells. They waited for several seconds before Tyler leaned across and rang the bell again.

"Hurry up, dude," he said over the Beethoven, as if Rex could hear him.

Again they waited. Again nothing.

Kitty felt a gurgling sensation in her stomach. Try as she might to blame it on car sickness, she couldn't ignore the fact that something felt eerily wrong.

Kyle took a step off the porch and tilted his head back. "Rex!" he yelled up to the second floor of the house. "It's us. Open the door."

"Maybe he's embarrassed," Kitty offered. "About the video."

Tyler snapped his fingers. "Good point." He reached out and depressed the door latch. It clicked and he swung the door open.

"Sweet," Kyle said. He took the two steps up to the porch in a single bound and barreled past Tyler into the foyer. "Rex! What the fuck, dude? Are you sleeping?"

"Put your pants back on," Tyler said as he followed his bromantic partner into the house. "And stop playing with yourself."

Kyle turned to him, fist extended. "Nice one, dude."

"Thanks." Tyler returned the bump, then headed up the stairs. "Let's check his room."

Kitty stood on the doorstep as the guys raced upstairs. Front door unlocked, the house silent. Something about it made her uneasy, as if she'd just stepped into a scene from a horror movie.

You're being ridiculous. Kitty stomped her foot against the doormat and forced the fear from her mind. Kyle and Tyler knew Rex better than anyone and they didn't seem apprehensive. Kitty was just tainted by the last few weeks. With shoulders squared, she stepped into the Cavanaughs' foyer.

She recognized the decor immediately. Apparently, not much had changed since Rex's thirteenth birthday party. The foyer was a massive space of gilt paint and marble, with a twenty-foot ceiling and a double-wide staircase that curved up one side. In front of her, an arched doorway led to the living room. She could see the fireplace flanked by floral vases and just a peek of sparkling chandelier above. It was the site of Rex's humiliation.

"His cell phone's here," Tyler shouted.

"Seriously?" Footsteps pounded above her.

"Yeah. See for yourself."

"Check the spare bedroom," Kyle said after a pause. "I'll hit his parents' room."

"'Kay." Tyler darted by the upstairs balcony. "Rex! This isn't funny. Come on, we need to talk."

There was an urgency in their voices that hadn't existed a minute ago. As normal as it had been for Rex not to answer the door, apparently this was the exact opposite. The gurgling in Kitty's stomach returned, only now it was more of a thundering wave. She wanted to flee the house, to wait outside and let Kyle and Tyler search for their friend, but she just kept staring into the living room.

It took her several minutes before she realized why. There was something on the floor behind the piano. Something that shouldn't be there.

Kitty blinked, her eyes focused on the object. It was a shoe, a brown Oxford worn by a fair number of Bishop DuMaine's male population. No, not just one shoe. There were two. Kitty took a few steps farther into the living room, rounding the piano, and froze in her tracks.

Not just shoes; there were legs attached. And a torso.

Kitty's mind screamed at her to stop, to look away, but her body had a mind of its own. Before she even realized what she was doing, she'd approached the figure on the floor and was hovering over it.

It was the motionless body of Rex Cavanaugh with a belt pulled tightly around his neck.

TWENTY-FIVE

SOMEONE POUNDED ON BREE'S BEDROOM DOOR, JARRING her from her nap.

"We go now," Olaf barked from the hallway. "You get in car. Olaf drive."

She slid out of bed, shoving her feet into her black biker boots as she pulled a striped sweater over her rumpled vintage dress. She felt almost as enthusiastic about her first group therapy session as she would be about a trip to the dentist. Except maybe the dentist would be less painful than listening to whiny girls bitch about their lives while trying to pretend like she was "participating in her rehabilitation."

Now, Bree, how do you feel about the choices you've made?

How do I feel about punishing bullies and asshats? Pretty darn good, actually.

She found Olaf waiting for her downstairs, holding the front door wide open.

"Won't the alarm go off the second I walk outside?" she asked.

"Olaf disabled alarm."

Of course he did.

Bree climbed into the backseat of the Escalade, so bleary-eyed she almost didn't see the manila envelope on the seat.

She wasn't surprised, really. In fact, she'd been expecting to find one of the hateful envelopes ever since she was sprung from juvie. It had been a pipe dream to think the killer would really leave them alone, and Bree couldn't help but think that the near accident and warehouse fire were merely preludes to what he had in store for them next.

With gritted teeth Bree broke the seal and slid a piece of paper from its sheath. Just a simple message: *I will destroy everything you love.*

Dammit.

She was still staring at the note as Olaf backed the car out of the driveway. Without thinking, she pulled the seat belt across her lap and shoved it into the buckle.

It clicked into place.

"Did you fix the seat belt?" she asked, eyeing Olaf's reflection in the rearview mirror.

"Was it broken?" he asked.

Bree twisted in her seat and squinted at the buckle. The scratches she'd seen two days before when they'd almost been run off the road were gone: the unit had been entirely replaced.

So the killer wanted to remove all evidence of attempted murder. Bree dug her fingers into the envelope. That could only mean one thing.

He was going to try again.

Dr. Walters's office was less ominous than juvie, and without the security bells and whistles Bree was half-expecting to see as she climbed the exterior staircase to the second floor, Olaf close behind in case she got any ideas about fleeing on foot.

But like the day room at juvie, her waiting room was intentionally cheerful. The walls were painted a pale shade of tangerine, and the waiting area was decorated with a mix of IKEA sleek and kid-friendly savvy. A low table with Crayola-colored plastic chairs sat in the middle of the room, complete with a wooden train set and some Duplo blocks. The "adult" chairs that lined the wall on three sides were plush and comfy, upholstered in a sunny floral print that matched the walls, and each of the three end tables held a lamp shaped like a pineapple surrounded by a bevy of teen-centric magazines including *Teen Vogue* and *J-14,* both of which showcased smiling, airbrushed photos of the heartthrobs du jour.

It all made Bree want to puke.

"May I help you?" asked an overly cheerful receptionist.

"Bree Deringer," Bree said, countering the receptionist's abundance of enthusiasm with a total lack of her own.

"Ah!" she said, checking a clipboard. "You're here for our group session."

"Unfortunately," Bree said under her breath.

The receptionist eyed Olaf, standing silently by the door, hands clasped behind his back so the defined muscles around his chest practically burst through his button-down shirt, and her body went slack. Her eyes traced the bodyguard from his face to his abs and back again. Slowly. Decadently, as if she wanted to make sure she absorbed every morsel of Olafiness. Then she touched her finger to her chin; Bree was relatively certain she was wiping away a line of drool.

"And how may I help *you*?" the receptionist said to him at last, her voice throaty.

Olaf merely nodded toward Bree, looking every bit like a caveman.

"He's with me," Bree said, smiling curtly. "Big Brother is watching."

"Yes," the receptionist said. "Your brother is . . . big."

Gross.

The receptionist's eyes never left Olaf's face as she pointed absentmindedly at the office door. "Room B down the hall."

And Olaf claims another victim.

Room B was three doors down on the left, and Bree could hear an undercurrent of movement from within as she approached. Chairs being positioned on a carpeted floor, bags being unzipped, jackets being stowed. Bree took a deep breath as she paused outside the room. *Here goes nothing.*

Seven or eight chairs had been circled up in the middle of a windowless conference room. Dr. Walters hadn't arrived, but four other girls had already taken their seats, leaving an empty chair between each of them. Bree had been hoping to avoid a neighbor, but no such luck. Without making eye contact with anyone, she chose an empty seat on the far side of the room, between a tiny blond who was fiddling with a smartphone and a curvy Hispanic girl who sat with one leg tucked underneath her and her arms draped over the back of the chair. The body language was an unmistakable "You can't break me!" and Bree hoped that sitting next to that kind of personality might take the spotlight off her.

Her immediate neighbors ignored her, and the other two girls, both brunettes, stared at the floor and the ceiling respectively, then switched almost simultaneously, as if they couldn't be zoning out in the same direction at the same time.

"Good morning, ladies." Dr. Walters breezed into the room wearing a gauzy floral skirt that billowed around her as she swirled into a chair. "And how is everyone this afternoon?"

Murmurs of "good" and "fine" filled the room, but since Bree felt neither, she remained silent.

Dr. Walters didn't seem particularly interested in anyone's response as she settled herself on the opposite side of the circle, notepad in hand, and smiled. "Bree, it's good to see you."

All eyes turned to Bree, as if the other girls had just now noticed that she was there.

"Welcome to your new therapy group, as mandated by the Juvenile Detention Department of Santa Clara County." Dr. Walters gestured to the brunette on her right, then continued around the circle. "This is Kaylee, Emma, Heather, and Jacinta."

Bree hoped she wouldn't be tested later.

Dr. Walters glanced at her watch. "We'll give our late bird just another minute," she said, "before we start without—"

Just then, a tall girl with dark auburn hair rushed into the room. "Sorry I'm late, Dr. Walters," she said breathlessly.

Dr. Walters turned to Bree. "And the last member of our group is Tamara."

Only Bree didn't need Dr. Walters to introduce the late-comer. She knew her face.

It was Tammi Barnes, DGM target number six.

TWENTY-SIX

BREE MISSED EVERYTHING DR. WALTERS SAID FOR THE NEXT ten minutes. All she could do was stare at Tammi Barnes.

It was a mission Bree remembered well, one of the most satisfying DGM had ever pulled off. Tammi was captain of the cheerleading squad, a model student, friendly and outgoing with teachers and faculty, the center of a large and inclusive group of friends—and an unholy she-bitch to the young cheer wannabes who crossed her path. DGM discovered that Tammi was behind a hazing ritual for all the incoming JV cheerleaders, which involved forcing freshman hopefuls to give blow jobs to the varsity football team in order to make the squad. Football players filled out scorecards, which were circulated throughout the student body, and every guy at Bishop DuMaine knew which girls got an A, and which got an F.

The revenge mission was a tough nut to crack. Tammi lived a seemingly perfect life with her mom, stepdad, and two sisters. She never got into trouble, never stepped out of line, and as far as everyone knew, never kept any secrets. She was, however, very proud of her dance skills. Tammi grew up in Beverly Hills before her mom remarried and moved the family to Palo Alto. She claimed that while in LA, she'd been some kind of dance prodigy, studying with top teachers and in demand for music videos, television, and film. Tammi would readily tell you that the only reason she wasn't a professional dancer already was because her strict mom wouldn't let her go to a single audition until she turned eighteen.

And that self-mythology remained unchallenged until DGM dug up proof to the contrary. The Tiny Dancer Hip Hop Academy in Hollywood, California, maintained an online database of their students, past and present, including a thirteen-year-old Tamara Barnes. Margot had managed to hack into the site and download a video of Tammi dancing in the academy recital. DGM submitted the video to a website called "Dance or Dud?" where viewers rate and share dance videos. The truly awful video of Tammi Barnes doing her interpretation of Beyoncé's "Single Ladies" routine quickly became one of the most watched, and lowest rated, hits on the site.

And DGM made sure that everyone at Bishop DuMaine knew it.

But Tammi Barnes deserved the shame. She was a ruthless bitch, even more dangerous than Amber because she had a decent brain to go along with her power, and a chameleonlike ability to hide it. But now, here she sat in Bree's juvie-mandated group therapy session. What the hell had happened to her?

"Shall we get started?" Dr. Walters said. "Remember, anything shared in this session is one hundred percent confidential.

If you are caught trying to use any of the information you learn here outside of group therapy, you will be in violation of your parole and/or probation. Do you understand the parameters of this agreement?"

"Yes," everyone mumbled. This time Dr. Walters was paying attention, and looked right at Bree.

"Yes," Bree said quickly, realizing her silence wouldn't cut it.

"Good." Dr. Walters flipped a few pages into her notepad, and took up her pen.

"Tamara, we made some excellent progress at the end of the last session, so I'd like to pick up where we left off."

"Okay," Tammi said with an affable smile.

"We'd been talking about your stepfather, and the verbal and physical abuse you'd witnessed in your home. Can you tell us about that?"

Tammi sat very still. "I think I mentioned my stepdad had a gambling problem?"

Dr. Walters nodded.

"Right," Tammi said. "Well, by last summer he'd lost all of our savings, and was about to lose the house. So he bet a load on game seven of the NBA finals." She shook her head and laughed quietly to herself. "He swore he could make up for the losses. He just needed one big score to break even and then he'd quit." Tammi dropped her eyes to her lap and fell silent.

"And what happened?" Dr. Walters prompted.

Tammi shrugged without looking up. "He lost."

The story only got worse from there and Bree found herself cringing as Tammi related in dispassionate detail how her stepfather had come home hours later, drunk and angry. Tammi had corralled her sisters in their bedroom, hoping he'd just pass out. No such luck. She could hear the argument escalate from the kitchen, listening as her mother tried in vain to calm him down. Then the telltale thump, as her mother hit either the ground or the wall from the impact of his fist.

"My sisters started to cry," Tammi said, staring into the middle of the circle. "I tried to soothe them, keep them quiet, because I didn't want him to hear and come after us. More banging from the kitchen. My mom was pleading with him to stop and suddenly, something snapped in me. Who was this asshole? What gave him the right to hit my mom?"

"What did you do then?" Dr. Walters asked.

Tammi swallowed. "I grabbed my sister's softball bat from her closet. One of those metal ones with a rubber grip. I slipped off my shoes so he wouldn't hear me coming, went down the back stairs and through the laundry room. Came up behind him. I didn't even look to see if my mom was okay, didn't wait for her to tell me to stop because, of course, that's what she would have done. I just swung at his head as hard as I could."

Bree fought back tears. Last year, Tammi Barnes had represented all that was awful about Bishop DuMaine: the powerful student who humiliated those weaker and less fortunate than herself. DGM had dug into Tammi's past to find that little nugget on which to base their revenge against her, but they hadn't discovered this terrible secret about her family.

Would it have mattered? If they'd found out that her stepfather was a monster, would it have changed the fact that she forced a dozen freshman girls to blow football players? Maybe not, but perhaps it did explain why Tammi was such a bitch at school. She was trying to exert power in the only place she felt she had any.

Tammi looked up at Dr. Walters, her eyes tight with confusion. "He didn't die, but I wanted to kill him. I really did. Is that bad?"

"We're not here to judge what's good or bad," Dr. Walters said. "Only to discuss how we feel, and find ways to manage our emotions going forward."

"I felt angry," Tammi said. "Really angry. And then as he lay unconscious, my mom screaming over his body, I felt strong for the first time in my life. Like I'd taken control."

"And where do you think that feeling came from?" Dr. Walters asked. "You've mentioned before that you'd always felt powerless in regard to your stepfather. What changed for you that day?"

Tammi stared back at the center of the circle, silent. Dr. Walters waited patiently, and Bree held her breath, desperate to know the answer. Game seven of the NBA finals would have been mid-June, just weeks after the DGM prank against Tammi her senior year.

"Something horrible happened at school," she began at last.

Bree clenched her jaw. Had what DGM did to her sent her over the edge and somehow landed her here?

Tammi paused and glanced up. "Actually, no. It wasn't horrible. I mean, it was at the time. I was totally humiliated." She smiled sheepishly. "But I was a bitch at school. Like, the worst. I don't blame anyone for getting back at me. I deserved it."

Bree's jaw dropped. Tammi Barnes was taking responsibility for her actions? It was as if Bree's world had changed in an instant. Before, DGM targets were criminals that had evaded prosecution, and DGM was the Mossad going after Nazis. It was almost impossible to wrap her head around the idea that Tammi might actually be a victim herself.

"So this event at your school . . . ," Dr. Walters prompted.

"I think it showed me that people can fight back when they feel victimized. That *I* could fight back. So when I picked up that softball bat, it was like I was acting on behalf of others. I didn't care what happened to my stepfather, I only wanted to make sure that he couldn't hurt anyone ever again."

"Thank you, Tammi," Dr. Walters said. "I know it's been a difficult few months for you, after your mom kicked you out of the house. How are things in the group home?"

Bree's mind raced. This was their fault. As much as she'd been a bully at school, at home Tammi was a victim, and the prank against her had been a catalyst for her to take action. Tammi had only graduated from Bishop DuMaine a few months ago, and since then, had defended her family by braining her stepfather, been arrested, kicked out of her house, and sent to live in a group home. All because of what DGM did to her.

"Bree, did you hear me?"

Bree's head snapped up. She was lost in her own thoughts, oblivious to everything else.

"Huh?" she replied lamely.

Dr. Walters sighed. "We're giving our 'I feel' statements about Tammi's story. How did it make you feel?"

"Oh, right." Bree licked her lips, which had suddenly gone bone-dry. "I feel . . ." Guilty? Responsible? Like a total asshole? "I feel sad."

It was the lamest response known to man. "I feel sad" was the therapy equivalent of "I'm good, how are you?" It meant nothing in the grand scheme of things because, hell, who in that circle didn't feel sad?

And yet it was the best word to describe how Bree actually felt at that moment. Sad for Tammi, sad for herself. Bree realized that she and Tammi had more in common than she'd ever imagined. They were both bullies, and they were both victims.

"I think," Dr. Walters began after scribbling some notes on her pad, "that we can all understand your 'I feel' statement, Bree. Since this is your first session, let's talk a bit about why you're here."

Bree's sadness vanished, replaced by white-hot panic. She was there because she'd admitted to being DGM. How was she supposed to talk about that with Tammi sitting right next to her?

"Go on," Dr. Walters said. "Remember, everything you say here is safe. I don't report to the courts or to your parents."

That so wasn't Bree's concern.

"Right," she said, trying to think how she could possibly get through this without mentioning DGM. "I'm here because—"

A trio of soft beeps emanated from Dr. Walters's watch. "Ah, I see we're at time already."

Saved by the bell. Literally.

"Next session is tomorrow, and we'll pick up where we left

off. Bree, be prepared to share your story."

Well, shit.

Olaf was waiting in the exact same spot he'd been an hour before when Bree had walked into her therapy session. He didn't say a word as she followed the other girls out of the room, merely held the door open for her and stepped aside, ushering her into the bright afternoon sunshine.

It was as if her therapy-mates had vanished the moment they left the building, so desperate were they to get the hell out of there. A flurry of car doors and revving engines, then Bree and Olaf were the only ones left. But as she followed Olaf to the car, she realized that wasn't entirely true. Tammi stood at a bus stop in front of the medical building.

"Hey!" Bree said, flagging Tammi down. "Do you want a ride?"

She wasn't sure why she did it. Guilt, curiosity, a sense of responsibility for Tammi's fate. More likely, a deep, desperate need to know how Tammi's life had turned out.

Tammi turned and stared at Bree for a few seconds, then her eyes shifted to the black SUV and the mammoth beast who drove it.

"Is that your dad?" she asked.

Bree snorted. "No. Just a driver."

Tammi continued to stare at her. "You went to Bishop DuMaine."

Tammi Barnes recognized her? That was about as surreal

as the Queen of England recognizing the fifth stable boy at her least frequented castle. Again, that didn't gel with the stuck-up, self-absorbed bitch Bree remembered from school.

"Yeah," Bree said. "I'm a junior."

"I graduated in June," Tammi said.

I know.

Tammi blinked rapidly. "I'm staying off Newbridge Street. Is that too far?"

"Nope," Bree said, without consulting Olaf. "Come on."

Tammi climbed into the backseat and gave Olaf the address. Without responding, he entered it into the GPS, and eased the SUV out of the parking lot.

"Nice car," Tammi said, gazing around at the leather seats and top-of-the-line technology.

"It's my dad's," Bree said, as if deflecting the ownership of something so ostentatious.

"Does the driver come with it?"

Bree smiled. "Package deal."

"Oh."

They fell silent. Only the sound of the local news radio station murmured in the background. Bree tried to think. She wanted to ask about Tammi's family situation, about what happened to her after the DGM prank, about what was going to happen going forward, but she was at a loss about how to begin. She knew more about Tammi than she could ever admit, which is what happens when you spend a week crouched in someone's backyard, sifting through their recycling. But apparently, the one thing Bree didn't find out was the most important of all.

"So what do you do now?" Bree asked, desperate to initiate conversation. "That you've graduated, I mean."

"I'm on probation," she said. "So I have to check in, and come see Dr. Walters three times a week."

"Fun."

"And I work at the mall. A little boutique place that sells accessories and stuff."

The kind of place you would have spent all your money at a year ago.

"Sounds cool," Bree said lamely.

"Not really. But I don't mind. At least I'm not relying on anyone. I can take care of myself and no one can tell me what to do. It's a good feeling."

Bree nodded. She could appreciate the point. Never in her life had she felt free, not from the expectations of her father nor the shame of her mother. On the flip side, she'd never had to work, never had to earn her own money. Would it be liberating or terrifying to tell her parents to fuck off once and for all?

"That's pretty brave," Bree said with a smile. "Being on your own."

Tammi raised an eyebrow. "Brave? Brave is when you have choices. I don't have any."

Olaf eased the car to a stop at a red light and Bree felt ill. Tammi was right. She didn't have a choice. While Bree had all kinds of options, and what had she done with them?

"I guess you're—"

"Could you turn that up?" Tammi interrupted, pointing to the radio on the dash.

Without a word, Olaf cranked the volume.

"The senior at St. Francis has been missing since yesterday. Wendy Marshall was last seen in the Menlo Park area driving a black 2012 Lexus IS 250, and the police are asking for anyone with information on her whereabouts to contact them immediately. This is Valerie Fujiyama for KGO News."

"Wow," Tammi said. "Do you remember her from school?"

"Yeah," Bree said as she slumped back in her seat, her hands trembling. "I think so."

Wendy Marshall, DGM target number one, was missing. That had to be a weird coincidence, right?

"Here's my place," Tammi said. Olaf stopped in front of an early-twentieth-century Craftsman in desperate need of a gardener, some gopher traps, and a coat of paint. A rusted swing sat on the porch and the garbage bin on the side of the house was overflowing. A far cry from the four-bedroom ranch that Tammi used to call home.

"Thanks for the ride," Tammi said. "See you tomorrow."

"Yeah," Bree said. "Tomorrow."

When she'd have to spill her DGM story in front of Tammi. Great.

TWENTY-SEVEN

OLIVIA WAS A PANICKED MESS BY THE TIME SHE GOT HOME from school. Peanut, her usual ride, had disappeared after school was dismissed, forcing Olivia to take the bus. Which was fine, except for the fact that every single underclassman taking public transportation home was watching either Rex's birthday video or Amber's fat-camp photo montage on their phones. She was literally surrounded by DGM. Her brain swirled with recent events: the new pranks, the warehouse fire, the envelopes. It was as if everyone on the bus was taunting her, and with every passing second, she became more and more desperate to escape. By the time she reached her stop, she wanted nothing more than to run to her room, dive into her stash of packaged baked goods, and hide under the covers for the rest of the night.

"Livvie!"

Her mom bolted across the living room and tackle-hugged Olivia the moment she opened the front door, squeezing her so hard, she had to gasp for air.

"You won't believe what happened today," her mom cried.

She broke away and gripped her daughter by the shoulders. "I've been offered . . ." She let her voice trail off intentionally, her eyes wide as she prolonged the drama of her announcement. "A one-woman show off-Broadway."

Olivia cocked her head. "But we're in California."

Her mom clicked her tongue. "I know that, silly. *The Lady's Curse* is previewing in San Jose. Charles says—"

"Charles?"

She laughed. "The producer. Charles says they're already guaranteed a month-long run at the HERE Arts Center in SoHo. Can you believe it?"

Actually, no. Olivia couldn't believe it at all. "How?"

Olivia's mom took her by the hand and dragged her to the sofa. "I was working the lunch shift and this guy approached me at the bar. Youngish, attractive. He said I looked familiar but, you know, that's every guy's line when they're trying to pick up the bartender. Anyway, I was like, 'Yeah, whatever,' but he was really persistent. Finally he snapped his fingers and said, '*Twelfth Night* at the Public, 1998. Am I right?'"

"He remembered you from like seventeen years ago?"

"Why is that strange?" her mom snapped. "It was a smash hit and my reviews were amazing. 'June Hayes entranced as Olivia . . .'"

"'A fantastic, exhilarating new face at the Public,'" Olivia said, completing the review. "I know. It just seems so . . ." Convenient? Unlikely?

"Don't be jealous," her mom said, pouting like a ten-year-old. "You're not the only one in this family with acting prospects.

How do you think it felt to have Fitzgerald Conroy see us living in this dump, me heading off to my shitty bartending job? I was supposed to be somebody."

Olivia recognized the frenzied tone of the voice, the way her mom's eyes darted around the room. She was on the upswing of one of her manic episodes, probably ignited by Fitzgerald's visit, and now the flame had been fanned by some hack producer promising the moon. Olivia would have to tread lightly.

"So, um, when do rehearsals start?" Olivia asked, trying to de-escalate the situation.

"Tonight!" She rushed to her bag and pulled out a thick, brad-bound script. "Then every evening for the next two weeks."

Every evening? Alarm bells went off in Olivia's head. "Did you permanently change to the lunch shift at Shangri-La?" she asked hopefully.

"Lunch shift?" Her mom laughed. "I don't need that horrible bartending job anymore. This is our ticket to the big time, Livvie! Back to New York. Back to midnight cocktails at Bar Centrale after performances, then sleeping till three in the afternoon before doing it all over again."

"Mom," Olivia said slowly, as if she was afraid to say the words out loud. "Did you quit your job?" *Please say no.*

"Of course!"

Olivia felt the room spin around her. Could this day get any worse? "How are we going to pay the rent?"

Her mom grabbed Olivia by the shoulders. "We'll have plenty of money! Once rehearsals are over, I'll be getting seven thousand a week. A week! Think of it, Livvie!" Her mom did a little pirouette, then sashayed into the kitchen, where she poured a glass of water from the filtered jug.

Seven thousand a week. As much as Olivia wanted to share in her mom's readiness to believe in the unexpected windfall, the entire situation seemed too good to be true. Which usually meant it was.

Olivia followed her mom into the kitchen and leaned against the counter. "So," she said, trying to sound casual and nonjudgmental. "Have you seen the contract yet?"

"Please. This is a business based on reputation."

Oh boy. "So you haven't seen a contract."

Her mom whirled on her. "No," she mocked. "I haven't seen a contract."

"Maybe you should ask Charles about it?" Olivia wanted to see this seven thousand a week and guaranteed run off-Broadway in writing before she let go of the tiny ball of stress forming in the middle of her heart.

"You know, Livvie, I don't like your attitude."

"*You* don't like *my* attitude?" Olivia blurted out. Who was being the child and who was the adult in this scenario?

She was instantly sorry for her outburst. Her mom's face turned beet red and her eyes practically sparked with rage.

"One standing ovation and you think you know more than I do?" she roared. "I clawed my way to the top of New York, honey, and then I sacrificed all of it for you. How dare you try and ruin my moment of success, you selfish little bitch!"

"Mom, I'm sorry. That's not what I meant."

But it was too late. Her mom stormed out of the kitchen,

picked up her script and her purse, and yanked open the front door.

"Where are you going?" Olivia asked.

"I'm going to learn my lines before rehearsal," she said, without looking at Olivia. "Don't wait up."

Olivia stared blankly at the door long after her mom had slammed it in her face. She was worried, angry, stressed beyond belief, and for some reason, she felt incredibly guilty. Her mom was right about one thing—she'd sacrificed her career for Olivia. A lot of actresses in her position wouldn't have had the baby at all, or at least wouldn't have kept it. Where would her mom be today if she'd never had Olivia? Tony winner? Oscar winner? Instead, she was stuck here, broken and forgotten.

Olivia's eyes shifted across the room to where almost a dozen pill bottles lay strewn across the coffee table. More? She was pretty sure there hadn't been that many yesterday.

Suddenly, her mom's recent mood swings came into focus. She stormed across the room, scooped up all the bottles, leaving only the two prescriptions she recognized, and marched into her bedroom. She had no idea where her mom had gotten all the pills, but something had definitely shifted in her mom's emotional state in the last couple of days, and the pills must be to blame. Olivia would stash them until she could talk to Dr. Kearns and find out what was going on.

But as Olivia searched her bedroom for a hiding place, she heard a sharp knock at the door.

Her mom must have forgotten her keys again. She dumped the pill bottles on her bed and rushed to the front door.

Only it wasn't her mother on the landing.

"Amber!" Olivia exclaimed. Amber didn't even make the short list of people who might have been knocking on her door in the middle of the afternoon. "What are you doing here?"

Without answering, Amber shouldered past Olivia into the living room. "So this is where you live," she said, eyeing the small interior. "I didn't know it was a one-bedroom."

Olivia stiffened. She'd been in Amber's gorgeous four-bedroom home more times than she could remember. The eight hundred square feet Olivia and her mom shared could have easily fit into Amber's room alone.

She was ashamed of the way she lived, afraid of letting her friends know just how poor she really was. But she wasn't going to let Amber see that.

"It's all we can afford," she said proudly. "My mom works double shifts to cover rent."

"Worked," Amber said. "Past tense. Right?" She turned and faced Olivia for the first time. "I ran into her out front and she told me she's doing a Broadway play?"

"It's previewing here," she said, holding her head high, unwilling to let Amber see the shame she felt over her mother's delusions of grandeur. "Before a possible run off-Broadway. My mom's a well-known figure at the Public Theater in New York so it's a perfect fit." Okay, slight exaggeration. But Amber wouldn't know that.

"I guess."

Olivia took a deep breath. She was tired of the mind games. "Why are you here?"

Amber looked Olivia dead in the eyes. "I want to ask a favor."

"From me?" Olivia blurted out. Amber had never admitted to needing anything from anyone in the history of their friendship. Maybe today's humiliation had affected her more deeply than Olivia realized.

"I know that Rex and I are broken up," she said by way of an answer. "But I'm asking you not to date him."

Olivia laughed. She couldn't help it. "I don't want to date Rex."

Amber took a step closer to her, scrutinizing her face. "Are you sure about that?"

Why didn't she believe that Olivia was in no way interested in her ex-boyfriend? "Absolutely sure."

"Because I remember the night of the bonfire. I saw how you kissed him."

Dammit. That stupid bonfire! Olivia desperately regretted the act of making out with Rex to make Donté jealous. That momentary lapse in judgment had caused her nothing but grief.

"Amber, I know what you saw that night," she started. She just needed to make a clean break of it. Get it off her chest. "But it's not what you think. I was only—"

A shrill, old-fashioned telephone ring ripped through the room. Amber's cell phone volume must have been on full blast. She whipped her phone out of her purse and quickly answered it.

"What is it, Kyle? I'm busy."

Olivia could hear the muffled, unintelligible syllables coming through the phone, but the only hint as to what Kyle said was in Amber's reaction. The color drained from her face, the hand holding the phone shook uncontrollably, and her eyes glassed over. Her arm fell away from her face; her phone clattered the floor.

"Amber?" Kyle yelled, so loud that Olivia could hear it. "Amber, are you there?"

"What happened?" Olivia asked. "What's wrong?"

Amber lowered herself to the arm of the sofa but didn't say a word.

Olivia snatched the phone off the floor. "Kyle? It's Olivia. What happened?"

"Oh, thank God you're with her," he said.

"What happened?"

TWENTY-EIGHT

BREE WAS PRACTICALLY CRAWLING OUT OF HER SKIN WHILE
she waited in her bedroom for John, desperately trying to keep
her mind off Tammi Barnes.

Everything she believed in had been turned on its end. She'd
cast herself as a hero, or at least a penitent sinner, attempting
to atone. Instead, she had just made things worse for Tammi.
And how many others? Coach Creed and Ronny DeStefano had
turned up dead. Now Wendy Marshall was MIA. Was that on
her head?

And then there was Christopher. His death would stay with
her forever.

Seriously, she was a menace. Maybe she should just join a
convent, like her dad kept threatening. She would be doing the
world a public service by locking herself away where she couldn't
do any more damage.

A loud thud from her window snapped her out of her self-
pity.

John's muffled voice floated through the pane. "Are you

going to let me in or should I just hang out here all night?"

Bree leaped out of bed and threw open the window. "Why are you here so early?"

John planted his hands on his hips in a fake pout. "If you don't want to see me I can just leave."

"No!" Damn, she wanted to see John more than anything else in the world. "But school's not out yet. Did you ditch gym?"

"School was canceled after fourth period."

"What?"

"Throw down your hair, Rapunzel," John said. "We have a lot to talk about."

Twenty minutes later, Bree sat on her bed, stunned. "Rex and Amber in the same day? Whoever did it is either incredibly smart or painfully stupid."

"What do you mean?" John asked.

Bree shrugged. "Pulling off a prank is the easy part. But not getting caught afterward? That's where it gets dangerous. This new DGM group pulled off two missions at once after just a few days of planning. That's not going to end well."

"I wonder who it is." John shifted onto his side and lay down next to her, propping his head up with his hand. "One person? Two people?"

"At least," Bree said. She thought of all the different roles she and the other girls had played during their missions. Recon, tech, contact, research, breaking and entering, decoys, red herrings. There was no way they could have pulled off any of their missions with fewer than the four of them. "Four was the perfect number for us." She paused, and considered the current state of DGM with its two newest members. "I guess six is even better."

John smiled up at her. "You're the DGM master."

"Yeah." A *Star Wars* quote popped into her head, oddly appropriate to her mood. "Only a master of evil."

"You're not blaming yourself for Tammi Barnes, are you?"

"Why not?" She flopped back onto her comforter. "DGM was the catalyst for everything that's happened to her. She went from being a normal teen to a homeless one, all because of me."

"Bree . . ." John eased his way up to her side and tilted her face toward him. "Did you ever think that maybe you helped her? Even though she's broke and living in a group home, maybe that's an improvement from what her life was like before?"

"Stop trying to make me feel better." She didn't want to be absolved.

"Yeah, yeah," John said, dismissively. "You crave the guilt. I get it, Catholic girl."

Bree scowled at him, not because he was wrong but because he was right.

"But beating yourself up over this isn't going to make up for anything. Not for what she did, and not for what you did."

Bree had to admit he had a point.

He leaned down and kissed her, soft and slow, and all thoughts of Tammi Barnes faded. She caressed his cheek, her fingers lingering on the square lines of his jaw. She felt so much calmer when John was with her. He was the only person in the world who cared about her, who really listened to her, and she knew that he would always be there when she needed him.

She arched her back and his kiss deepened. Right now she needed him. Badly.

John shifted his body and Bree slid her hands down the back of his pants, pulling his hips closer. He moaned into her mouth, the hum buzzing her lips, then he moved lower, kissing her chin, her neck, her collarbone. She lifted her arms over her head as he slid her dress up and—

A sharp knock on the door jarred both of them from the moment.

"Bree?" her mom said. "Are you in there?"

"Shit!" Bree whispered. Her mom hadn't been in her room since she got out of juvie. Why now? She glanced at the window, where the rope ladder still hung. Dammit, she'd forgotten to haul it up. Had the neighbors noticed and called her mom?

John rolled off her onto the floor and began to shimmy under the bed.

"No," Bree hissed. She pointed at the window.

"No time," he said, and slithered his skinny torso under the frame.

"Bree, did you hear me?" Her mom jiggled the door handle. "Why's this locked?"

The last thing she wanted was for John to witness the horror of drunk Mrs. Deringer, but she didn't have a choice. She dashed to the window and pulled the curtains closed, then quickly unlocked the door.

"Heeeey, Mom," she said, hand on her hip in what she hoped was a casual pose. "What's up?"

Her mom stood in the hallway, arm braced against the

doorjamb, and peered over Bree's shoulder into her bedroom. "Why did you take so long to answer?"

"I was sleeping." And to illustrate the point, Bree stretched an arm over her head and faked a massive yawn.

"Mm-hm." Her mom's eyes lingered on the drawn curtains. Bree held her breath. "And why was the door locked?"

"There's a strange guy living in our house," Bree said. "My door is always locked."

"Olaf is not a stranger," her mom said with a huff. She breezed past Bree into the bedroom, eyes still searching. "He's practically part of the family."

"Right." Bree folded her arms across her chest. "And I'm sure your intentions toward him are purely maternal."

Her mom's head snapped around, eyebrow raised. "Purely."

The curtains fluttered in the breeze, exposing the hooks of the rope ladder. Bree casually moved to the other side of the room to keep her mom's focus away from the window.

Her mom strolled around, examining the band posters tacked up on the wall. She paused at the dresser and her eyes swept across the framed photos. They were all of Bree and her brother, Henry, at various stages of childhood through his high school graduation. Bree wondered if her mom even processed the fact that there were no photos of either parent in the montage.

Finally, her mom sat down on the edge of Bree's bed. "I wanted to continue our conversation from yesterday."

"Are you going to give me my phone back?" Bree asked.

"No."

"Let me have internet access?"

"No."

"Allow visitors?"

Her mom pursed her lips. "I can't do that."

Bree set her teeth. "Then we have nothing to talk about."

"Bree," her mom said. She sounded almost sad. "I know you think I'm a horrible mother . . ."

That's because you're a horrible mother.

" . . . and that I've abandoned you here in Menlo Park. But did you ever stop to think that maybe you're better off without me?"

Every single day.

A faint buzzing sound emanated from beneath the bed. John's phone! He muffled it immediately, but Bree held her breath, praying her mom didn't hear it.

"I realize," her mom began, oblivious to the cell phone, "I haven't been particularly . . . motherly. You have to realize, Bree, that I was raised to be selfish. To think only of myself. I was miserable here, playing the dutiful politician's wife. I didn't want to feel like that, and I certainly didn't want you to see me like that."

Bree snorted. "Are you trying to tell me that you did me a favor by taking off for France?"

"In a way, yes."

Lady, you are out of your mind. She wanted to say it, but starting a fight with her mom was not going to get her out of the room faster. Better to just play along.

"You know what, Mom? You're right. I think you made the right decision."

"You do," she said drily.

"Absolutely." Bree put her arm around her mom's shoulder and guided her toward the door. "We learned in therapy today about processing our emotions and looking for noncombative solutions. So I think, right now, the best thing for me is to have some alone time to process what you've said."

"Okay."

She practically shoved her mom into the hallway. "I'll see you at dinner. Bye!"

Bree twisted the handle, locking it firmly, and rested her forehead against the smooth, cold wood of her bedroom door. "That was close."

John dragged himself out from underneath the bed. "I'm sorry."

She turned and smiled. "It's not your fault you got a text."

"Not that." He walked purposefully toward her and enveloped her with his arms. "About your mom."

"Oh."

"Why didn't you tell me she lived in France?"

Bree avoided his eyes.

"So if your dad's in Sacramento all the time, that means you're here alone in this house. Is that even legal?"

Bree shrugged. "There's Magda."

"Who?"

"The housekeeper."

He took her face in his hands and tilted it upward. "You should have told me."

"How could I? Just blurt out, 'Oh, my parents both abandoned me once my brother went off to college. Isn't that awesome?'" She shook her head. "Not exactly lunchtime conversation."

He leaned closer. "From now on," he said softly, "you tell me this kind of stuff, okay?"

She nodded. "Okay."

John's cell phone buzzed again. "Crap, I forgot about that." He pulled it out of his pocket and swiped the screen. After a second, he gasped.

"What?" Bree asked.

John's body went rigid. "Oh my God."

"What is it? Who's it from?"

John glanced up at her. There was fear in his hazel eyes.

TWENTY-NINE

KITTY WAS STILL SHIVERING THIRTY MINUTES AFTER THE POLICE arrived. She wasn't cold. Or maybe she was? She honestly couldn't tell. "Numb" was a better word. She sat halfway up the staircase, leaning against the wall, her back to the living room.

She wasn't even sure how much time had passed since Kyle and Tyler raced downstairs and found Kitty standing over the lifeless body of Rex Cavanaugh. She couldn't speak, couldn't scream, couldn't even look away until Kyle grabbed her by the shoulders and guided her back to the foyer. One of them must have called 911 because she remembered the sound of sirens. Then bodies bustling in and out of the front door while voices shouted in the distance, at once angry and afraid.

Kyle and Tyler had disappeared; maybe they'd been asked to leave? Or were being questioned by the police? She had no idea, only knew that no one had bothered her. She probably should have told someone that she was there, that she'd been the one to discover the body, but she didn't have the energy to peel herself off the soft, plushy carpet. She leaned her head against the wall and closed her eyes. Maybe if she was very quiet, they wouldn't remember she was there.

People had been talking nearby, their words indistinct and muddled. Then she heard footsteps, strong and clear against the tile floor, and an authoritative voice broke through the white noise.

"Dr. Choudhary, do we have a time of death?" he asked.

Kitty knew that voice. Not daring to move lest he notice her, Kitty opened her eyes and strained to get a view of the foyer. Sergeant Callahan's back was to her. He stood, hands on his hips, with two women in matching coveralls.

"The body had been there for quite some time," Dr. Choudhary said, peeling off a pair of rubber gloves. "I'd say time of death is between eight and ten o'clock this morning."

The body? He has a name. Kitty hated Rex, but she felt a knee-jerk reaction to the way the medical examiner stripped him of humanity. Maybe that was just how they managed to do their jobs, staring at death every day.

Sergeant Callahan nodded. "Accidental?"

Dr. Choudhary arched an eyebrow. "Not unless he broke his own neck."

"I'm sorry?"

"The straight-line bruising is postmortem, plus there are signs of a struggle."

"You're saying it was murder."

She nodded. "My best guess is that the murderer surprised our vic and attempted to strangle him with the belt. Vic fought back, causing the abrasions around his neck, which probably snapped during the struggle. Death was instantaneous."

The news that Rex had been murdered came as no surprise to Kitty. She pictured Rex's face—purple and bloated, eyes open, mouth frozen in a silent scream. It was a look of terror.

Her hands began to tremble again.

Sergeant Callahan inhaled deeply then let out his breath in a slow, controlled whistle. "Anything else?"

"We found several different hair samples on the victim. They'll go to the lab for DNA analysis."

Several different hair samples? Kitty wasn't an expert but it seemed kind of odd that Rex, who had been home alone since before first period, would have had contact with enough people to accumulate that many strands.

Dr. Choudhary nodded to her assistant, who held out a plastic bag. "And we found this tucked into his shirt pocket."

"You've got to be kidding me." Sergeant Callahan held the bag up to the light and Kitty's breath caught in her throat. She could see the white card printed with clear, black letters. DGM.

"Does it mean anything to you?" Dr. Choudhary asked.

"Unfortunately." Sergeant Callahan tucked the bag under his arm. "Forensics is going to take over. Call me if you find anything else."

"You're not staying?" Dr. Choudhary asked.

He shook his head. "I need to check out a missing persons report. A Mrs. Gertrude Hathaway called this morning in a panic. Said her nineteen-year-old son Xavier was kidnapped from his bedroom last night."

Kitty's eyes grew wide. Xavier Hathaway was missing too?

"Another one?" Dr. Choudhary asked. "Do you think they're related?"

"Not sure," Sergeant Callahan said as he turned toward the door. "But I'm keeping all options on the table."

Ed sat in his car and stared at Olivia's text message.

Rex Cavanaugh was dead.

He thought of what Olivia and Kitty had told him: about Ronny DeStefano, who'd tried to blackmail Christopher; about Coach Creed, who'd made Christopher's life hell at Archway; and about Rex Cavanaugh, who shared a secret with Christopher, and who'd bullied him mercilessly as a result.

He thought of Christopher Beeman, placing the noose around his own neck in the boiler room of Archway Military Academy. Now three of the people responsible for driving him to suicide were dead with him.

Maybe there was justice in the world after all.

He checked the time on his phone, then laid it on the passenger seat and picked up a pair of mini binoculars, training them on a house at the end of the tree-lined residential street on which he was parked.

Should be any minute now.

After two hours of stakeout, the block was familiar now—the luxe gardens and expansive lawns, the mix of natural wood and white-washed fences delineating one property from the next, the luxury SUVs in every driveway. The house he gazed at through the binoculars seemed exactly like its neighbors, indistinct in every way. But that was only on the surface. Inside, Ed knew that house had been marked by tragedy.

A charcoal-gray sedan rounded the corner at the end of the street and pulled into the driveway of Brant and Wanda Beeman's Palo Alto home. Ed was tense with anticipation as Wanda climbed out of her car and walked to the front door, then stopped dead in her tracks.

He could practically see her thought process as she stared at her front door, which Ed had broken into and left wide open. *Did I forget to lock the door? It doesn't look like someone broke in. No, I'm pretty sure I locked it. Is Brant home early from his business trip? No, the flight from LA was delayed.*

Ed held his breath. Would she do it? Would she take the bait? After a few seconds, Wanda pulled out her cell phone and hurried back to her car.

Bingo.

If Ed had guessed correctly, and he was pretty confident that he had, Wanda Beeman was, at that very moment, calling whatever friend or family member had graduated from the police academy twenty years ago. He'd been very careful in his breaking and entering: he didn't want it to look as if the house had been burglarized, because that would send Mrs. Beeman dialing 911 in a hot minute. No, he wanted it to be a disturbing but possibly innocuous event. She couldn't be sure she had closed and locked the door behind her, but she couldn't be sure she hadn't. Not wanting to clog the emergency lines, she'd call whoever it was she knew in local law enforcement.

The wait seemed to take forever. Ed had been unable to find any Beemans in the local police force directories, and this was his last, best chance to follow this line of investigation. Maybe he was being paranoid? As if a cop would really be involved in this DGM murder mess. Still, a cop with a personal tie to Christopher Beeman? It was a plausible motivation.

Finally, a car turned the corner and Ed crouched down in the driver's seat as a black-and-white police cruiser pulled up in front of the Beemans' house. Ed peered through the binoculars, barely able to breathe as an officer stepped from the car, giving Ed a close look at his face.

"Oh shit."

THIRTY

KITTY LOOKED AROUND OLIVIA'S LIVING ROOM, THE LATEST DGM meeting place, and prayed that her teammates had been more successful in their investigations than she had been.

"Are we all ready?" she asked.

Ed the Head grinned at her. "Ready and able."

Olivia nodded, her face grim.

John leaned forward and spoke into Kitty's phone, which lay faceup on the coffee table. "Can you hear us, Bree?"

Bree's voice crackled through the speakerphone. "Loud and clear."

"Awesome idea to leave your phone with her," Kitty said, smiling approvingly at John. As uncomfortable as she'd initially been to have him in on their little secret, she had changed her tune. They were going to need all the help they could get.

"Oh my God!" Bree's heavy exhale rustled the speaker. "It's so good to hear you guys."

"I know how much you've missed me," Ed said with a smirk.

Bree snorted. "Yeah, and I'm sure the feeling's mutual."

Kitty shook her head. "Chitchat later, kids. Olivia's mom will be back from rehearsal in a few hours. We've got limited time."

"When do we not?" Ed asked.

"Kitty," Bree said, her voice full of concern. "I'm so sorry about your uncle's warehouse. Will the insurance cover everything?"

The image of the fire came rushing back to her, the words "I'm back" glowing in the darkened alley as the warehouse burned to the ground. "The fire was ruled arson," Kitty said. "If they prove my uncle set it, the insurance is void and he'll probably go to jail."

"Damn," John said.

"We'll find out who did this," Bree said. From the harshness in her voice Kitty could picture the fierce look on Bree's face. "And prove that your uncle is innocent."

"Thanks." It was sweet of Bree to say, but the last thing Kitty wanted to do right now was linger on her personal stakes. It wasn't going to help them. "The medical examiner was pretty clear: Rex was murdered."

Ed fidgeted in his seat. "And a DGM card was left on the body."

Kitty stood up and walked behind the sofa. She needed to think, which meant she needed to move. "Rex Cavanaugh, Coach Creed, Ronny DeStefano. What do they have in common?"

Ed the Head snorted. "Other than being Grade A douche bags?"

"And connected to Christopher Beeman," Bree said.

"I think the Beeman connection is overhyped," Ed said.

"We've found nothing tangible connected to him."

"They're also all former DGM victims," John suggested.

DGM victims. "Speaking of," Kitty said with a heavy sigh, "I overheard Sergeant Callahan say that Xavier Hathaway has been listed as a missing person."

Ed folded his arms across his chest. "Good riddance."

Kitty ignored him. "And according to Logan, the Gertler twins have also disappeared."

"What?" Olivia cried.

Kitty nodded. "Logan told me and I confirmed it today. They disappeared from the surf shop last night. No trace of them."

Olivia slumped in her chair. "Oh my God."

"Logan thinks you might be involved," Kitty continued, looking pointedly at Olivia. "But I told him it was just a coincidence."

"I've got even worse news," Bree said. She sounded alarmed. "Wendy Marshall is missing too."

"What?" Olivia repeated.

"Yeah, I heard it on the radio."

"Xavier Hathaway, Wendy Marshall, and the Gertler twins." Kitty felt her breaths coming faster. She'd known it couldn't be a coincidence when she heard about Xavier, but she hadn't wanted to believe it. "Four missing persons, all connected to DGM."

"And all people we personally investigated this week." Ed the Head whistled. "That's no coincidence."

Kitty's mind raced. She pulled a piece of paper from her duffel bag, the list she'd made with Ed and Olivia in the computer lab just days ago, and began to read off the names.

"Number one—Wendy Marshall," she said. "Missing. Two—Christina Huang, East Coast. Xavier Hathaway, missing. The Gertlers, missing. Melissa Barndorfer, in Europe. Tammi Barnes . . ." Kitty looked up at her phone. "Bree, you saw her this morning, right?"

"Yeah," she said. "And again tomorrow."

"We'll list her as not missing for now." Kitty returned to her list. "Then we've got Ronny, Coach Creed, and now Rex Cavanaugh."

"All DOA," Ed added, stating the obvious.

"If our killer is a former DGM target," Kitty said, looking at the phone on the table, "then Tammi is the only possible suspect."

"It's not Tammi," Bree said quickly.

Ed snorted. "How do you know?"

Kitty bit her lip, waiting on Bree's silence. She could almost see her flecking off bits of her nail polish on the other end of the line.

"I just don't think it's her," she said at last.

"I'm so glad you've found this deep love for Tammi Barnes," Ed said, sarcasm dripping from every word. "But may I remind you what she did to earn the scorn of DGM? I saw those blow job scorecards. Nasty stuff."

Olivia scowled at him. "Yeah, and weren't you taking side bets on which freshmen would score the highest?"

"I'm a businessman." Ed snapped his fingers. "Oh, and how did Tammi attack her stepdad? With a baseball bat?"

"The same way Ronny was killed," Olivia said slowly.

216

"She didn't do it!" Bree repeated.

Ed shrugged. "You willing to bet your life on that?"

"Okay," Kitty said. This bickering wasn't going to get them anywhere. "If Tammi's not involved, then she could be the next one to disappear."

"I'll talk to her tomorrow," Bree said quickly, sounding somewhat placated.

"And don't forget Amber," Olivia added. "She's a DGM target too."

"Tammi Barnes and Amber Stevens," Ed mused. "Victims or killers? News at eleven."

"Hm." John was staring at the ceiling.

"What?" Kitty asked.

He stretched a long arm behind his head and grabbed the back of his chair. "I was just thinking. There's got to be some way we can use this to our advantage."

"What do you mean?"

"Well," he said, bouncing his head against the crook of his arm. "You've never known exactly where and when the killer was going to strike next, right? This might be our chance to set a trap."

"You mean use one of them as bait." Ed slid to the edge of his seat. "I like this plan already."

Kitty saw both the positives and the negatives of this approach. On the one hand, they might be able to lure him out into the open. On the other, they'd be putting someone's life in danger. "I like the idea of going on the offensive."

"Yeah," Bree chortled. "Cuz that worked out so well the last time."

"Wasn't it *your* idea last time?"

"Semantics."

"I don't think I can convince Amber to help us," Olivia said. "Unless John asks her."

"Oh, hell no," Bree said.

"You got a better idea?" Ed asked.

Bree paused. "Tammi. I think I can get Tammi to do it."

"I wish Margot was here," Olivia whined. "She'd know what to do."

"What would Margot do," John mused. "I like it. We need wristbands or something."

What *would* Margot do? It was a more helpful question than perhaps John realized. Margot always took the direct, logical route. Nothing crazy, nothing with a low probability of success. She weighed the pros and cons, evaluated the weak points, calculated the various pieces of each and every plan. Why couldn't they do the same?

"Okay." Kitty sat down, her body tense. "Bree, see what you can do with Tammi, but if it doesn't work, we move to plan B."

"Plan B?" Bree asked. "What the hell is that?"

"That," she said slowly, "is where we put on a show."

THIRTY-ONE

BREE'S PULSE RATE SPIKED AS OLAF CAREENED THE SUV INTO the parking lot at Dr. Walters's office. In the next sixty minutes she had to avoid mentioning her involvement with DGM, satisfy Dr. Walters's requirements for "adequate group participation and sharing," and find out if Tammi Barnes would help her find a killer.

No problem.

Tammi was already seated around the circle when Bree entered the therapy room. She smiled and dipped her head toward the chair next to her, inviting Bree to sit. *Here goes nothing.*

"Hey," Tammi said, a furtive smile threatening her face. "How's it going?"

Bree shrugged. "Same old, same old." She thrust out her leg so Tammi could see the anklet. "Not much to do when you're trapped inside all day," she lied.

"So you can't leave at all?"

"Just to come here."

"For how long?"

Until my dad takes the leash off? "Until my hearing."

Tammi's eyes grew wide. "Wow. What did you do?"

"Um . . ." Shit. Great job, dumbass. You haven't even been here thirty seconds and you've already walked into the one conversation you don't want to have. "It was stupid, really."

Tammi smirked. "Stupid like stealing a car stupid? Or stupid like clocking your stepdad over the head with a softball bat?"

"I'd call that last one more ballsy than stupid." Ballsy in a way that Bree admired, though as she pictured Tammi standing over the unconscious body of her stepfather, he suddenly morphed into Ronny DeStefano.

"Okay, everyone!" Dr. Walters chimed as she breezed into the room. "I'm glad to see we're all here on time today. Let's get started, shall we?" She flounced into an open chair, her voluminous peasant skirt billowing around her, and opened her notebook. "I believe we were going to start with Bree today?"

Bree nodded and took a slow, deep breath. *You can do this.* "Can we talk about my parents?" she asked, taking control of the conversation.

Dr. Walters's face lit up, her eyes glistening. Bree guessed that volunteering to discuss her mommy and daddy issues would be like waving a red flag in front of an angry bull, and she wasn't wrong. "Of course! Where would you like to start?"

Bree launched into a monologue that she'd been carefully going over in her head all morning. She started with her father, how his political career had always been the driving force in his life, dominating all of his decisions, from whom he married (an heiress with a recognizable name) to where he lived (a district where said wife's family had a stellar and well-known reputation) to where he sent his kids to school (established Catholic institutions with long histories of Ivy League placements). Then she brought up her mother, the spoiled, infantile socialite who hated her life as a wife and mother so much that she'd run away to the South of France as soon as her darling son had left for college.

It made a great story, Bree had to admit. And the best part was that it was all true, every last detail. She couldn't have written a movie script this believable. Her tragic, neglected little life made for excellent therapy fodder, and Dr. Walters hung on every word, scribbling endless notes as she asked Bree repeatedly how it all made her feel, how her home life influenced her decision making, and where she hoped she'd be at the end of her time in therapy.

And so Bree jumped into her feelings of abandonment and anger. At first she really thought she was playing them up, exaggerating her resentment for the sake of her audience, just like she'd practiced. But as she was relating the story of her brother's high school graduation, long-buried memories came racing back into her mind, tumbling out of her mouth before she could edit them. The obvious pride displayed by both of her parents that day, the way they fawned over Henry Jr., parading his valedictorian honors in front of her father's political associates and her mother's society contacts during a lavish reception at the country club. She remembered how small she felt, how secondary. It was as if her family unit consisted of her parents and her brother, and she was merely some changeling who had appeared on the Deringer doorstep.

Bree loved her brother. Despite the four-year age difference, they'd been pretty close growing up. He was funny and kind and affectionate, all attributes her parents lacked. But as Dr. Walters drew feelings out of her, Bree's face grew hot, and her eyes stung with the effort to suppress the tears that threatened to blind her vision and swamp her mind.

Which is when she walked into a trap.

"Now, Bree, do you think this desperate need for attention and approval from your parents is what prompted your association with DGM?"

Bree caught her breath. Her head jerked up, aware suddenly of her carelessness. Beside her, she could sense Tammi's body go rigid, hear her breaths as they came faster and faster.

"I . . ."

Dr. Walters's alarm dinged with perhaps the worst timing in the history of the world.

"And we can pick up with that on Monday. Thank you, ladies."

Tammi bolted from her chair and raced out the door before Bree could say anything.

Dammit.

Bree ran down the hall and into the lobby, just in time to see Tammi disappear through the door.

"Tammi!" she cried.

"Where you go?" Olaf said, as Bree dashed through the lobby.

But she didn't wait to explain. Tammi was already hurrying down the street. "Wait!" Bree cried.

Tammi didn't slow down or even glance back as Bree

thundered after her, just continued doggedly forward as fast as she could go without breaking into a run.

"You have to listen to me," Bree said, as she began to overtake her prey.

"Why?" Tammi asked over her shoulder. "So I can make an idiot of myself again?"

Gah. This was not how this was supposed to go down. And after being outed as DGM, she couldn't exactly lead with "Hey, would you like to play possum for a killer?" So she tried a different approach. "Tammi, you might be in danger."

"I live in a halfway house," Tammi said with a laugh. "How much more dangerous can it get?"

"Wendy Marshall," Bree said, panting. "Xavier Hathaway. Maxwell and Maven," she paused for air, "Gertler."

Tammi stopped, right in the middle of the sidewalk, and half-turned back to Bree. "What about them?"

"They're all missing," Bree said.

Tammi stared at the pavement, her mouth working up and down as if she were literally chewing on Bree's words. "Why are you telling me this?"

Why *was* she telling Tammi this? If she was the killer, she was tipping her hand. And though in her heart Bree didn't really believe that Tammi was responsible for three murders, an attempted murder, and four kidnappings, she had tried to kill her stepfather. And DGM had kinda ruined her life. How big of a leap was it to actually finish the deed and get back at her enemies at the same time?

No, she couldn't believe it. This Tammi Barnes was a

different person than the one Bree had known in high school. And Bree was willing to bet her life that Tammi wasn't a killer.

"Look," she said at last. "Everyone in the area who's been a victim of DGM is either dead or missing."

Tammi's face clouded. "And you felt the need to warn me, right? Out of the goodness of your heart?"

"Tammi," Bree said, the sting of her words hitting hard. "I just want you to be careful. Whoever is doing this is . . ." Insane? Relentless? "Dangerous."

Instead of a look of fear or concern passing over her face, a slow grin crept up her cheeks. "I know what dangerous is," she said in a raspy voice that made the hairs on the back of Bree's neck stand up at attention. "And you don't have a clue." Then she turned and disappeared around the corner.

Okay. So maybe Bree had been wrong.

A horn blared as Olaf screeched the black SUV to a halt beside her. "Get in car!" he bellowed. "Does Olaf need to carry you?"

"No." Bree opened the door and climbed into the backseat.

"That better."

"Olaf," she said, "I need you to follow that girl I was just talking to. She went down Maple. Can you—"

Olaf pulled away from the curb and blew past Maple Street so fast Bree couldn't even catch a glimpse of any pedestrians.

"What the hell?" she said, grappling with her seat belt. "I need to find out where she went."

"Home," Olaf said.

"It's a matter of life and death."

But instead of his usually quick response, Olaf paused this time and snuck a glance at her over his shoulder. For a split second, she thought the big beast would show some humanity for once and throw her a bone.

"Olaf have orders," he said instead.

"Yeah," Bree muttered, slumping in his seat. "I bet you do."

But as he sped off toward home, his eyes fixed on traffic, Bree slipped John's cell phone from her bra and sent a quick, silent text.

Time for plan B.

THIRTY-TWO

OLIVIA FIDGETED UNCONTROLLABLY AS SHE SAT IN THE bleachers. This was the third all-school assembly in a month. The last two had been showstoppers: first DGM's prank against Coach Creed, then Bree turning herself in with the whole school and half the Menlo Park Police Department in attendance. And today? Today would be no different.

Well, slightly different. Olivia scanned the bleachers as the last of the students and teachers filed into the gym. Instead of bursting at the seams as it usually did with the entire student body crammed inside, today the Bishop DuMaine gym was barely half-full. Three deaths had been enough for most parents, and almost the entire freshman and sophomore classes, plus a smattering of upperclassmen, hadn't shown up for school.

No matter. There were enough eyes watching for what Olivia had planned.

She swallowed, and recrossed her legs for the billionth time. Was this going to work? Or were they about to make another colossal blunder?

"What's wrong with you?" Jezebel asked. "You're so jumpy."

"Have you seen Amber?" Olivia asked by way of an answer.

"Nope."

Where is she? Olivia reached into her tote bag, searching for her phone, when she remembered it wasn't there. Part of the new security measures on campus. Since both Rex's video and Amber's photo montage made the rounds online, where every student with access to the internet in the palm of their hand could stream them in a matter of seconds, Father Uberti had banned all portable cellular and wireless devices from campus. First thing that morning, all Bishop DuMaine students had been greeted by uniformed police officers, who confiscated phones and tablets and forced everyone to open their mouths and give a DNA swab sample. Olivia was pretty sure that violated a half-dozen First Amendment rights, but whatever. She'd managed to stash her phone in Peanut's car, and she just hoped that Kitty and Ed had managed to stash theirs before the cops bagged them.

Olivia shifted her body again, eliciting an irritated grumble from Jezebel, then her attention was drawn to the far side of the gym as Kyle and Tyler marched through the door. They wore matching black armbands over their blue 'Maine Men polo shirts, a tribute to their fallen comrade. They'd been handing out the armbands around campus all morning, and much to Olivia's horror, the gesture had spread like wildfire. Their fellow 'Maine Men wore them, of course, but others had joined in. Rex Cavanaugh was more feared than revered at Bishop DuMaine, but in the end, he was one of them. And he had been viciously murdered.

Father Uberti arrived next, followed by a half-dozen priests. Representatives from the archdiocese. Two of them wore the same black hooded cassocks as old F.U., with matching cinctures around their waists. Must be members of his order. The rest wore the usual black pants and jackets with stiff white collars around their necks.

Father Uberti walked more slowly than usual, and his air lacked its usual cocky self-importance. His shoulders sagged, and he stroked his beard with an almost manic energy. For the first time in Olivia's high school career, Father Uberti looked insecure.

He took the microphone with a heavy sigh. "I will assume by the marked drop in attendance," he began unceremoniously, "that news of Mr. Cavanaugh's death has been made public."

He paused briefly, and Olivia noted the total silence in the gym.

"I'll take that as a yes," Father Uberti continued.

Jezebel nudged Olivia's arm and nodded toward the door. "There she is."

Olivia turned and saw Amber in the doorway, her perfect spiral curls framed in the morning sunshine. She stepped into the gym and Olivia could see that her face was turning red, her body tense and clenched as if she was barely containing her rage. Her eyes swept the bleachers, searching. Then they landed on Olivia.

"You bitch!" she roared. Every head in the gym turned toward Amber as she extended her arm, pointing at Olivia. "This is your fault."

Olivia looked behind her, as if Amber could possibly be

referring to someone else. "What did I do?"

Amber stormed to the middle of the gym floor. "Don't act like you don't know!"

Olivia stood up and held her hands in front of her as she walked down the wooden stairs. "I seriously have no idea what you're talking about."

Amber met her at the base of the steps. "Don't you?"

"No, I—"

Amber's hand came out of nowhere, smacking Olivia cleanly on the cheek. The sting rippled through her flesh and stars shot in front of her eyes from the force of the strike. The students in the gym let out a collective gasp.

"Miss Stevens!" Father Uberti cried into the microphone. "How dare you strike another student."

But Amber wasn't listening. "I know the photos came from you. What do you have to say for yourself?"

Olivia righted herself, her palm pressed to her cheek. "I had nothing to do with it, Amber."

"That's not what I heard."

"Miss Hayes, Miss Stevens!" Father Uberti sounded helpless. "Take your seats this instant."

"Then you heard wrong," Olivia shouted back. "I didn't even know you went to fat camp."

That was the tipping point, apparently. Olivia watched with some satisfaction as Amber's face turned bright red, her lips pulled tight against her teeth. Then, without warning, she hurled herself at Olivia, arms stretched toward her neck.

Olivia hit the hardwood floor, and rolled over, then under,

Amber, locked in a death grip. She landed on top of her former best friend, both sandals lost in the melee, dress hiked up to her hips.

The crowd cheered as if they were in the gym for a basketball game instead of an assembly, and their fervor seemed to spur Amber on. She screamed and lunged for a fistful of Olivia's pixie-short hair, managing only a half inch or so of length, then yanked Olivia off her. Olivia lashed out with her arms as she tumbled over, and caught Amber's head with her elbow. Amber howled and reared back, releasing Olivia's hair, and she was able to scramble to her feet. Olivia lunged at Amber, still hunched on all fours, but a hand was around her waist, pulling her away.

"What the fuck is your problem?" she screamed at Amber, straining against Kyle's arm.

Tyler plucked Amber off the ground and pinned her arms behind her back. "You're my problem," she yelled. "I hate you."

"I hate you too!"

Father Uberti stormed across the gym, the priests from the archdiocese following in his wake. "What in the name of God is wrong with you two?"

Amber went limp in Tyler's arms. "She started it."

"Me?" Olivia gasped. "She attacked me, Father Uberti. Unprovoked."

"Unprovoked my ass." Amber turned to the priest. "She told DGM about the photos of me."

Olivia narrowed her eyes, struggling against Kyle. "I have no idea what she's talking about."

"You want to find DGM?" Amber pointed directly at Olivia. "Ask her."

Father Uberti's eyes trailed from Amber to Olivia. "In my office. Both of you."

"No," Amber said, her voice strong but calm. "You know what, Father Uberti? No, I won't go to your office." She wiggled herself free of Tyler's grasp. "I'm going home."

And without another word, she stormed out of the gym.

THIRTY-THREE

KITTY SLOUCHED LOW IN THE DRIVER'S SEAT, KEY READY AND waiting in the ignition, and watched the side door of the school.

"You sure this is going to work?" John asked from the back.

"No."

"Awesome."

She didn't elaborate. Kitty's stomach was already doing backflips, and she didn't need to be reminded that plan B wasn't exactly the most well-thought-out strategy in the history of secret missions.

Before she had time to further worry herself into an ulcer, the school door flew open and Amber raced down the stairs to the parking lot. Her face was beet red, her blouse disheveled, hair a tangled mess. It looked as if Amber had been in one hell of a catfight.

"You should see the other guy," John mumbled.

A squeal of tires pierced the silence of the parking lot, and before Kitty could even turn over the ignition in her old Camry,

Amber had peeled her Mercedes out of the lot.

Seconds later, the "other guy" appeared as Olivia scampered down the stairs. Like Amber, her clothes were in disarray and her pixie-short curls a rat's nest. She hurried to Kitty's car and climbed daintily into the front seat.

"How did it go?" Kitty asked.

A satisfied smile lit up Olivia's delicate features. "It was amazing."

Kitty held up her hand and gave Olivia an enthusiastic high five.

"It was the best acting performance Amber's ever given," Olivia added. "By far."

"Yeah," John said, "because she wasn't really acting."

Kitty grinned. "Neither was Olivia."

It had been remarkably easy to get Amber onboard with the plan . . . as long as John was involved. Kitty had approached Kyle and Tyler with the idea before school, doubling down on her new position as leader of the 'Maine Men. She suggested they go on the offensive and try to catch the killer themselves, then laid out the plan to use Amber as bait.

Meanwhile, John recruited Amber via text, playing up his concern over her safety, and his wish that they could do something about it. He'd even managed to get Amber to suggest the staged catfight herself.

To Kyle, Tyler, and Amber, today's plan seemed to be their idea. No one suspected DGM at all.

Not bad for a morning's work.

"Stay with her," Olivia advised. She fumbled with her seat belt as she tried to put it on. "But not, you know, too close."

"Fly casual?" John suggested.

Olivia glanced back at John. "Am I supposed to know what that means?"

"Nope," John said.

"Stay on target," Kitty said as she released the parking brake. John and Bree weren't the only ones who knew *Star Wars* by heart.

In the rearview mirror, she saw John nodding in approval. "Nice one."

"It's like you're speaking a language I don't understand," Olivia said.

John leaned forward. "How can you not understand the best movie trilogy ever made?"

"*American Pie*?" Olivia asked.

John shook his head in bewilderment. "I don't think I can talk to you right now."

"Good." Olivia turned back around. "Can we hurry up and catch Amber?"

Kitty gritted her teeth as she sped after Amber's black Mercedes coupe, trying to ignore Olivia's nonstop stream of passenger-seat driving. *Run that light. She's switching lanes. Watch that pedestrian. You're too far behind. Now you're too close.*

"Why do we have to tail her, Kojak?" John asked as they sped through an intersection, barely avoiding a red light. "Haven't you been to her house like a million times?"

234

Kitty saw Olivia's body tense up. "I don't want anything to happen to her."

John snorted. "Between school and here?"

The light mood of a few moments ago had evaporated. Kitty knew exactly why Olivia was so worried, and she needed John to understand that the risk factor here was very, very real. She caught his eye in the mirror as they stopped at a light. "Remember what he's capable of."

Amber was four or five cars ahead of them when the light turned green. According to Olivia's directions, Amber should have turned at the intersection, but instead, she kept going straight.

"What's she doing?" Kitty asked.

Olivia bit the inside of her lower lip. "I don't know. Stay with her, though."

Kitty followed the line of cars, her eyes peeled for the shiny black coupe in case Amber realized she'd missed her turn and flipped a bitch in the middle of the street. They'd gone almost a mile before Amber veered off the road into the Coffee Clash parking lot.

"She wants a latte?" John asked as Amber hurried up the steps and into the coffeehouse. "Now?"

"An iced triple-shot nonfat vanilla soy latte with two Splenda," Olivia corrected.

"This is ridiculous." Kitty pulled into a spot at the far end of the mini-mall and looked around. There were three other cars in the lot, plus a silver SUV at a meter in front. It was pretty deserted for a Friday afternoon, and Kitty could see through the glass doors into the café, where Amber was paying for her drink.

"At least we know no one's following her," Olivia said. "That's something."

Kitty pursed her lips. "I guess."

Two minutes later, Amber strolled out of the café, iced coffee concoction in hand, and rolled her car out of the lot. Without a word, Kitty followed, again leaving a few cars between them. They'd gone three blocks before Kitty noticed a car close behind them. The same silver SUV that had been parked in front of the Coffee Clash.

Amber pulled into the left turn lane, but instead of following her, Kitty switched lanes to the right, keeping an eye on the SUV. She was probably imagining things, but she just wanted to make sure they weren't being followed.

"What are you doing?" Olivia asked as they passed Amber's car.

Kitty glanced at the rearview mirror. "Checking something."

Olivia twisted in her seat and stared out the back window. "Is someone following us?"

"I don't know," Kitty answered. The SUV hadn't followed them into the new lane. They drove a few more blocks in tense silence, then Kitty let out a slow breath. "I think we're fine."

Olivia relaxed back into her seat. "Thank God."

Kitty made a U-turn at the next intersection and headed back toward Amber's house.

"Was it the silver SUV you were worried about?" John asked from the backseat.

"Yeah," Kitty said. "Why?"

"Because it just made a U-turn to follow us."

"Are you sure?" Olivia asked.

Without waiting for an answer, Kitty slammed on the accelerator. The aging engine strained, the RPMs rocketing into the red zone. She zigzagged around cars, weaving in and out of lanes like a race-car driver. If the SUV was actually following them, he'd have to match her speed and her course. To her horror, she saw the SUV accelerate rapidly, and whiz around several cars in an attempt to keep up with her.

"Shit."

"Oh my God!" Olivia cried. "It's him!"

Whether or not the killer who'd been terrorizing them for weeks was, at that very moment, tailing them through the streets of Menlo Park, Kitty couldn't say for sure. There was a logical argument against it, but at the moment, the logical-argument part of her brain wasn't working. Just the panic reflex.

"Can you get the license plate?" Kitty asked.

John spun around in his seat. "Looks like California, but I can't get digits. He's too far away."

"Dammit!"

Kitty scanned the road ahead, looking for an escape route. Her eyes landed on a large delivery truck in the far right lane two blocks ahead.

"Hang on!" she said. The engine roared as Kitty coaxed even

more speed out of the old Camry. They careened through a yellow light, then just as she passed the truck, she zipped in front of him, slammed on the brakes, and made a dangerous right turn onto a side street. With any luck, their pursuer had lost sight of them for a split second when Kitty pulled in front of the truck, and didn't see her turn off the main road.

Foot back on the accelerator, she raced through the suburban neighborhood, praying no one stepped into the street, then turned into someone's driveway and cut the engine.

"Everybody down!" she ordered.

Seat belts off, Kitty and Olivia crouched low in the front seat while John flattened himself in the back.

"Do you think we lost him?" Olivia whispered.

"I hope so." Even if he did see them turn onto the side street, Kitty was counting on the fact that her nondescript Camry was a pretty common car, and whoever was following them might not notice one parked in a driveway.

"I don't understand," John said. "I thought we wanted the killer to show up at Amber's house. Why were we trying to lose him?"

"I . . ." That was a good question, after all. But Kitty couldn't explain the abject terror she felt at the idea that the killer had been following them. It was like an instinctual reaction to flee.

Before Kitty could answer, she heard a sound that made her blood run cold. A car pulling up alongside.

She held her breath as a car door opened, then slammed shut. Maybe it was just the homeowners? Footsteps on concrete as someone walked up to the door and knocked on the window.

"What are you guys doing?"

Kitty knew that voice. She sat up and found the slightly confused face of Logan Blaine on the other side of the glass.

THIRTY-FOUR

OLIVIA LET OUT THE BREATH SHE'D BEEN HOLDING, THEN opened the passenger door and tumbled out of Kitty's car. "Logan!"

But instead of his usual smile, Logan's face was hard, his eyes narrow. "What the hell is going on?"

Kitty scrambled out of the driver's side, closer to Logan. "It's okay," she said, trying to calm him down. "I can explain."

Olivia had no idea what she was talking about. "Explain what?"

Logan yanked his cell phone from his pocket. "I should call the cops right now. Tell them what you've been up to."

"Dude, calm down." John placed his hand on Logan's arm.

"Calm down?" Logan cried, shaking John off. "Your girlfriend tried to kill my girlfriend. Don't tell me to calm down, dude."

John shook his head. "It's not like that."

Logan pointed at Olivia. "And I told you about those Gertler guys and now they've disappeared."

"Logan," Kitty said, her hands held up before her. "You don't understand."

"Damn right I don't understand."

But Olivia understood perfectly. Logan thought they were the ones behind the killings, the ones who had attacked Margot. It was so ridiculous, especially since until about twenty seconds ago, they thought the killer was behind the wheel of Logan's silver SUV, that she burst out laughing.

"Really?" John said, turning to her.

"I'm sorry," Olivia gasped, gripping her stomach. "Can't help it. He thinks we're the killers!"

"Why is that funny?" Logan asked with complete sincerity.

"Because we thought *you* were the killer," John said.

Logan's eyes grew wide. "Me?"

"Well, whoever was chasing us," Kitty explained. "By the way, why were you chasing us?"

"Um . . ." Logan scratched his chin. "I guess I don't really know. I saw the fight in the gym and then Olivia followed Amber outside. I saw her get into your car and . . ."

"And you thought we were all in it together," Kitty said, completing his thought.

"Aren't you?"

"Yes," Olivia said, coming around the car and taking Logan by the arm. "But not in the way you think. We're all on the same side."

"Same side of what?" Logan asked.

Olivia tugged him toward his SUV. "Come on," she said. "I'll explain on the way. We have a date to keep."

◆ ◆ ◆

"So you're using Amber as bait to try and find Rex's killer?" Logan asked as he halted his SUV down the hill from Amber's house.

"That's the plan," Olivia said. She'd kinda sorta filled him in on the drive, leaving out key information, like the fact that she, Kitty, and Margot were members of DGM. Best not to bring him into the fold without Margot's permission.

Logan stared at the steering wheel. "If it's the same dude who attacked Margot . . ." His voice trailed off, and Olivia watched the tendons around his jaw ripple as he clenched his teeth.

"Then we'll hand him over to the police," Olivia said softly, finishing his sentence.

"And Margot will be safe," he added.

Olivia could see the mix of emotions playing themselves out in the minute changes in Logan's facial features. Tightly pressed lips denoted his anger, his furrowed brow showed the worry, and hints of loneliness and confusion could be found in his searching brown eyes and wrinkled forehead, respectively. There was nothing else Olivia could say without giving away too many of DGM's secrets, so instead she patted his hand and opened the door. "Come on."

Olivia and Logan climbed out of the car just as Kitty pulled up behind them.

"Dude," John said, with a nod at Logan. "When you're not chasing someone, you drive like my grandma."

Logan smiled, and all traces of his earlier worry vanished. "My mom threatened to yank my car if I get a ticket. So I try to drive like she does." His smile deepened. "When I'm not in car chases."

Kitty linked her arm through Olivia's and started up the street. "Which one's her house?"

"This way."

Olivia and Kitty hurried ahead, separating themselves from the boys. "What did he say?" Kitty whispered as soon as they were out of earshot.

Olivia spoke low and fast. "He's figured out that the attack on Margot is somehow related to the murders, but he doesn't know how."

"Did you tell him?"

Olivia shook her head. "Not about DGM. Just that we were trying to protect Amber."

"Okay." Kitty squeezed her arm. "Hopefully, in a few hours, this will all be over."

Olivia nodded, and turned into a steep driveway. "Here it is."

The boys jogged up behind them as they hiked to Amber's front door, which flew open before Olivia even had a chance to knock.

Amber rushed out and threw her arms around John's neck. "I'm so glad you're here," she said, holding him close.

"Er, yeah," John said, playing along. "We want to keep you safe."

"And Kyle and Tyler are coming too?" Amber asked.

Kitty nodded. "They should be here any minute."

Amber leaned into John, who stiffened at her touch. "I'm

lucky to have so many strong men here to protect me."

"So now what do we do?" Logan asked, peering out the window.

Kitty followed his line of sight. The living room had a bird's-eye view of the driveway and the winding street below. If anyone came looking for Amber after she'd declared she was going home, alone, they'd see him or her coming. Kitty just prayed the killer took the bait.

"Now," she said calmly. "We wait."

Olivia curled up in the corner behind the sofa, hidden from sight by a large plastic ficus, and kept her eyes on Amber. She lounged amid the sofa cushions, languidly flipping channels on the television. Olivia was pretty sure she'd fallen asleep at some point, but despite the tediousness of the afternoon, Amber hadn't complained once. She sat as she was supposed to, calm and casual, seemingly alone in a well-lit house. The bait dangling at the end of the line.

Olivia, on the other hand, had been a fidgety mess. She'd sat opposite Kitty at the dining room window for the first two hours, but had so much trouble keeping her body still, Kitty banished her to the other side of the room where her restlessness wouldn't rustle the curtains and give away her presence.

It was the silence more than the waiting that was getting to her, and she was almost grateful when Amber finally opened up the conversation.

"No one's coming," she said softly.

"We don't know that."

"They'd be here by now."

"We don't know that either."

"This sucks."

At least Olivia could agree with that.

"He'll come," Olivia said, trying to sound confident. "And we'll get him."

They had lookouts at every entrance. Kyle had taken the sliding door that led from the kitchen to the backyard. Tyler staked out the laundry room, which opened to the side of the house. John and Logan took the upstairs, where they could command a view of the entire block. They had every angle covered, every entrance to the house accounted for. If the killer did show up, they'd see him.

Only he hadn't.

"I know Rex could be an asshole," Amber said. "But I loved him."

From where she sat, Olivia couldn't see Amber's face, but her voice was sad, an emotion Olivia had never seen in her before.

"The night of the bonfire," Olivia began. She needed to get this off her chest. "What you saw, me and Rex, it wasn't what you thought."

She paused, but Amber didn't say anything.

"I know I told you that I broke up with Donté, but that's not how it went down. He dumped me."

"What?"

"Yep," Olivia said. "So I was just trying to make him jealous. Rex was so drunk he didn't know what he was doing."

She decided to omit the fact that Rex, even when sober, was

a pig who hit on her at every opportunity. He was dead, and Amber deserved to remember him in any way she chose.

"He knew what he was doing," Amber said softly. "When it came to you, he always knew."

Olivia wasn't sure what to say.

Amber took a deep breath, then exhaled loudly. "Rex was always talking about you. Whenever he was trying to get me to do something I didn't want to do, he'd make a comment about how hot you looked, or how talented you were. I'd give in every time."

Something she didn't want to do? Olivia thought of Ronny DeStefano and how, at one point, she'd thought Rex and Amber might have killed him.

"I'm sorry," Olivia said.

Amber laughed, drily and without a hint of mirth. "He even tried to use me to pay off a debt."

"What?" Olivia cried. She couldn't help herself.

"Shh!" Kitty whispered from across the room.

"Yeah," Amber said, her voice lower. "This guy wanted money from Rex for . . ." She paused, and Olivia wondered if she'd spill Rex's biggest secret. "For something," she said instead. "And he offered the guy a night with me as payment."

"Oh my God, Amber," Olivia said, shocked. Rex was even more of a monster than she'd realized. "I'm so sorry."

"I didn't do it," Amber said. "Gave him some jewelry instead. But that was Rex."

Olivia pushed herself to her knees and crawled to the edge of the sofa. She didn't care if she could be seen from the street; she needed to look Amber in the eyes. For all the bad blood between them, Olivia wouldn't have wished Rex on her worst enemy, and she was just now beginning to understand what Amber's relationship with him had been like.

"Amber," she said, staring at her friend in the growing twilight. "You deserve better than that."

Amber's smile was tight. "Do I?"

"Yes," Olivia said. "And don't ever forget it."

Kitty crouched on the dining room floor, hidden behind the silk damask curtains, knees hugged tightly to her chest, head resting against the wall as the sun gradually shifted across the horizon.

Several cars had passed on Amber's secluded block. None had so much as slowed down, let alone stopped. She'd seen three nannies pushing their wards in strollers, cell phones fixed to their ears as they walked. Two joggers, one with dog accompaniment, one without. A FedEx truck had caused a brief flurry of anxiety as it squealed to a stop in front of the house, but the driver merely checked his GPS before he roared up the street.

From the pocket of her jeans, Kitty's phone vibrated. The noise sounded so loud in the tense silence of Amber's living room, she jumped.

"Do you see something?" Olivia whispered. She scrambled to Kitty's side.

Kitty shook her head. "Cell phone."

"Oh."

The message was from Mika.

Where are you? Practice started half an hour ago.

Kitty hadn't told anyone she was bailing on school, let alone volleyball practice two days before a huge tournament. She thought about responding, coming up with a lie about food poisoning or something, so Mika wouldn't worry about her, but then a second message came in.

Or are you at some special 'Maine Men meeting?

Kitty could practically hear the derision in Mika's voice, and suddenly, she didn't care if her best friend knew where she was or not.

Fifteen minutes later, a flurry of texts lit up her phone.

Donté: Mika said you didn't show up for practice. Is everything okay?

Mika: Seriously, where are you? Coach is biting through nails she's so pissed.

Coach Miles: Wei! You'd better have a good excuse for missing practice or I'm benching you for Sunday's tournament.

Coach Miles: This is not NCAA behavior.

Donté: I'm worried. Please let me know you're safe.

Coach Miles: Especially after I did you that favor, getting Vreeland on the team at Gunn. I am not impressed, Wei.

Donté: Kitty?

Enough! She typed two quick words to Donté so he didn't call the cops and report her as a missing person. **I'm fine.** Then she powered off her phone and shoved it back in her pocket. She needed to be on her game for something much more important than a volleyball tournament. People's lives were on the line and if she wasn't—

Kitty froze. Out of the corner of her eye, a shadowy figure

crept across the neighbors' front lawn.

"What?" Olivia asked. "What do you—"

Kitty held up her hand and Olivia fell silent.

Had she really seen something or was it just a trick of the departing light? Kitty stared out onto the front lawn, hardly daring to breathe.

It felt like an hour as she sat there, body rigid, waiting to see if something moved outside the window. Her quads ached from crouching, and in the lengthening late-afternoon shadows, her eyes began to play tricks on her as every tree, bush, and mailbox seemed to move when her eyes were fixed elsewhere. She was just about to give up and call the whole thing quits when she saw it again.

This time there was no mistaking the darkened figure that darted from behind the garbage bin across the street and disappeared into the hedges at the edge of the Stevenses' property.

Someone was outside.

"Oh my God!" Olivia gasped.

"You saw it too?"

A creak from the floor above, then John's head appeared at the top of the stairs. "Did you guys see that?"

"What?" Amber asked. There was a catch in her throat.

Kitty knew exactly what she was feeling. Panic. Even though they had superior numbers and the element of surprise, their anonymous stalker had killed three people. They couldn't take him lightly.

"Kyle!" Kitty said, her voice hushed. "Get ready."

"On it!"

She turned back to the window in time to see the dark mass dash across the front lawn to the door. Kitty fought the instinct to lunge at the door and lock it, even though they'd intentionally left it unlocked for the ambush, and as she crouched behind the curtain, legs ready to pounce, she couldn't help but think they'd all made a horrible mistake.

Her heart pounded in her chest, so loudly she almost missed the imperceptible click of the handle. There was a rush of air as the door silently swung open, then closed, and a hooded figure tiptoed into the living room.

"Now!" Kyle yelled.

Bodies flew from every direction. Kyle, Tyler, Logan, and John all seemed to tackle the intruder at once, smothering him. Olivia dashed to the wall and switched on the overhead lights, while Kitty slowly rose to her feet and approached the dog pile of tangled limbs.

"I've got him!" John cried.

Logan groaned. "That's me, dude."

"I called 911," Kyle barked. "The cops will be here any second. Don't even bother trying to escape."

"I'm not trying to escape!" came a familiar voice.

"Ed?" Kitty said.

Kyle, John, and Logan peeled away to reveal Ed the Head, who had Tyler in a half nelson.

"Let me go!" Tyler roared.

"Fine." Ed released Tyler, who rolled off him and collapsed onto his side. "You were too easy to pin anyway."

"What the hell is he doing here?" Amber asked.

Olivia was pale as a sheet and still trembling. "You're supposed to be keeping an eye on Tammi Barnes."

"What's wrong?" Kitty asked.

Ed climbed to his feet, as the blare of sirens grew louder outside. "Tammi Barnes has disappeared."

THIRTY-FIVE

SERGEANT CALLAHAN SLAPPED HIS PALM AGAINST THE TABLE in the interrogation room so fiercely that Kitty jumped in her chair.

"What were you thinking?" he bellowed. His countenance was dark and glowering, and the jolly bedside manner he used with underage suspects had completely vanished.

"We were trying to help," Kyle said lamely.

Sergeant Callahan pointed at Amber. "By putting her life in danger?"

"Um . . ." Kyle looked at Kitty as if hoping she'd supply the answer. So much for the big man on campus.

"We didn't think you'd listen to us," she said. Once again, it was her job to take control. "And Amber wasn't in any danger with all of us in the house."

"Do you really believe that?" Sergeant Callahan asked. It was a loaded question, but Kitty had no choice but to answer.

"Yes."

"Then you're stupider than I thought, Kitty. What if the

killer had shown up with an automatic weapon? What would you have done then, huh? Disarmed him with your extensive hand-to-hand combat training? I'll tell you what would have happened. You'd all be dead." He pointed to each of them in turn. "Every single one of you."

"But," Kitty said, unable to help herself, "the killer's never used a gun. Don't you think it would be out of character?"

Sergeant Callahan's eyebrows shot up. "I'm so glad your FBI profiling experience has come in handy here. I'm so glad you kids think you know more than those who risk their lives every single day."

"To protect and serve," Ed said. Despite his glibness, Ed looked markedly uncomfortable as he drummed his fingers against the table.

Sergeant Callahan smacked the table again. "This isn't a video game. Real lives are at stake."

"We know that," Kitty said. *Better than you can imagine.*

"Do you?" Sergeant Callahan asked. His eyes narrowed as he glared at her. "Do you really?" He paused, a hint of a smile tugging at the corners of his mouth. "Because if I was the killer, you'd be the next victim on my list."

Kitty's mouth went dry as Sergeant Callahan's eyes continued to burn a hole through her head. There was something hard in those eyes, a fierceness Kitty had seen only once before in her living room. *If I was the killer . . .*

"They did more tonight than you've done in a month," Amber said.

Sergeant Callahan laughed, breaking eye contact with

Kitty. The grim look on his face vanished. "More harm, you mean."

Only Amber didn't find it funny. She shot to her feet and screamed in Sergeant Callahan's face. "It's your fault Rex is dead!"

Sergeant Callahan's face grew red. "I'm sorry?"

"Locker searches," Amber sneered. "Assemblies. Stupid, pointless questioning. On TV they'd have brought in a profiler, a CSI team, something professional. You just sat there and let this guy kill again." Her voice faltered. "You let him kill Rex."

A tear rolled down Amber's cheek, and for the first time in her life, Kitty actually felt sorry for the meanest girl in school.

Silence fell as Amber glared at a surprised Sergeant Callahan, her chin quivering as tears welled up in her eyes. Kitty watched as Olivia reached out and gripped Amber's hand. All this time Amber had been the enemy, the symbol of what DGM fought against at Bishop DuMaine. But in the end, she was just as scared and vulnerable as the rest of them.

The quiet was jarred by the sharp pounding of footsteps outside the door, followed by the indistinct swell of voices, quickly muted, then sharp staccatos as officers in the station barked out orders.

Sergeant Callahan shook off his stupor and strode to the door. "What the hell is going on out there?"

Before he reached it, the door burst open, held by an enormous arm. It was attached, as best as Kitty could tell, to a WWE wrestler with flowing blond locks and pecs the size of dinner plates. He stood at attention as a trim woman with sun-streaked hair and an expensively tailored suit strode purposely into the interrogation room.

"Brendan," she said, addressing Sergeant Callahan. "Is there a reason you're holding these children for questioning without parental consent?"

Sergeant Callahan straightened up immediately—shoulders back, eyes forward—as if his superior officer had just arrived for inspection. "Mrs. Deringer!"

Kitty's eyes grew wide. Mrs. Deringer? As in Bree's mom?

At the other end of the table, she saw John wriggle in his chair.

"They're not being questioned, Diana," he said. "There are no charges at this time."

Mrs. Deringer laughed. Her entire face lit up, and she looked like a teen herself with her perfectly smooth skin and dancing brown eyes. Kitty had a difficult time reconciling her with her angry, sarcastic, and totally non-designer-label-wearing daughter.

Mrs. Deringer laid a hand on Sergeant Callahan's arm, and he visibly relaxed at her touch. "Are you really going to tell me that you were attempting to scare these poor children?"

"Diana," he said, clearly flustered. "What are you doing?"

"I'm here in my official capacity as the children's rights advocate for the students of Bishop DuMaine," she said, smiling.

Kitty pinned her lips together. An official children's rights advocate? Was that even a thing?

"But I thought—"

"So unless you're planning to charge them with obstructing

justice or interfering with a police investigation, I suggest you release them all into my custody."

"No, Mrs. Deringer." Sergeant Callahan shook his head, confused. "I mean, yes. I mean, at once."

Mrs. Deringer smiled, her dancing eyes fixed on Sergeant Callahan's face. "I knew you'd understand." Then she spun around, winked quickly at Kitty, and snapped her fingers. "Children," she said, turning toward the door. "Follow me."

Ed paused outside the interrogation room as the others filed past him, his spidey sense tingling. Something was wrong.

At first, it just sounded like background voices, distant and fuzzy, as if someone had left the TV on in the break room. But as they neared the double doors that led outside, the noise began to swell, and Ed could clearly hear the angry shouts of a large crowd.

"Quickly," Mrs. Deringer said out of the corner of her mouth.

"What's going on out there?" Ed asked, trotting after her.

"It sounds like a mob," Olivia said.

Mrs. Deringer paused before the doors and turned to face them. "It appears that some parental members of the community have gathered outside the precinct to express their, er, disapproval of the investigation. So if you'll just stay close to Olaf, we should be fine."

Ed shimmied up behind Olaf's bulk. "Done and done."

As soon as the door opened, a wave of sound crashed into them. About forty people had gathered outside the station, kept at bay by a line of noticeably inadequate metal barriers, and two uniformed officers who looked as if they weren't sure how to handle the situation.

"If you could all just go home," one officer pleaded.

"The police are idiots!" a woman screamed, followed by supportive cheers.

"Ma'am," the officer said patiently, "this is a complex situation, and we are—"

"My son is missing!" the woman cried. She pushed herself to the front of the crowd, and Ed instantly recognized Xavier Hathaway's mother. "And you've done nothing to find him."

"We're doing everything we can."

"Really?" a man asked, his voice full of sarcasm.

"Yes," the officer said, clearly offended. "In fact, Sergeant Callahan is questioning suspects right now."

"It's that DGM group!" someone else yelled.

Another voice agreed. "Yeah. They're the ones behind it."

"Is that them?" Ed saw a finger pointing in their direction. "Are those the suspects?"

Uh-oh.

"They're the ones! They're the killers!"

There was a rush of rage and motion as the crowd pushed forward, hardly contained by the two officers who attempted to form a wall between them and the crowd. Ed was wondering if they'd have to make a break for it, when Mrs. Deringer stepped forward.

"Ladies and gentlemen," she said, her voice commanding and utterly calm. "These children are not murderers. They were witnesses to the most recent string of crimes, and their presence here this evening is merely to help the investigation."

"Who the hell are you?" someone asked. "Their lawyer?"

"I represent the students of Bishop DuMaine Preparatory School," she said, keeping up her bluff. Good call. If they found out she was Bree Deringer's mom they'd probably tar and feather her. "And we want to find out who is behind these killings and disappearances as much as you do."

The crowd stalled, their angry momentum derailed. Mrs. Deringer spun back to Ed and the rest with a guilty smile. "Quickly," she said under her breath. "To the cars."

They walked as fast as they could without breaking into a run, glancing back over their shoulders every few seconds just to make sure the mob hadn't changed its collective mind.

"How did she know where we were?" Kitty asked.

"I used Logan's phone to text Bree," John said. "To tell her what happened in case we got arrested."

"I had no idea her mom was such a badass," Olivia said, her eyes wide with wonder. "And fierce. Did you see that Burberry jacket she has on? A-mazing."

"I wonder if she'll let us see Bree," John said to no one in particular.

"I wonder," Ed the Head chimed in, "if we should talk about what the fuck actually happened tonight!"

"Can we at least get out of the police parking lot first?" Kitty said drily. "In case you missed it, there's a mob back there calling for blood."

Ed rolled his eyes. "Fine." It wasn't like he wanted to talk in front of Logan anyway. How he managed to weasel his way into the plan at Amber's house was beyond him.

They rounded the building where two cars waited: a tank-like SUV, black with tinted windows, and a Lincoln Town Car with a livery tag on the back bumper. A driver stood at the passenger door and whipped it open as they approached.

"Sweet," Ed said, starting for the Town Car. "I've always wanted my own private driver."

Mrs. Deringer held out her arm. "Not you, twerp," she said under her breath. Then she turned to Kyle and Tyler, once again all charm and smiles. "Do you think you boys could escort Amber home? After all she's been through, I think she could use the support of two strong, sensitive men such as yourselves."

Tyler puffed up his chest. "Anything you say, Mrs. Deringer."

"And on behalf of the students of Bishop DuMaine," Kyle said, attempting to out-brown-nose his friend, "we're lucky to have you as our rights advocate."

"Yes," Mrs. Deringer said with a twinkling smile. "Aren't you?"

Amber, however, didn't look as pleased. She reached out to John. "I want to go with him," she whined.

But Mrs. Deringer intercepted her, draping an elegant arm around her shoulders and guiding her toward the Town Car. "I know, my dear. But now isn't the right time. You know they say that relationships based on intense experiences never work."

"Isn't that from *Speed*?" Ed asked under his breath.

"You need to give this one a little space after tonight," Mrs.

Deringer continued. She squeezed Amber's shoulders as they reached the car door. "Trust me. I bagged a senator." Then she pushed Amber into the car and slammed the door.

When she straightened up, she was all business. "The rest of you, come with me."

"Hold up," Ed said, eyeing Logan. "Don't you think 'Girl-friend in a Coma' here should go ride in the clown car?"

"Huh?" Logan asked, looking confused.

"Ed!" Olivia cried. "That's awful."

Ed shook his head in mock contrition. "I know, I know, it's really serious."

John stared at him in disbelief. "You're a total dick some-times, you know that?"

Ed smiled. "Sometimes?"

"I'm not sure what you're talking about," Logan said, "but I can hitch with Amber back to her house. No worries, dude."

"I think that's best," Ed said.

Kitty and Olivia had other plans. After exchanging a hurried glance, Kitty stepped forward. "Actually," she said, "I think you should come with us."

"Why?" Ed asked. "What could he possibly bring to the table?"

"He's got as much of a stake in all this as you do," Olivia said.

That's not true.

The Town Car drove off, sealing the deal, and Ed resigned himself to having Logan along for the ride. "Fine." He grabbed Logan by the wrist and dragged him to the center of the group. "But he has to swear the same oath John and I did. It's only fair."

"Oath?" Logan asked.

Ed rolled up his sleeves like a proctologist about to perform an exam, then thrust his arm forward. "Just relax and let it happen, big guy. It only hurts for a second."

THIRTY-SIX

BREE STOOD AT THE FRONT DOOR AND STRETCHED HER UPPER body outside as far as she could, careful to keep her anklet within the perimeter of the house. Her mom and Olaf should have been back by now. What if Sergeant Callahan had refused to release her friends? What if the killer had somehow gotten to them first?

She imagined John's lifeless body, beaten and bloodsplattered, like the crime scene photos of Ronny. *I will destroy everything you love. . . .*

Bree squeezed her eyes shut, desperately trying to banish that thought from her mind. They were fine. She just needed to be patient.

The roar of a car engine broke Bree from her pity party. Her eyes flew open and she saw John sprinting up the walkway toward her.

"Bree!" He wrapped his arms around her and kissed her on the lips.

Bree felt her face burn. Out of the corner of her eye, she

saw her mom ease out of the SUV. John seemed to realize the situation at the same moment. He pulled back, blushing scarlet from chin to hairline, and faced Bree's mom. "Mrs. Deringer, I'm sorry. Bree and I . . ."

"Have been humping like rabbits in my daughter's bedroom? Yes, I know."

Bree's stomach dropped. "How?"

Her mom looked at her with pity. "Darling, it will be a cold day in hell before I fail to recognize Old Spice in any of its various forms. And unless you'd suddenly taken to dousing yourself in aftershave, the only explanation is that a boy had been in your room."

"Oh."

"Now," her mom said, shushing them toward the open door. "If we could all go inside, there is, apparently, a great deal you have to discuss."

Her hand held firmly in John's, Bree led them through the foyer, down the hall, and through the formal dining room to the kitchen.

Ed the Head whistled as he examined the decor. "Sweet digs. Senator Deringer has excellent taste."

"Thank you!" Bree's mom cooed from behind them.

Bree and John took seats at the far end of the farmer's table while everyone else filed in, Logan bringing up the rear. "Um . . ." Bree looked from Kitty to Olivia.

"It's okay," Kitty said. "Logan knows."

"Can I get you kids something to drink?" Bree's mom asked.

She puttered around, aimlessly opening the refrigerator and the cabinets as if searching for something domestic to do. "Water? Soda? Cocktail?"

"Mom . . ."

"You know," Ed said, his voice smarmy, "Bree never told us she had an older sister."

"Seriously?" Bree said.

Her mom giggled. "You, twerp, are a charmer."

Bree rolled her eyes. Damn, she really would flirt with anything with a pulse. "Okay, Mom. We've got business to discuss."

"Fine." Her mom sighed dramatically. "I'll be in my room if you need me."

Even after her mom's incredible act of faith in busting her friends out of the pokey, Bree couldn't stand the attention-seeking behavior.

"It *was* pretty awesome of her to come rescue us," John said, as soon as Bree's mom was out of earshot. "How did you pull that off?"

"I tried calling everyone after I got your text," Bree said. "When no one picked up I figured it was serious and called in reinforcements."

Kitty nodded. "All of our phones were off."

"Except his," Bree said with a nod to Ed. "But he didn't pick up."

Ed the Head folded his arms across his chest. "I turned off my ringer while I was trying to clean up your mess with Tammi Barnes."

"Some good that did," Olivia said.

Bree sucked in a breath. "What happened with Tammi?"

"I went to the mall to keep an eye on her like you asked, but she never showed up for work," Ed said. "Then I drove over to her place, but she never came back. The supervisor at the half-way house must have called the police when she didn't show up because a couple of squad cars rolled in just after sunset. I think technically she'd broken her parole."

Bree gritted her teeth. "You were supposed to keep an eye on her."

Ed threw his arms wide. "I tried my best! Maybe if you hadn't blown it at therapy, this wouldn't have happened."

Logan turned to Kitty. "Who's Tammi Barnes?"

"We've got two possible scenarios here," Kitty said, barreling forward. "Either Tammi's the killer, or our homicidal friend got to her just like the rest of them."

"Who are the rest of them?" Logan asked Olivia.

Olivia slumped back in her chair. "Now what?"

"I don't think you'll like the answer to that one." Bree walked to the kitchen and pulled four manila envelopes from a drawer. "I found these on the doorstep when I got home from group therapy."

"Shit!" Kitty and Olivia said in unison.

Ed shook his head. "You've got to be kidding me."

Bree passed out the envelopes labeled "Olivia," "Kitty," "John," and "Ed."

"What was in yours?" Kitty asked, fingering the flap on her own envelope.

Without a word, Bree pulled out a photo and held it up for them to see. It was a candid black-and-white shot, slightly grainy as if taken from a distance, of John shinnying up the rope ladder outside her bedroom.

She watched John's face as he examined the photo. He didn't freak out, just calmly processed the details. "That was from yesterday."

"Yeah."

Without hesitating, John broke the seal on his envelope and removed a similar black-and-white photo. Bree swallowed as she stared: it was of her, climbing out of the car at Dr. Walters's clinic.

"There's another note too," Bree said, hoping her voice didn't tremble as she read the killer's threat out loud. "'Each of you will lose something you love more than life itself. This started with you and it ends with you, so tune in for Sunday's big finale. P.S. I'm not getting mad, I'm just getting even.'"

"Sunday?" Olivia said. "Why Sunday?"

"Oh God," Kitty gasped.

"What?" John asked.

Kitty looked at Bree. "Sunday is the volleyball tournament at school. The one with all the college scouts."

"A big finale," John mused.

Olivia's face was hard-set as she stared at her envelope. "I don't want to open this." Bree didn't blame her. The idea that the killer was targeting John made her sick to her stomach.

"We'll do it together," Kitty said. "On three."

"Fine," Olivia said with a toss of her short curls. "You too, Ed."

Ed snorted. "Unless he's wiping out my bank account, there's nothing in here that can scare me."

Kitty counted down. "One. Two. Three."

She and Olivia broke the seal on their envelopes at the same time while Ed shoved his, unopened, into his bag. Kitty's hand began to tremble as she stared at her photo.

"What is it?" Bree asked. She reached under the table and laced her fingers with John's.

"It's . . ." Kitty paused, her voice catching. "It's my sisters. Walking home from school."

As with the other photos, this one looked as if it had been shot with a telephoto lens. It showed a set of identical twin girls, backpacks slung over their shoulders, walking arm in arm down the street. The photo had caught them in a moment of levity: both girls were laughing hysterically as if one of them had just cracked a joke. They looked so young—eleven, maybe twelve years old.

"*I will destroy everything you love*," Ed said quietly.

"Well," John said with a heavy exhale, "at least he knows what that is."

Bree squeezed John's hand fiercely. She couldn't lose him. "We have to stop him before he hurts someone else."

"I think . . ." Olivia began. The quiver in her voice made Bree look up immediately. She was trembling, and her face had gone deathly pale. "I think he already has."

She stared at the piece of paper on the table that had come in her envelope. It was a printout of an email, sent to June Hayes. Olivia's mom.

Dear Ms. Hayes,

I regret to inform you that due to unsatisfactory performance, you have been replaced in the production of *The Lady's Curse*.

Sincerely,

Charles Beard

THIRTY-SEVEN

OLIVIA LEANED FORWARD IN THE FRONT PASSENGER SEAT OF the Deringers' SUV as if willing the large Scandinavian driver to go faster.

Not that he could have. The tires shrieked in protest as they rounded each bend, yellow lights were a signal to accelerate, and she had to grip the "oh shit" handle at every turn. But it wasn't enough.

She glanced down at her phone and hit Redial for the thirtieth time. Four rings, then the voice mail picked up.

"I'm terribly sorry, I can't get to the phone," her mom said in rounded, dulcet tones. "I'm in rehearsal for my new—"

Olivia ended the call and immediately hit Redial.

"I'm sure she's fine," Kitty said. "Just asleep or maybe at work?"

"She quit her job," Olivia said. The voice mail kicked in and she ended yet another call. "Because of this play."

If Kitty had anything else to add, she kept it to herself. Piled into the back with Logan, John, and Ed the Head, none of them said a word.

How could she have been so stupid? Testing out a one-woman show in San Jose for an Off-Broadway run was ridiculous, let alone her mom's involvement. Twelfth Night *at the Public, 1998. Am I right?* Her mom's ego was so wounded after her visit from Fitzgerald Conroy, she would have fallen hard for a line like that. She wanted so badly to believe that "June Hayes" would once again be up in lights, a name bandied about in *Playbill* and the *New York Times* theater review. Her mom had probably already rehearsed her Tony acceptance speech.

Olivia should have realized this was actually the work of a killer hell-bent on revenge.

Olaf hit the brakes and Olivia momentarily went airborne between her seat and the safety belt, before her head smacked back against the headrest. "Here," Olaf said simply.

She took the stairs to her apartment two at a time, keys gripped tightly in her hand, hardly even aware of the pounding of footsteps behind her.

"Mom!" she cried as she unlocked the door. "Mom?"

There were bottles of red wine everywhere. One on the kitchen table—open, but only half-consumed—one on the counter—also unfinished—then two on the coffee table, both overturned. Next to them, the framed photo of June Hayes as Olivia from the opening of *Twelfth Night* at the Public Theater in New York. The glass was smashed.

Her mom lay on her side on the sofa, facing the television. Olivia heaved a sigh of relief. It had been an angry, drunken night, but no worse than Olivia had seen before. It would be followed by days of tearful self-pity alternating with marathon sleep sessions, and hopefully sometime next week, her mom would snap out of her funk, ask for her old job back at the Shangri-La, and life would go back to normal.

"Is she okay?" Kitty asked at Olivia's shoulder.

Olivia winced, suddenly aware that her friends were bearing witness to the bipolar chaos that was Olivia's home life.

"She'll be fine," Olivia said, trying to sound cheerful. She marched into the living room, righting the wine bottles on the table and shifting some broken glass from the photo. "Lick her wounds and move forward. Right, Mom?"

She turned to her mom and all the warmth drained out of her body. Cuddled in her lap were almost a dozen pill bottles. Her mom's jaw hung limply open and a trickle of vomit snaked out from the corner.

Kitty dashed to her side. "Call 911," she said to Ed. "Now."

"What's wrong?" John asked. "Is she okay?"

Before anyone could answer, Olaf bounded across the room. He scooped up Olivia's mom, cradling her in his arms, and was halfway to the door before Olivia could respond. "What are you doing?"

"Olaf faster to hospital," he said, already heading down the stairs. "Bring pill bottles. Hurry."

Kitty sat next to John in the hospital waiting room and stared at the clock on the wall. In the movies, emergency rooms were always romantic places, where gorgeous, well-dressed actors awaited news of their loved ones.

This ER looked more like a prison visitation room: uncomfortable wooden-armed chairs with stained gray upholstery, pale yellow walls with an informational poster about heart disease, a selection of magazines four months out of date, and a pathetic vending machine that looked as if it hadn't been restocked since Kitty was still in diapers. Bar None? Did they even make that candy anymore?

Ed and Logan had disappeared soon after arriving at the hospital, but John sat stoically beside her, completely still. He rested his head against the wall, arms folded across his chest, eyes closed. How could he nap? Kitty was crawling out of her skin, wondering if Olivia's mom would be okay. She'd used what little battery power was left on her phone to call home and check on Lydia and Sophia, who thought it was positively hilarious that their older sister was worrying about them. Still, she made them promise to stay put and keep the doors and windows locked.

Now, with the battery on her phone nearly dead, she couldn't distract herself with mindless games or Facebook stalking. She would have killed for a good book, or even a crappy one, but had to settle for the small television set in the corner, now showing local news, with no sound. A couple of talking heads gabbed silently on and on, and Kitty's eyelids began to flutter, a slow blink transforming into prolonged seconds of darkness.

"Look!" John said, nudging Kitty awake. Her eyes flew open. John was pointing at the television set, where a photo of Tammi Barnes filled up the screen.

Kitty rushed across the room and hit the volume button on the set, desperate to hear what the reporters had to say.

". . . last seen in the eight-hundred block of Willow Road. If you have any information as to the whereabouts of Tamara Barnes, we ask that you call the Menlo Park Police Department immediately at the number on your screen." Then Tammi's photo vanished and the talking heads reappeared. "And now for a sports update, we go to Chip Peterson. Chip? What's going on with those Niners?"

"Anything?" John asked as Kitty slumped back to her seat.

"Just what we already knew. She was last seen leaving the doctor's office."

"Damn."

Kitty gazed up at the water-stained ceiling tiles. "At least the police are looking for her."

John snorted. "Right, because they've done such a great job finding the others."

She had to admit he had a point.

Ed the Head breezed into the waiting room and took a seat opposite Kitty and John. "What's shakin', bacon?"

"Where have you been?" Kitty asked.

Ed laced his fingers together and cracked his knuckles. "Getting the scoop on Olivia's mom."

John cocked his head. "I thought we were banned from updates since we're not immediate family."

"Please," Ed snorted. "When has that ever stopped me?"

Kitty glanced at John. "Never," they said in unison.

"Prognosis is good," he said with a smile. "Looks like we got to her just in time. Another hour and she'd have slipped into a coma."

Kitty grimaced. "How's Olivia?"

Ed held his hand flat, and wiggled it from side to side. "She's meh. But she's a trouper. Won't leave her mom's side."

John pulled out his phone. "I'll update Bree."

"Is there anything we can do?" Kitty asked.

"Doubt it. Olivia will be here all night."

"Can we see her?"

Ed shook his head. "Getting through Checkpoint Charlie to the hospital rooms is easier said than done."

"Okay," Kitty said, eyeing the admittance desk. Would it be worth it to try and make a dash for Olivia's mom's room? Probably not. The last thing she wanted to do was cause her friend more stress. "I can come back in the morning and bring breakfast or something."

She should probably get home. Bad enough that Coach Miles was on her case about missing practice; now her parents would be freaking out over her late return. What would she tell them? She was on a date with Donté? The mere thought of her probably-by-now ex-boyfriend made her eyes instantly tear up. She'd been able to push their unresolved confrontation from her mind during the chaos of the day, but now it rushed back to her afresh. Would she be able to get over the fact that he wouldn't trust her after asking her to do the same?

She wasn't sure.

"Olaf can take us home," John said, reading from his screen. "Bree says he's still outside in the parking lot."

"Kinda nice to have Thor around," Ed said. "It's like we're the Avengers or something."

John stood up and stretched his arms over his head. "Yeah," he said with a laugh. "You can be Ant-Man."

"I'm totally Hawkeye."

Kitty cocked her head. "Didn't Hawkeye spend like half the first movie as a bad guy?"

Ed gave her one of his finger pistols. "Yep. He's a complicated man. Kinda like—"

But Ed never finished the sentence. Logan came tearing into the lobby, his face lit up like fireworks.

"What is it?" Kitty asked, instantly on alert.

"It's Margot," Logan said, trying to catch his breath. "She's awake."

THIRTY-EIGHT

KITTY PAUSED JUST OUTSIDE MARGOT'S ROOM, OVERCOME with emotion. Margot was sitting upright in her hospital bed. Her skin was ashen, her features frail and doll-like. Her father stood on one side of her bed, his hand gripping Margot's shoulder so fiercely Kitty could see his knuckles whitening, and her mother's face was buried in Margot's lap, weeping.

Logan edged his way past Kitty into the doorway and Margot's face lit up. "Logan!"

Mrs. Mejia's eyes flashed. "This area is for family only. How did you get in here?"

Logan swallowed. "The nurses let us in."

More like couldn't stop the tidal wave of her friends as they barreled into Margot's hospital room, but Kitty didn't correct him.

"Who are you?" Mrs. Mejia asked, her voice steely.

"I'm Logan, Margot's boyfriend." It was a simple statement, utterly lacking in sarcasm, but it seemed to ignite Mrs. Mejia's rage.

"What!" she cried, jumping to her feet.

"Mom," Margot said, reaching out. "It's okay."

Her mom didn't even look at her. "Get out of here, all of you. And forget you ever met my daughter."

"Margot wants us here," Logan said with utmost confidence.

"Margot is a minor," Mr. Mejia said, more calmly than his wife. "And as her legal guardians, the decision as to whom our daughter can and cannot see is ours to make."

"And we don't want you here," Mrs. Mejia added. "I'm calling security."

"Stop!" Margot roared. Her body lurched with the force of her voice, as if she wasn't used to the physical exertion of shouting.

"*Mija*," her mom said, her tone softer. "You're not well enough to see all these people."

Margot closed her eyes, took a deep breath, and stared at her mom with hard, stern eyes. "Mom, I'm fine. More than fine. And besides, I want to see them. These are my friends." She glanced nervously at the door where Ed, John, and Kitty crammed into the opening behind Logan. "I need them here."

"I forbid it!" Mrs. Mejia was either so used to her rules going uncontested, or so paranoid about her daughter's safety, that she was willing to alienate her affection completely.

"I'm not a child anymore, okay?" Margot thrust her arms forward, exposing several long, dark lines from wrist to elbow. "Do you know why I did this? Have you ever bothered to ask me why?"

Kitty flinched at the sight of Margot's scars and the memory of what had driven her to it.

"Do you?" Margot prompted. "Do you think it's because you were too lenient? Because I had too much freedom? Too many friends?"

"These friends of yours," her mom said, reaching out for her daughter's hand. "They'll take advantage of you. They'll hurt you."

Margot's gaze shifted to Kitty's face. "No," she said quietly. "No, they won't."

"But—"

"I want to talk to my friends," Margot said firmly. "Alone."

Mrs. Mejia opened her mouth to protest, but her husband draped an arm around her shoulders. "I think we could use some coffee." He guided his wife toward the door. "Let's see if the cafeteria is still open."

As soon as Margot's parents had disappeared down the hall, Kitty rushed to her bedside, threw her arms around Margot's neck, and squeezed her. "I'm so glad . . ." she started, her voice catching in her throat.

"I'm okay," Margot whispered in her ear.

Kitty released Margot's neck, taking a moment to wipe a stray tear from her cheek as her hair fell before her face. "Good."

"But how . . ." Margot started. "I mean, why are you all here?"

"We just happened to be on a little field trip to the ER," Ed said. "You know, typical Friday-night fun."

Margot stiffened. "Is everything okay? Where's Olivia? And Bree?"

"Slowly," Logan said, stroking her hair. "We'll explain." Margot smiled at him gratefully, then he leaned down and kissed her on the lips, gentle and slow, as if he was afraid she might break.

Kitty's body tensed as if she was in pain: it reminded her of the way Donté used to kiss her.

"I've been so worried about you," Logan said as he pulled away.

Their reunion was sweet, but Kitty couldn't wait any longer to ask the burning question. "Did you see anything?" she blurted out. "Before you were attacked? Do you know who did this?" Finally, there was a chance for a clue, something to put a face on the killer.

"I . . ." Margot's brow clouded. She stared at the foot of her bed, eyes searching, as if the answer to Kitty's question was somehow lurking in the bedsheets. This could be it, the moment they discovered who was behind all the murders at Bishop DuMaine. If Margot had seen anything before she was attacked, anything at all, it could be the break they'd been waiting for.

Logan seemed to sense the import of the moment as well. He leaned forward, one hand clasped in Margot's, the other on her shoulder. Even John and Ed the Head had moved farther into the room, ringing Margot's hospital bed in silent anticipation.

"I don't remember," she said at last.

"Nothing?" Logan asked.

Her eyes sought him out. "I remember the finale. You were dancing. You smiled at me."

"Anything else?" he prompted. "Anything after that?"

She shook her head. "I can't." Her eyes shifted to Kitty, then

Ed, and landed on John. Kitty could see the question passing over her face. *What is he doing here?* "You're John Baggott," she said. "Right?"

Kitty laughed. Despite a week in a coma, Margot's security instincts were just as strong as ever. "It's okay," she said. "He knows."

Margot's eyebrows shot up. "What?"

"They all do," Kitty added.

"A lot has happened since you took your little nap," Ed said. His words were flippant, but his voice was deadly serious. "We've all been sworn in."

"All of you?" Her eyes lingered on John, and Kitty remembered with a pang of guilt that at one point, John had been a suspect.

John, bless him, sensed Margot's uneasiness and backed toward the door. "You guys have a lot to discuss."

"You don't have to leave," Kitty said. She felt bad, after all John had done to help them, that he was being banished from the inner circle.

He held up his hand. "It's okay. I'll go check on Olivia." Then he slipped into the hallway, closing Margot's hospital-room door behind him.

Margot's eyes grew wide. "Olivia?"

"She's fine." Kitty drew a chair close to Margot's bed. "But John's right. We have a lot to talk about."

Olivia sat at the edge of her chair, one arm draped around the unconscious body of her mom while she rested her head on June's shoulder. She could almost imagine she was a child again, curled up in her mother's lap for comfort after a bad dream or a rough day at school. It had always been just the two of them, ever since Olivia could remember. They never talked about her dad, only enough for Olivia to understand that he was not and never would be a part of her life, and that she was probably better off because of it.

As difficult as her mom could be at times, she'd always been there for Olivia. She'd sacrificed her own career so that her daughter could have every opportunity in life. And though keeping her mom on her antidepressants had always been a struggle, Olivia knew her mom loved her very much. And the feeling was mutual.

Besides, they really didn't have anyone else. Just each other. So the depth of pain her mom must have been feeling earlier that evening . . . Olivia could only speculate. She'd seen her mom in some dark places, going days without showering, twenty-hour sleep marathons, and then the drinking. But they had always passed, always gone away and been replaced by happier, more hopeful periods. Why had this time been different?

"How's she doing?" John smiled at her from the doorway.

"She hasn't woken up yet," Olivia said, surprised by the cragginess of her voice, "but they told me she should be okay."

"Awesome," John said. "That's the second piece of good news we've gotten tonight."

"Second?"

John smiled. "Margot's awake."

Olivia shot to her feet. "How is she? Is she okay? Oh my God, does she know who—"

"She doesn't remember anything," John said, shaking his head.

"Shit."

"Sorry."

Olivia looked down at her mom, tubes sticking out of her arm and her nose, her chest rising and falling at an unnatural pace. Her hands balled up into fists and she fought the urge to punch something.

"He did this to her," Olivia said.

"Olivia," John said softly. "Isn't your mom . . ."

"Crazy?" Olivia said, raising her eyebrows. "Is that what you meant?"

"No."

"The word is 'bipolar.' And yes, she is. But I meant he drove her to this. The pill bottles—those weren't her usual prescriptions. She said the pharmacy called her to say she had a pickup. It had to be the killer."

"Damn."

"She'd put everything on the line for that play and that email would have been enough to send her over the edge. Charles Beard," Olivia said, remembering the name on the email. "Christopher Beeman. Not a coincidence."

A doctor breezed into the room, his white coat fluttering behind him like a cape. "Miss Hayes?"

"Yes," Olivia answered. Oh no, what now?

He held something in his hand that he began to pass to her, then paused, eyeing John. "I'm sorry, but visitors aren't allowed."

"This is my brother," Olivia lied, without missing a beat. "John."

"Oh." The doctor looked back and forth between Olivia and John, trying to find some resemblance between the strawberry blond, blue-eyed girl and John's dark hair and hazel eyes. Eventually, he gave up. "We found this in your mother's pocket," he said, handing the piece of paper to Olivia. "It's addressed to you."

Olivia took the note with a trembling hand. "Thank you."

The doctor gave a nod and withdrew from the room.

The note was written on a plain piece of computer paper, folded in quarters with the words "For Olivia Hayes Only" written on the front in her mom's messy, frantic scrawl.

"Do you want me to go?" John asked.

"No." Olivia turned the note over in her hands without opening it. She didn't want to be alone when she read it. What was she going to find inside? A suicide note? An explanation as to why her mom felt her life was so not worth living that she'd abandon her daughter to the foster care system? Because that's what it meant. Olivia had no one—no siblings, no grandparents, and no idea who her father even was, let alone where. Did she want to know her mom's last thoughts?

Not really. But she needed to read it anyway.

Livvie,

You were right. I'm a fool. An old, washed-up fool who believed somehow this time would be different. But it's not. I'm a fuck-up. A loser and a bad mother. And you'll be better off without me.

But I'm not leaving you alone. You've got your father now and he'll take care of you. He might not believe you, but I had a DNA test done to prove it. It's in my dresser drawer.

He'll take care of you, Livvie. I know he will. You have his eyes. I thought of him every time I looked at you.

I love you so much. You know that, right? But I'm so bad for you, Livvie. You'll be happier when I'm gone.

If they try to take you away, show them this. I, June Hayes, relinquish custody of my daughter Olivia Hayes to her biological father, Fitzgerald O'Henry Conroy.

THIRTY-NINE

ED WATCHED MARGOT'S FACE INTENTLY AS KITTY FINISHED catching her up on everything that had happened in the last week: the copycat DGM, Rex's death, a half dozen or so missing persons, and the bombshell revelation that Christopher Beeman was dead.

Her poker face was impressive. She took it calmly, dispassionately, the only glimmer of emotion coming when Kitty mentioned Olivia's mom's suicide attempt.

As Kitty fell silent, Margot stared at the blank wall on the far side of the room, and Ed knew that her brain was hard at work, analyzing and cataloging all the information she'd just downloaded.

"The footage from Rex's birthday party," she said at last, eyes still fixed on the wall. "What grade was he in?"

Kitty glanced at Ed for confirmation. "Sixth?" she said.

Detail-oriented she was not. "It was Rex's thirteenth birthday," Ed said. "Which would make it eighth grade."

Margot nodded to herself. "And the photos of Amber were from a fat camp?" Again, no hint of emotion, but Ed couldn't help wondering what Margot was feeling. Amber had tormented her ruthlessly about her weight in junior high, and the revelation that Amber had been a fat kid herself just a year or two earlier should have elicited a mix of anger and glee. Or at least it did in him.

"Yeah," Ed said.

Finally, Margot turned to Kitty. "Was Donté pissed off about you joining the 'Maine Men?"

Kitty flinched. Once again, Margot's scientific mind had hit the nail on the head. "Yeah," she said. "Mika too."

"I see." Margot pressed her palm to her temple, grimacing, and Logan launched to his feet, hovering over her protectively.

"Are you okay?" he asked breathlessly. "Maybe you should rest. We can come back later."

Margot leaned into Logan, and Ed's stomach knotted up. Why couldn't that be him?

"I'm fine," she said. "I just can't believe Donté, Mika, Theo, and Peanut are the new DGM."

"What?" Kitty cried.

"How could you possibly know that?" Logan asked.

"Mika went to St. Alban's with Rex," Margot began. "Shouldn't be too difficult to trace that video back to her. You said yourself that she and Donté freaked out when you joined the 'Maine Men. I'd guess that Theo went to Camp Shred. Not at the same time as Amber, but soon after. I think we already knew they were two of DGM's biggest fans."

"I caught Theo logging in to the school email server in Coach's office," Kitty said, nodding as she suddenly put the pieces together. "He looked nervous as hell when I barged in on him."

"He was probably setting up the fake email account," Margot said.

"What about Peanut?" Kitty asked.

"Based on what I've seen of their interactions, she hates Amber Stevens as much as I do." Margot blinked and her eyes softened. "As much as I *did*. And she would have been in a position to steal the opening-night video from Mr. Cunningham's office and tape over it with Amber's montage."

Ed applauded enthusiastically. "Nicely played, Sherlock Holmes."

"Donté . . ." Kitty slowly rose to her feet and began to pace in a tight circle. "He and Mika were so pissed at me. And they've both been distant lately." Then she laughed, manic and uncontrolled. "Oh my God, Margot. You're right! It's because they were keeping this secret. From *me* of all people. Isn't that freaking hilarious?"

"Less hilarious," Ed said, "if the cops figure out that they're involved."

Margot looked up at Logan and opened her mouth to say something, but Logan cut her off. "Don't apologize."

Margot blushed. "I didn't want anything to happen to you. The less you knew about what was going on, the safer you were."

"Now it's my turn to keep *you* safe."

Ed wanted to strangle him. "And how are you going to do that?" he asked, unable to keep the sarcasm out of his voice.

"For starters," Logan said, squeezing Margot's hand, "I'm not letting her out of my sight ever again."

"I'm sure Mr. and Mrs. Mejia will have something to say about that," Ed replied.

"What's your damage, dude?" Logan asked. "You've been on my case all freaking day."

"I—"

"You have got to be kidding me!"

Kitty's head whipped around to the doorway, now occupied by the scowling figure of Sergeant Callahan. He wasn't in uniform, instead comically out of place in dress slacks, a striped button-down shirt, and a sports jacket.

"You guys again?" he said.

"Sergeant Callahan." Ed raised his hand for a high five. "Long time, no arrest!"

Sergeant Callahan glared at him. "Don't tempt me."

Ed grinned. "That is a nice business-casual look you've got going on."

"It was date night with Mrs. Callahan," he said, then added under his breath, "who is going to kill me." Then he turned to Kitty. "You want to explain to me what you're doing here?"

"We were here helping a friend," Logan answered, "when we heard Margot was awake."

"Well, now I'm going to need you all to vacate," Sergeant

Callahan said sternly. "I have some important questions to ask Margot."

"Will do, sir," Ed said. He grabbed Kitty and yanked her toward the door.

"Sergeant Callahan," Kitty said, shaking Ed off. She looked to Margot, who nodded her head quickly, decisively. She seemed to know exactly what Kitty was thinking: spill everything to Sergeant Callahan once and for all before someone else gets killed.

Sergeant Callahan sighed impatiently. "Yes?"

"We need to talk to you about the murders."

"For chrissakes!" Sergeant Callahan planted his hands on his hips. "What did I tell you guys about interfering? I've got three unsolved murders, five missing persons, and as we speak the FBI has taken over my office at the station. So the last thing I need is you guys coming to me with crazy theories."

"But we know who the killer is!" Kitty cried.

"Kitty," Ed said with a nervous chuckle. "I'm not sure we should be bothering the nice police officer with this."

Sergeant Callahan arched an eyebrow. "Really? What's his name? A description of what he looks like? Home address? Maybe the kind of car he drives? Do you have any of that information?"

"Er, no," Kitty said. "But we know—" She paused. Something on his wrist glittered in the harsh overhead lights, drawing her eye. It appeared to be a very expensive watch. Like the one Amber Stevens might have given to Ronny DeStefano.

If I was the killer, you'd be the next victim on my list.

"Yes?" Sergeant Callahan said. "I'm waiting. What is it you know?"

"Nothing," Kitty said, forcing a smile. "You know, you're right. We're way out of our league here." She grabbed Ed by the arm and hustled him toward the door. "I'm sorry we wasted your time."

"It's okay," he said, clearly taken aback by the radical shift in the conversation. "I suggest you kids go home, go to sleep, and keep your noses out of this before you wind up in custody on federal charges. Do you understand me?"

"Can Logan stay?" Margot asked. "He was there that night, you know. In the theater."

"Mr. Blaine has already answered my questions," Sergeant Callahan said with a softer tone than he'd used since his arrival. "And I do think we should be alone."

"It's okay," Logan said, standing up. He leaned down and kissed her tenderly on the cheek. "I won't go far."

Kitty felt Ed's arm tense up.

"Promise?" Margot asked.

Logan smiled. "From now on, I'll always be right by your side."

"Why didn't you tell him?" Logan asked, hurrying down the hall after them.

Kitty paused in front of the elevator and released her grip on Ed's arm. "He's not going to listen to us."

"He might have," Logan said, "if you showed him the photo

and the note. They need to know about Sunday."

Kitty shook her head. "Sergeant Callahan isn't going to do anything about Sunday."

"Why not?" Ed asked tentatively.

"Because he's wearing Amber's dad's Rolex."

"The sergeant is the killer?" Logan asked, clearly confused.

"Oh, come on," Ed said. "You can't really believe Sergeant Callahan is behind all this. That's ridiculous."

"Is it?" Kitty's mind raced. "Amber was right at the station today. We've done more productive research than the entire police department. Why? Because someone on the inside is thwarting the investigation." Without even realizing it, she'd begun to pace. "If he's not the killer, then he's protecting someone. Either way, he's involved."

"Who are we going to tell?" Logan asked. "Should we go to his boss?"

"No!" Ed cried.

Kitty arched an eyebrow. "Why not?"

"I just meant that his captain isn't going to listen to us," Ed said. He cleared his throat. "And if Sergeant Callahan finds out we're on to him, it would be a disaster."

Kitty nodded. "Good point." Every once in a while, it was good to have Ed around.

"We can't do nothing!" Logan cried.

Kitty stopped abruptly and glanced down the hallway toward Margot's room. Going up against Sergeant Callahan was dangerous, but for once they had the upper hand. If they struck now, they could catch him in the act. But they were going to need reinforcements.

"What?" Logan asked, sensing her excitement. "What are you planning?"

Kitty slowly turned back to them. "Time to call in the cavalry."

FORTY

KITTY SAT IN HER CAR OUTSIDE DONTÉ'S HOUSE, A TEXT TYPED into her phone but not sent. She reread it for the billionth time: **I'm out front. Need to talk to you. Really important.**

It was dry, to the point, and revealed none of the emotions currently spinning around inside her like an emo whirlpool. Even with the bombshell she was about to drop on Donté, she wasn't sure if she'd blown her chance with him. His texts that afternoon had escalated from worried to concerned to frantic, but her only response had been "I'm fine" followed by radio silence as she switched off her phone. How did he interpret that? As a rejection? Did he think she'd gone completely cold?

Probably. It's what Kitty would have thought if the roles were reversed. Still, she hoped that he'd at least be curious enough to hear her out.

She hit Send, then shivered. A thick layer of fog had rolled down from the bay, and the whole neighborhood felt damp and cold.

She wasn't sure how long she'd have to wait: Donté wasn't

much of a late-night person, but at midnight on a Friday, he should still be awake.

She was right. As she stared at the screen, she saw the telltale dots indicating that Donté was typing a response. She held her breath as her phone vibrated.

Be right down.

Thirty seconds later she saw the front porch bathed in warm yellow light as Donté stepped outside. He wore a pair of blue-and-green plaid flannel pajama pants, a black T-shirt, and slippers. He must have been getting ready for bed, and as she watched, he lifted the hem of his shirt to wipe his face, exposing a rock-hard eight-pack that disappeared into his PJ bottoms.

Kitty's stomach did a backflip as she remembered those abs pressed up against her own. *Focus*, she said to herself. *You're here on business*. She took a deep breath, and let it out in three short bursts, then swung the door open and stepped out of the car.

As soon as Donté saw her, he jumped off the porch and raced down the driveway. She didn't even get a word out before he wrapped his arms tightly around her.

"Baby," he said, his breath tickling her ear. "I'm so sorry. I was a total asshole and I don't know if you can forgive me but—"

Kitty giggled. She couldn't help herself. The happiness inside bubbled over, and she felt herself shaking with the futile effort to keep from laughing.

"What's so funny?" Donté asked. He sounded hurt.

She broke away and looked up at him. "I'll forgive you if you'll forgive me."

Donté shrugged. "There's nothing to forgive. You didn't do anything wrong."

"Neither did you."

He reached out and ran his fingers through her hair, his eyes tracing the lines of her face. "Not true. There's been something going on, something big, and I let it get in the way of us. I wanted to tell you, but it might put you in danger, so I had to keep it a secret."

Kitty nodded. "I know."

"No, you don't."

A wicked smile broke the corners of Kitty's mouth. "I know that you're a part of the new DGM," she said softly.

Donté's eyes grew so wide Kitty thought they might pop out of his head. "How—?"

"Because I've been keeping the same secret from you." She waited and let the meaning of her words sink in. She could actually see the moment when Donté realized what she was saying. His jaw fell open and his shoulders sagged.

"You?"

"Yes"

"DGM?"

Kitty laughed again. "Yes."

Donté ran a hand over his closely shaved head. "But . . . but you're the student body vice president. You joined the freaking 'Maine Men!"

"I had to. We were trying to figure out who'd been carrying on in our name. They were a resource."

"We?"

Oh, this was going to blow his mind. "Bree Deringer," she began.

"We assumed."

"Margot Mejia."

"Also assumed."

"And Olivia Hayes."

Donté inclined his head. "You're kidding me."

"Nope."

Donté took a step back, then walked in a tight circle, processing what he'd just heard.

"And now it's you," Kitty continued, bringing it all back home. "And Mika. Peanut Dumbrowski and . . . Theo?"

Donté stopped walking and looked up. "Are you a mind reader or something? How the hell could you know that?"

Where was she supposed to start? It was a ridiculously long story, one that she and the girls only partially understood. And there was one thing she needed to know first.

"How did you decide to take over for DGM?" Kitty asked. "How did the four of you come together?"

Donté arched his left eyebrow. "You don't know?"

Uh-oh. Was she supposed to? "No."

"You aren't the one who recruited us?"

Kitty slowly shook her head.

"Oh." He pulled his head back, his lips pressed together. "It was the morning after the assembly where Bree turned herself in. We all found notes on our doorsteps."

Kitty's stomach tightened. "In plain manila envelopes?"

"Yeah!" Donté gasped, then tilted his head to the side.

"Wait, how did you know that?"

"I'll explain later." Her mind raced as she slowly realized the killer's plan. "What did they say?"

"That it was time for a new team to step up and take over where the first DGM had left off. And that if I was interested, to meet on the tennis courts that night at eight o'clock. It was signed 'DGM.' When I got there I found Mika, Theo, and Peanut, and we just kind of jumped in."

Kitty stared blankly at Donté's house. The killer recruited a new version of DGM. *I will destroy everything you love.*

The photo, the anonymous invitation to be the new DGM. There was only one reason the killer would have involved their friends. "I think you guys are in a lot of danger."

Donté gripped her shoulders, his worried eyes fixed on hers. "Tell me what's going on. Please."

"We need to get everyone together," Kitty said. There was no time to lose. "First thing tomorrow morning. Your team and mine."

"Okay. Why?"

She took his hands in hers and squeezed them tightly. She wasn't going to let anything happen to him. "Because I think someone's going to try and frame you for murder."

FORTY-ONE

KITTY ADJUSTED HER LAPTOP SO THE CAMERA CAPTURED THE entire corner of the patio next to the Dumbrowskis' pool, then backed away. "Can you see everyone?"

Bree nodded. Her face pixilated, and jerked slightly as the stream buffered. "I think so." She pointed at the screen, moving her finger around the semicircle. "Damn, this is a lot of people for a secret DGM meeting."

"I know." Kitty glanced back over her shoulder. Bree was right. Olivia, Ed the Head, Peanut, Theo, Mika, Donté, John, and herself. Plus Bree via the internet. So much for their tightly kept secret.

"I've got kale chips, tofu cheese puffs, and savory quinoa cakes," Peanut said, placing a tray of snacks down on a metal table beneath a large umbrella.

Ed leaned in to Olivia. "Is that food or a science experiment?"

Theo dove into the quinoa cakes, munching happily. "These are awesome. Did you make them?"

"I helped," Peanut said, blushing.

"Where's Margot?" Bree asked.

"Still at the hospital," Kitty said. "But Logan's with her."

"He's pretty much refusing to leave her side," John added, "until this psycho is behind bars."

Ed grunted. "Isn't that sweet."

"Good," Bree said, ignoring Ed. "If the killer finds out she's awake, he might try and take her down."

Theo froze midbite and exchanged an uneasy glance with Peanut, while Mika squirmed in her chair. Kitty winced. She, Olivia, Bree, and Margot had been living with the threat of their anonymous stalker for over a month, but today was the first time the newbies learned that their lives might be in danger, and she didn't want to completely freak them out.

"You guys are going to be okay," Kitty said firmly. "No one's going down."

Ed the Head elbowed John in the arm. "That's not what I heard."

"Ew?" Olivia and Peanut said in unison, then smiled at each other.

Oh well. At least the mood was still on the light side. "I know this has all come as kind of a shock to you guys," Kitty said, looking at the new DGM members in turn. "It's a lot to process."

Peanut stared blankly at Kitty. "I don't understand."

Ed reached across Olivia and patted her hand. "We know."

"If you didn't ask us to take over as DGM," Peanut said, "then who did?"

Kitty tapped the side of her nose with her finger. "That's

exactly why you're here this morning."

Mika smiled broadly. "I should have known you were involved," she said. "I can't believe I didn't see it!"

Kitty preened a little. "I'm pretty good at keeping a secret."

Ed rolled his eyes. "You're not the only one. The killer seems to be pretty good at it too."

Great. Bree was usually enough of a smart-ass for the group; now they had two. "You're not wrong," Kitty said, using his one-liner to drive home the gravity of their situation. Donté, Mika, Theo, and Peanut needed to understand the danger.

"This guy we're dealing with," Olivia said, inching to the edge of her lawn chair, "is deadly."

"Three murders already," Kitty said. "And five former DGM targets have gone missing."

"He's been one step ahead of us all along," Bree added.

Kitty picked up the manila envelope that had been left for her boyfriend. "Even in recruiting you guys."

"Why would he get us involved?" Mika asked.

"It's not enough just to destroy our lives," Olivia explained. "He wants to destroy everything we love, too."

"Which means us," Donté said, addressing his team. "Kitty thinks he might try and frame us for something."

"For what?" Theo asked, his eyes wide. "Rex's murder?"

Ugh. Kitty wasn't going to suggest Rex's murder—and certainly not Sergeant Callahan's involvement—until they had more information. She didn't want anyone to panic. "Not necessarily. It might—"

"Oh my God!" Peanut cried. Her hands flew to her face.

"We'll go to juvie. I can't go to juvie. Do you know what happens to girls like me there?"

"Damn," Bree said with a shake of her head. "Do you and Olivia share a brain or something?"

"Just half of one," Ed mumbled.

Olivia stuck out her tongue at him.

"No one's going to juvie!" Kitty cried.

"I've heard that before," Bree said.

Kitty sighed. Wrangling her own team was hard enough. This was like herding cats.

"Guys," Donté said, pushing himself to his feet. He strode to Kitty's side. "We need to stay calm. We don't know anything for sure, other than that the killer is planning something for tomorrow."

"Planning what?" Theo asked, his face white as a sheet.

Kitty took a deep breath. "We don't know, but we think it has something to do with the volleyball tournament."

"Like, dude might go full *Heathers* on Bishop DuMaine," Bree said.

Donté set his jaw. "We have to stop him."

"We should tell the police," Peanut said.

Kitty cringed. This was going to send them over the edge. "That might be a problem."

"Why?" Mika asked.

"Because we think Sergeant Callahan is involved." Kitty took a deep breath. "He might be the killer."

Mika opened her mouth to say something, then snapped it shut. In fact, no one said a word. The only sound was the gentle lapping of the water against the edge of the pool, and a rustling of leaves overhead.

"What are we going to do?" Peanut shot to her feet and flapped her hands up and down in a full-blown panic. "I can't handle this. We just wanted to put Amber and Rex in their places, you know? We didn't want anyone to get hurt."

"Someone always gets hurt," Bree said. "Sometimes they deserve it. Sometimes they don't. But don't think for a minute that we're one hundred percent innocent."

Kitty knew Bree was talking about Tammi Barnes. They didn't know what was going on in Tammi's home life or how that affected her behavior at school. All they saw was a cold-hearted bitch who forced some fourteen-year-old freshman girls into a pretty skanky situation. Did she deserve what DGM did to her? Yes. But could they have helped her if they'd known what was really going on? Probably. And that was the part that haunted all of them.

"Look," Kitty said. "We're on our own for this one."

"What did you have in mind?" Donté asked.

"We all show up at school on Sunday," Kitty said. "We'll outnumber him and, hopefully, be able to stop whatever he has planned."

"You realize he's a cop," Ed said. "With a side arm."

Kitty scowled. "The thought has crossed my mind."

"And that's not actually a plan," Ed continued. "That's more like half a plan. Maybe one third."

"I don't think I want to . . ." Peanut started.

Kitty held up her hand. "You can stay home if you want. You

can try and hide from this. But I guarantee he'll find you."

Peanut bit the nail on her pinky finger. "But—"

"Ronny DeStefano," Kitty interrupted.

"Coach Creed," Bree said.

"Rex Cavanaugh," Olivia added.

"Someone has to pay for that," Donté said. "We're all in this together now."

Donté's support gave her strength. They had to see this through, no matter the outcome. Last time they tried to make a stand against the killer, Kitty had let her fear and her bitterness control her decisions. But this time it was all about the team. There was strength in numbers, even more so with Donté by her side.

"It's time to decide," she said, gazing around the semicircle. "Who's in?"

"We're in," John said, before Bree even had a chance to answer.

"We?" Bree asked.

"Don't start," John said. "You can't leave the house, jailbird. So I'm taking your place on this one."

Bree jolted in her chair. "John, you can't."

"Too late," he said.

"But—"

John reached over and silenced the volume on Kitty's laptop as Bree continued to talk, then gestured to the group. "Who's next?"

"We have to do this, Peanut." Theo placed his hand over hers.

Peanut sighed. "Fine."

"I'm in," Olivia said. "After what he did to my mom, I need payback."

Kitty gazed around the room with a smile on her face, which dropped when her eyes landed on Ed the Head.

"I know you swore an oath," she said, ready to give him an out. "But this goes above and beyond. Ed, if you want to bail, no one will blame you."

Ed laughed. "You think I want out? Hell no! I'm in this, Kitty Wei. Don't think you can get rid of me now."

Kitty was taken aback. "I wasn't going to kick you out, I just thought—"

"You thought wrong," he said.

"So we're all agreed?" Kitty said, bringing them back around. "We're going to do this together?"

There was a brief pause and Kitty held her breath. Finally, heads began to nod around the circle and a single word rang out across the patio.

"Together."

FORTY-TWO

KITTY SAT ON A BENCH IN THE GIRLS' LOCKER ROOM, ELBOWS resting on her knees. Her right leg bounced furiously against the tiled floor, creating a rapid, high-pitched squeak from the rubber sole of her cross-trainers. It sounded like a mouse caught in a centrifuge, a manifestation of the adrenaline-fueled anxiety raging within her.

The adrenaline part was normal. She was used to the rush she got when she jogged out onto the court for warm-ups before a game. It was a feeling she loved, a feeling she embraced like an old friend. It meant she was about to do the one thing she loved more than anything else in the world, and the one thing she was really, really good at.

Of course, an exhibition tournament for a whole panel of college scouts upped the ante, but representatives from all the top collegiate volleyball programs weren't the reason her pulse was skyrocketing and her stomach was in knots. She had a bigger fish to fry.

The bench jostled, and Kitty's head snapped around. Mika

sat next to her, her dark skin sallow and her large brown eyes puffy, telltale signs of a sleepless night.

"Hey," Mika said, manically picking at the cuticles around her thumb.

"You okay?" Kitty asked.

"No." Then Mika laughed, short and breathy. "I'm scared."

Scared was an understatement. Kitty thought of the photo of her sisters walking home from school. She was glad they were safe with their mom on the other side of town at their piano lesson. "So am I."

Mika spun on the bench to face Kitty. "I can't stop thinking about everything. Like what if—"

Kitty held up her hand. "Don't. You can't think about that right now. We have to trust that everyone else is going to do their job."

That was the plan. The best one they'd been able to come up with. Kitty and Mika were to suit up and play in the tournament and Theo to assume his managerial role as if nothing was wrong. It seemed like the easiest assignment, since they weren't combing the gym from rafters to basement looking for signs of foul play. That was left to John, Ed, and Donté. Kitty wasn't playing lookout from the stands with Peanut and Olivia. She wasn't stuck at home like Bree, or the hospital like Margot and Logan. Nope, she was a decoy, a passive player in the game that was about to unfold. It was a role Kitty hated.

"I don't know how you guys dealt with it for so long," Mika said after a pause.

"Dealt with what?"

"The stress. I mean, there was this awesome rush after we outed Rex and Amber, but afterward, I was so paranoid we'd get caught. It wasn't fun anymore."

Kitty nodded. She understood exactly what Mika had been feeling. Every time they pulled off a prank, she swore it would be her last one. She'd spend days convinced that Father Uberti was on to her. But then the paranoia would wear off, and they'd find out about something awful one of their classmates had been doing, some innocent being victimized by their peers, and the whole process would start again.

Kitty pictured the video of Mika and Ronny, the DGM mission that started them down the rabbit hole of death and fear.

"I just wanted to say that I'm sorry." Mika stared at her lap.

"For what?"

"For telling Donté you joined the 'Maine Men."

Kitty placed her hand on Mika's shoulder. "It's okay." She smiled out of the left side of her mouth. "I didn't exactly deal so well with you and Donté sneaking around."

Mika's eyes grew wide. "You thought I was messing with Donté?"

"Not exactly," Kitty said, feeling foolish for doubting her best friend and her boyfriend. "But I knew you were keeping something from me."

Coach Miles rounded the row of lockers. "There you two are!" she said, her booming voice echoing off the tile. "Everyone's on the court for warm-ups. You gonna get your asses out there or what?"

"Yes, sir!" Kitty pushed herself to her feet.

"Wei," Coach said, narrowing her eyes. "You got your head in the game today? I need you to be the focused team captain I've known for two years, not the flaky space cadet from the past two days."

"She's focused, Coach," Mika said. "Trust me."

Kitty smiled at Mika, thankful for her support. She'd missed it.

"Good!" Coach barked. "Oh, and Wei? I saw the roster for Gunn. Barbara Ann Vreeland is starting today."

A wave of relief swept over Kitty. Finally! She'd been able to do something to mitigate the damage she'd inflicted on Barbara Ann. At least the scouts would get to see her talent.

"Thanks, Coach."

"No problem." She shoved her whistle in her mouth and gave it a sharp toot. "Now, move it!"

Kitty and Mika jogged out of the locker room down the long hallway to the gym. "You had Coach get Barbara Ann on the team?" Mika asked.

"Yep." Of course, that was before Kitty knew she might actually be putting Barbara Ann's life in danger by having her play in the tournament, but whatever. Nothing she could do about that now.

They hit the highly polished court. Mika paused and smiled at Kitty. "That just might make this whole day worth it."

According to the doctors, Olivia's mom had been asleep for thirty-two hours. This, apparently, was normal in the case of barbiturate overdoses, one of the new and magical facts Olivia had learned since her mom had been admitted to the hospital. Ironically, while thirty-two uninterrupted hours of sleep was abnormal for the majority of the population, Olivia had watched her mom knock off for a whole day before, and she expected that June could go into hibernation for an entire weekend if her bladder were big enough.

While her mom had been asleep for a day and a half, Olivia hadn't slept a wink in at least as long. She'd tried, curled up in what passed as an easy chair in her mom's room, a seventies pleather monstrosity, barely wide enough to span her hips. She managed to rig a kind of lounger, by dragging the chair in front of a table so she could at least prop up her legs, and she ended up catching fitful naps all night long, nodding off every few minutes, then snapping awake when her head would loll to the side.

She hadn't been home to shower, hadn't done her hair or makeup, hadn't left her mom's side except for the DGM meeting at Peanut's, and only then because the nurses promised that her mom wouldn't regain consciousness for at least another six hours. Olivia couldn't bear the idea of her mom waking up alone and scared, unsure of where she was or what had happened.

And now she was going to have to leave again. The volleyball tournament started in less than an hour, and Olivia couldn't abandon her friends. Not now. But as she gazed at the sleeping figure of her mom, she couldn't help but wonder if this was the last time she'd ever see her.

"Knock knock."

Olivia knew the lilting British voice even before she saw Fitzgerald in the doorway. He was meticulously groomed as always, wearing his signature black turtleneck under a black sports jacket, his white pompadour hair expertly molded into place. He was all smiles as he stood there, but his light blue eyes—so like Olivia's own, she now realized—lacked their usual sparkle, and there was tension in his features that Olivia had never seen before.

"Hi," she said. It sounded so lame, but how were you supposed to start a conversation with the father you'd never known?

Fitzgerald appeared equally at a loss for words. Totally out of character. He opened his mouth to say something, then winced, as if whatever lines he'd rehearsed in his head suddenly seemed trite. Instead, he shifted his gaze to Olivia's mother.

"How is she?"

"Sleeping." Really, Liv? Like he couldn't tell that already? "But she's going to be okay."

Fitzgerald nodded absently as he continued to stare at her mom. Was he searching for the young actress he'd had an affair with so long ago?

"The hospital called me last night," he said after a long pause. "About the note your mother left." He glanced at Olivia. "It's true, then?"

"That my mom tried to kill herself?" Olivia said.

"Em . . ." He wrinkled his mouth, grasping for words. "No. The other part."

He really couldn't bring himself to say it, could he? *That I'm your father.*

In the bed, Olivia's mom stirred. Olivia rushed to her side, hopeful that June was finally regaining consciousness, but her eyes didn't flutter open, and her breath continued slow and steady. Still sleeping.

"Perhaps I should come back later," Fitzgerald said.

That was probably a good idea. The last thing Olivia wanted was for her mom to wake up with the estranged father of her child looming over her hospital bed. But she needed to talk to him.

"Let's go into the hallway," she suggested.

In the stark fluorescent light of the hall, Fitzgerald scanned Olivia's face. "I can see it now," he began. "Before, I only saw your mother, but you have my eyes, and when I was younger, my hair was that same shade of strawberry blond."

It definitely explained why Olivia's fairness was so different from her mom's dark beauty.

"She never told you, did she?"

Olivia shook her head. "She never talked about my dad. I mean, you. I mean, who you were." *Way to babble, Liv.*

"I can't pretend that I'd have been Father of the Year if I *had* known about you," he said. "I don't think I'm particularly parental. But I would have been able to help. I could have made your lives more comfortable."

Olivia wondered what that would have been like. Maybe her mom wouldn't have had to work as hard? Maybe she would have had more time for acting and been happier?

"I have something for you," Fitzgerald continued. He reached into the breast pocket of his blazer and retrieved an envelope. "This doesn't make up for all the years I've missed, but it's a start. I realize I'll see you this summer, but I thought, perhaps, you could use it now. To help you through this crisis." Fitzgerald placed the envelope in Olivia's hand, kissed her swiftly on the forehead, and then hurried down the hall.

Olivia stood there lamely for several seconds before her brain kicked in, then she broke the seal on the envelope with her index finger and peeked at the contents.

Inside was a check for ten thousand dollars.

FORTY-THREE

KITTY AND MIKA JOGGED INTO THE GYM. THE REST OF THE team was already on the court, running through warm-up drills. As Kitty dropped her towel on the bench, Coach Miles raced up to her.

"Have you heard from Theo?"

Kitty tensed. Theo should have been at the gym hours ago. "No."

"I've called him a dozen times with no answer." She pointed at Kitty, dead between the eyes. "When you see Baranski, tell him he's fired."

"Yes, Coach." She could have pointed out that you can't fire someone from a class they're not getting graded in, but Coach Miles's mood was the least of her problems at the moment. Where was Theo?

She walked to the edge of the court, volleyballs flying around her as both the Bishop DuMaine and St. Francis teams practiced their sets and kills, and scanned the bleachers. Maybe Theo was with Donté? Her boyfriend should have been easy to spot in the crowd, since he was taller than the majority of the population. But as she searched row by row, the hairs began to stand up on the back of her neck. No Theo. No Donté.

Where could they be?

"Kitty!"

Kitty spun around and all the warmth drained out of her body. In the front row, waving like lunatics, were her little sisters, Sophia and Lydia.

"Shit!" Kitty sprinted across the court in a blind panic. "What are you guys doing here? You have piano lessons today."

Sophia smiled. "Miss Radovansky had to cancel our lessons."

"Some kind of family emergency," Lydia added.

"So now we get to see you play!"

"Isn't that awesome?"

Family emergency. Yeah, right. She remembered the photo the killer had sent, of her sisters walking home from school. Somehow, he'd managed to get the twins to the tournament.

"Where's Mom?" Kitty said quickly. She had to get them out of there. "She needs to take you home. Now."

Lydia's face dropped. "But we want to see you play."

"It's not fair," Sophia said, crossing her arms over her chest.

"Mom said we could stay."

"We're not kids anymore."

"And you're not the boss of us."

"Enough!" Kitty shouted. "Where is Mom?"

Lydia and Sophia stared at her blankly. She'd never yelled at them before, never been anything but an upbeat and patient big sister, and the girls looked as if they were going to burst into tears right there on the gym floor.

"She's . . . she's not here," Sophia sniffled.

"She's having lunch with Aunt LuLu and Uncle Jer," Lydia said.

"To talk about the fire."

"And she's not picking us up till two."

"Dammit," Kitty muttered under her breath. What was she going to do? It was too far for the twins to walk. She glanced around, looking for someone who could take them home. But how was she supposed to explain it?

"Wei!" Coach Miles barked. She tooted her whistle. "I need you. Now."

Something in her voice made Kitty take notice. She turned and found her coach on the far side of the gym near the entrance to the locker rooms, gesturing to her frantically.

Now what?

"Okay." She took each of her sisters by the hand and dragged them toward the main exit, where she plopped them down on a bench in the first row. Closer to the exit meant closer to safety. At least she hoped. "Sit here."

"But I want to be higher up," Sophia moaned.

"Yeah," Lydia said. "These seats suck."

"They're the best seats in the house," Kitty lied. She crouched down to eye level. "Because I can see you both through the whole game. Which will make me play better. Okay?"

That seemed to mollify the twins. They exchanged a look, then smiled. "Okay."

Then Kitty threw her arms around her sisters and hugged them so tightly she could feel them gasping for breath. "I love you guys," she said.

"Ew!" they groaned in unison.

With a tight smile, Kitty pulled herself away and jogged across the gym to Coach Miles. As soon as she got close enough to see the tense lines of her coach's face, Kitty knew that something was wrong.

"Coach?"

"Come with me." Coach grabbed Kitty roughly by the arm and hustled her down the corridor, past the entrance to the locker rooms, and outside into the courtyard. There she saw Donté, Theo, and Mika, surrounded by a half-dozen police officers. Kitty registered immediately that Sergeant Callahan was not one of them.

Donté and Theo had already been handcuffed, and a female officer was in the process of securing Mika while another Mirandized her.

"If you cannot afford an attorney, one will be provided for you. Do you understand the rights I have just read to you?"

"Kitty!" Mika cried. Her voice trembled.

"Do you understand?" the officer repeated.

Mika's voice caught in her throat. "Yes."

"Can someone please tell me," Coach Miles began, "what the hell is going on here?"

"This is a police matter, ma'am," the lead officer said.

"We're under arrest for Rex's murder," Donté said. "Peanut too. They said there's DNA evidence linking us to the crime scene."

Kitty's heart thundered in her chest. DNA evidence? She flashed back to the day Rex was killed and the conversation she'd overheard between Sergeant Callahan and the medical examiner. What had the doctor said? Several hair samples had been found on the body?

Sergeant Callahan had planted that DNA evidence on Rex's body. That's how he framed them. If he wasn't the killer, then he was definitely the accomplice.

"We'll notify your parents once we reach the station," the officer said. He nodded to his colleagues. "Let's head out."

Coach Miles dashed in front of them, blocking the exit. "You can't just arrest my team manager and one of my star players."

"Yes, ma'am," he said. "I can. Now will you please stand aside?"

"Where is Sergeant Callahan?" Kitty asked. "I thought he was in charge of the investigation."

The lead officer sighed impatiently. "Day off." He took Donté by the shoulder and led him toward the exit.

Kitty ran to his side, pacing him as they hurried across the lawn. "I'll find out who did this," she cried. "We'll fix it."

The officer guided Donté's head into the backseat of the squad car. "Kitty, don't," Donté said. "It's too dangerous."

"I'm not letting you take the fall for this."

The officer slammed the door, and then they were gone.

Coach Miles threw her clipboard to the ground. "What is going on at this school?"

You have no idea. But Kitty didn't have time to explain anything to her coach. Without a word, she sprinted back to the locker room. She needed to call Bree.

Bree listened, speechless, as Kitty rapidly told her about the arrests of the other DGM members.

"What are we going to do?" Kitty asked. Even over the phone, Bree could sense her hopelessness.

"John's leaving now," Bree said calmly. "Ed should be there already and Olivia will be on her way. Just keep your eyes open, and don't be afraid to scream bloody murder if you see anything suspicious, okay?" Ed had been right. This was a horrible plan.

"Okay."

"We'll figure this out," Bree said, not entirely sure it was the truth. "We'll clear their names. Somehow."

"Thanks, Bree."

Bree tossed her phone on the bed and stared at it as John rubbed her back. "You catch all that?"

"So much for our plan," John said.

"It wasn't really much of a plan to begin with." Bree turned and slipped her hand into John's, holding it tightly. "I don't want you to go."

"I know. But I have to." He patted the phone in his pocket. "Ed already texted. Asked me to meet him in the courtyard behind the gym."

"The whole point of us showing up en masse was to overwhelm him." Bree shook her head. "How are you and Ed and Olivia supposed to manage that alone?"

John leaned in closer. "You'll find I'm full of surprises."

"Didn't Luke Skywalker get his hand cut off like two minutes after uttering that line?"

John pursed his lips. "Huh. Yeah, not my best quote." He stood up and grabbed his jacket from the back of a chair. "I'm going to check in every fifteen minutes." Then he smirked. "If you stop hearing from me, it means I'm dead."

Bree shot to her feet. "That is *not* funny."

"I'm sorry." He walked back and planted his hands on her hips. "But I'm scared, and this is how I deal."

Bree nodded. She was scared too, even though she was the one trapped at home and out of danger. But her heart ached for John, and the idea that he was taking her place and putting himself in danger made her want to cry.

"I love you," he said.

"I know."

Ed parked his car across the street from the Bishop DuMaine gym and stared at the exterior. *So here's where it's all going to end.*

He'd managed to keep Sergeant Callahan out of the mix, to keep his connection to Christopher Beeman hidden, and now it all came back to Bishop DuMaine, a place Ed both loved and hated. There was something kind of delicious about the irony.

With a heavy sigh, he reached to the passenger seat and unzipped his backpack, then pulled a plain manila envelope from its depths. He opened it carefully, lovingly, barely gripping the sides of the photo as he slid it onto his lap.

It had been taken two days ago. Or maybe three. It was kind of hard to tell, considering how little changed in Margot's hospital room while she was still unconscious. She was sound asleep, not yet awoken from her coma, her brown eyes closed, her face serene. This was what mattered most to him. This was what someone had tried to take away.

He gazed at Margot, taking in every detail. The photographer had stood inside the room, just to the left of the doorway, angling the camera to capture the length of the hospital bed as well as most of the get-well tokens that littered the far corner. Even though the photo was black-and-white, Ed had been in Margot's hospital room enough times to picture the vivid colors: pinks and yellows of floral bouquets, beige and white teddy bears, cards of bright orange polka dots and swaths of rainbows, the reflective surface of the Mylar balloon.

Ed paused, his eyes darting back to the balloon. Suddenly, his fingers crumpled the cherished photo, viciously mangling it into a ball, which he dropped onto the seat as if it was too hot to touch.

Then without another thought, he bolted from his car and sprinted toward the gym.

FORTY-FOUR

OLIVIA LEANED AGAINST THE WALL, PRESSING THE SMALL OF her back against the smooth, hard surface. She stared at the check in her hands. Ten thousand dollars. For the first time in a week, a weight had been lifted. Ever since her mom had announced that she'd quit her bartending job, Olivia had been keeping the panic at bay. What were they going to do for rent? What if they got evicted? Would they end up homeless? In a shelter? If nothing else, Fitzgerald offered her a reprieve from the nagging fear of poverty, at least until Olivia turned eighteen. And then who knows? Maybe she'd be able to bank on his name. The daughter of the world's foremost stage director? It had worked for Rebecca Hall.

She shook her head. No. If she was going to succeed as an actress, it needed to be on her own terms.

Olivia turned to go back into her mom's room, when she heard someone yelling at the end of the hall.

"What do you mean she disappeared? Wasn't anyone on duty?" A pause, presumably while someone answered, then the woman's voice again, growing more and more hysterical by the second. "Sixteen-year-old girls don't just disappear in the middle of the night! Where's the security guard?"

A petite woman with dark wavy hair stormed out of a room at the end of the hall, two doctors and a nurse trailing after her. "Mrs. Mejia," one of the doctors twittered. "Are you sure your husband didn't take your daughter home?"

Olivia sucked in a breath. *Mrs. Mejia?*

"Of course not," Margot's mom said. She blew past Olivia without looking at her, then stopped at the nurses' station by the elevator, where two guards were scrambling around a computer screen. "I demand to see the security footage from last night."

"It appears to be missing, ma'am," one of the guards said.

"Missing?" Mrs. Mejia roared.

She pulled a phone from her bag and quickly dialed. "Central Station? This is Racquel Mejia. My daughter has been kidnapped by a boy claiming to be her boyfriend. I want an APB put out on Logan Blaine immediately."

Olivia stood frozen in the hallway. Margot and Logan were missing. Could Sergeant Callahan have gotten to them? Had he gotten to everyone? His big finale? Olivia felt a creeping sensation race down her spine like a mass of spiders set loose on her skin. Was she the only one left?

Her hands trembled as she fished her cell phone out of the pocket of her skinny jeans. She tried Margot's number first. No surprise when the call went straight to voice mail. Kitty's phone rang at least, but it too went to voice mail.

She's playing in the tournament, Olivia told herself, trying to control the panic. *That's why she's not picking up.*

She said a silent prayer as she dialed Bree.

"How's your mom?" Bree asked the moment she answered.

Olivia let out a sigh of relief. At least the killer hadn't gotten to her. "Have you heard from Margot?"

"No," Bree said. "Why?"

Olivia dropped her voice. "All hell has broken loose at the hospital. Margot and Logan are missing."

"You've got to be kidding me."

"I wish," Olivia said. "I tried Margot's phone but it goes straight to voice mail."

"We have a major problem," Bree said. "The other DGM has been arrested for the murder of Rex Cavanaugh."

"What?" Olivia felt her chest seize up. "All of them?"

"All of them."

"Oh God . . ." Peanut would be absolutely freaking out.

"Sergeant Callahan must have done all of this. It's the only explanation."

Olivia swallowed. "Now what do we do?"

"John and Ed the Head are on their way to school."

"I'll meet them there."

"Okay," Bree said. "And, Olivia?"

"Yeah?"

"Be careful."

Olivia had just shoved her phone back into her pocket when it vibrated. A text. She whipped it out again and saw that it was from Margot's phone. *Oh, thank God!* she thought. *They're okay.*

But as soon as she saw the message, Olivia's stomach dropped.

It was a photo of Margot and Logan, bound and gagged in what looked like an industrial basement. Margot's eyes were pleading, Logan's defiant and angry. And there was a caption below the photo.

Where it all began. Come alone or they die.

Tears welled up in Olivia's eyes. Donté, Mika, Theo, and Peanut had been arrested, and now Sergeant Callahan had Margot and Logan, and would use them to lure the rest of the girls to the school, where he'd exact his ultimate revenge.

Part of Olivia wanted to flee, to grab her mom and Fitzgerald's check and take off running. They could change their names, find a new home, and start over.

Olivia wiped heavy tears from her cheeks. No, she couldn't do that. Wouldn't do that. She wasn't going to abandon her friends when they needed her most.

It was time to end this, once and for all.

She hurried down the hall to her mom's room. She'd just leave a note, and with any luck, by the time her mom woke up the nightmare of the last month would be over.

She rounded the doorway into the room and found her mom awake. "Mom!" she cried.

Olivia's mom smiled. She sat upright in the mechanized bed, with her cell phone in her hand. "Oh, Livvie, I'm so sorry."

Tears erupted afresh from Olivia's eyes as she threw herself into her mom's arms. Her chest heaved with body-racking sobs and the croaking moans that accompanied them sounded unnatural and beastlike as they filled the silence of the room. She realized in a moment that she hadn't allowed herself to cry since she'd found her mom splayed out on their living room couch. Now, the weight of her sorrow combined with the joy of relief came crashing down on her at once.

"There, there," her mom said, running her hand over Olivia's short curls. "It's okay, baby girl. It's going to be okay."

"Why would you leave me?" Olivia managed through the tears. "Why would you leave me all alone?"

Her mom was amazingly calm, the crippling depression of the other night evaporated. "I thought you'd be better off without me."

Olivia pulled away. "I'd never be better off without my mom."

Her mom swept a stray curl from Olivia's forehead, then wiped the tears from both of her cheeks. "I know. But in that moment . . ."

In that moment her mom had believed it. Olivia knew that reality all too well. It was one of the greatest trials she'd struggled with through her mom's bipolar episodes. No matter what she said, no matter how rational or passionate or upset Olivia got, she knew she couldn't combat the perceived reality in her mom's head. All she could do was wait until the episode passed and hope her mom didn't do anything to harm herself in the meantime.

A tactic that had worked . . . right up until it didn't.

Olivia wasn't sure how long she lay there with her head on her mom's shoulder before she realized there was some kind of music playing in the room. It was tinny and weak, but Olivia recognized the sound right away. It was Bangers and Mosh from the finale of *Twelfth Precinct*.

She sat up and looked at her mom's phone. There was a video playing on the screen.

"Where did you get that?" Olivia asked.

"I know we weren't supposed to film it," her mom said sheepishly. "But I figured since my daughter was the star of the show, I was entitled."

Olivia stared in silence. Her mom had zoomed in on her and Logan as they executed part of the final dance number together, then separated to opposite sides of the stage. The camera stayed on Olivia, now doing some cutesy pantomime with Donté. *Oh my God!* This was exactly what Olivia had been looking for. Peanut and the new DGM had erased the original, which meant Olivia was looking at the only video footage of that night. Possibly the only proof of what had happened to Margot.

"Don't be mad, Livvie," her mom said, misinterpreting her silence. "I only filmed a few scenes."

"Which ones?" Olivia asked anxiously.

"Your scene with Amber at the end of act one. The monologue in act two. The duel with Sir Andrew. Finale and bows. That's it, I swear!"

The music crescendoed, then applause roared from the tiny speakers on her mom's phone. Olivia turned back and saw the lights on the stage go out. That was the final tableau, where she and Logan embraced, with all the characters in their respective pairings. When the lights came back up, everyone broke their poses and moved into a straight line at the back of the stage to begin the curtain calls.

Her mom had zoomed out as far as the camera would go, then

panned from left to right across the stage as the minor characters took their bows. The camera lingered for a moment on Olivia, dead center between Logan and Amber, then continued to pan. When the camera reached the far end of the stage, Olivia held her breath. Just beyond that curtain stood Margot's prompter's stand. Had she already been attacked at this point? Or was she still sitting there, clapping along with the band, enjoying a successful opening night? She strained her eyes as the shaky video reached the end of the cast line, desperate to see something, anything, that would help to put a face on their anonymous stalker. No such luck.

The picture went haywire, sideways then black, though the sound continued.

"Sorry," her mom said. "Mr. Cunningham got up to go backstage and I tried to hide the camera. It comes back in a minute."

"Oh."

Sure enough, her mom had retrieved the camera from her lap, following Mr. Cunningham's pinstripe jacket as he edged out of the row to the side aisle near the stage door.

That's when she saw it.

Just a split second, a blurred image of someone hurrying up the aisle past Mr. Cunningham as the camera zipped away, back to the stage. But there was something familiar about the fuzzy profile.

Olivia grabbed the phone out of her mom's hand and paused the video.

"What are you doing?" her mom asked. "Your curtain call is next!"

But Olivia didn't care about her curtain call. She didn't care about the standing ovation, or about Amber's upcoming hissy fit. All she wanted to see was that blurry figure in the aisle. She walked the video back frame by frame, then paused.

"What is it?" her mom asked. She sounded alarmed. "Livvie, are you okay? What's wrong?"

Even though the image was dark and out of focus, Olivia knew right away who had been in the theater that night. Someone who couldn't have been there. Shouldn't have been there.

She was staring at Ed the Head.

FORTY-FIVE

BREE FELT UTTERLY HELPLESS AS SHE STARED AT THE PHOTO of Margot and Logan. That son of a bitch had them, and here she was, trapped at home, waiting for John to check in. He shouldn't be there. He should be home, safe and sound, not facing a maniac in Bree's place. She felt like a one-legged man at an ass-kicking contest: totally and completely useless.

"Darling, you're going to walk a hole through the carpet." Her mom stood in the doorway of Bree's room, a small plastic water bottle in hand.

"Sorry," Bree said. "I'm just anxious."

"Oh!" her mom cooed, perking up. "Why didn't you say so?" Without another word, her mom hurried to her room and returned a moment later with a plastic pill organizer. "Let's see . . . How about a Klonopin? That's always a good start. Or maybe a Xanax? No, that will make you sleepy." She glanced up at Bree. "Do you want to be sleepy?"

"No."

"I didn't think so." She returned her focus to the medication cornucopia. "I find a Celexa-Cymbalta cocktail has a nice one-two punch, or if you want to cut to the chase, I can give you a Haldol and be done with it."

Should she be concerned that her mom was apparently a one-stop shop for mood-enhancing prescription drugs? "I'm fine, thanks."

"Are you sure there's nothing you need?"

Bree thought about asking for her mom's help. Maybe if she sent Olaf down to the gym, they'd stand a chance? She opened her mouth, but before she could get a word out, her cell phone rang. She grabbed it from the table and answered it without looking.

"You're late," she said with a nervous laugh.

"What?" Olivia asked.

"Oh!" Bree said. "Sorry. I thought you were—"

"It's Ed!" Olivia yelled into the phone.

"What do you mean?"

"Ed is the killer. He lied to us. It was him all along!"

"That's impossible," Bree said. She had no idea what Olivia was talking about, and yet she could feel the panic in her friend's voice. "He has an alibi."

"Fuck the alibi!" Olivia screamed. "My mom has video from opening night of *Twelfth Precinct* on her phone. I just saw the curtain calls and Ed was there, in the theater, leaving through the stage door."

"Are you sure?" Bree asked.

"Positive." From Olivia's end of the phone, a horn blared. "I'm heading to school. You've got to warn everyone."

Bree froze. Had it been Ed the Head all the time? But Sergeant Callahan had the watch. How was that possible? Her brain had difficulty processing it all. Ed's alibi was a fake. He'd been at the theater that night. He'd murdered Ronny and Coach Creed and Rex. Not to mention the other DGM victims. Now Logan and Margot, and . . .

Oh God. John was meeting Ed at school.

"Hello?" Olivia cried. "Did you hear me?"

Bree forced her voice to work. "He's with John. At school. Ed has him."

Olivia was silent for a moment. "I'll find Kitty."

Bree wasn't sure what Olivia and Kitty could do by themselves, but she was in no position to argue.

"Call the police," Olivia said. "And don't panic. I'm sure John is fine."

Bree hung up and immediately dialed John's number. Without even ringing, his voice mail picked up. She dialed again, hoping it was just a cross call, but again voice mail. Again. And again.

Bree dropped the phone to her bed and squeezed her eyes shut, forcing the image of a dead or wounded John from her mind. No, she wasn't going to picture it. John was smart, and John was tough. He'd figure some way out of this.

"Bree?" her mom asked, her voice firm. "What is wrong?"

"I . . ." It would take too long to explain. "Hold on." She needed to try and convince the police that a serial killer was at the Bishop DuMaine gym. Yeah, that wouldn't sound crazy at all.

"Santa Clara County 911, please state your emergency."

"Um . . ." Bree swallowed. What was the fastest way to get the police to respond?

"Is this a prank call?" the operator said, clearly annoyed.

"I'm calling to report a . . . a suspicious package at the Bishop DuMaine gym." Bomb threats always worked with the cops, didn't they? "I'm here for a volleyball tournament and I saw a guy walk into the gym with a large bag, drop it by the door, and leave."

"Mm-hm," the operator said. "You said Bishop DuMaine, right?"

"Yeah."

"Interesting. This is the second call we've gotten today claiming that there's a bomb at that school. Kind of convenient considering just yesterday we got a memo from Sergeant Callahan at Menlo PD."

Bree groaned. She didn't like the sound of this.

"And he warned us," the operator continued, "to expect some prank calls from high school students in regard to Bishop DuMaine."

"Ma'am," Bree said, trying to communicate the appropriate amount of seriousness in her voice. "I promise, this is not a prank. This is—"

"Young lady," the operator said, interrupting her. "Do you have any idea of the penalty for making false statements to emergency response? The list of offenses is—"

Bree didn't wait for the rest of the lecture before ending the call.

"Bree Deringer," her mom said, hands on hips. "You tell me what is going on this instant."

"I think we screwed up. Bad."

Her mom sighed. "Obviously. What can I do to help?"

Short of convincing her buddy Sergeant Callahan to send the entire Menlo Park police force down to Bishop DuMaine, she didn't know . . .

Bree caught her breath. There was one way, one foolproof way to make sure the police went exactly where she wanted them to.

"What is it?" her mom asked.

Bree smiled at her. "I need to borrow the car."

Her mom arched an eyebrow. "You want Olaf to disable the house alarm and take you somewhere?"

"Nope. I just want the car."

"But the alarm will go off as soon as you leave the house. The police will trace your GPS signal."

Bree smiled. "Exactly."

FORTY-SIX

AS OLIVIA SCREECHED HER MOM'S CIVIC TO A HALT IN FRONT of the school, she was greeted by the sight of hundreds of people pouring out of the Bishop DuMaine gym.

Spectators and volleyball players alike exited through the two exterior doors, moving onto the lawn in a leisurely, unhurried kind of way. What had happened?

She sprinted across the grass toward a group of blue Bishop DuMaine athletic uniforms. The girls' volleyball team. She spotted Kitty behind the team, talking to two girls.

"Stay here," Kitty was saying to the girls as Olivia raced up to her, "with Coach Miles until Mom arrives. Do you understand?"

"Yes, Kitty," the girls said in unison. Kitty's twin sisters.

She caught sight of Olivia and her eyes grew wide. "Good," she said to her sisters. "I'll be right back." Then she grabbed Olivia by the arm and moved them out of earshot.

"What's going on?" Olivia asked, panting. "Why are you all outside?"

"Someone pulled the fire alarm," Kitty said.

Ed was trying to clear the Bishop DuMaine gym. Why?

"You won't believe it," Olivia said, panting. "But I know who the killer is."

Kitty eyed her. "Um, yeah. Sergeant Callahan, remember?"

Olivia's stomach clenched as she slowly shook her head.

The words tumbled out of her mouth as she quickly and calmly explained Ed's betrayal. She watched the same series of emotions pass across Kitty's face that she'd felt when she realized what had happened: confusion, surprise, anger, and finally, fear.

"I saw John with Ed about ten minutes ago," Kitty said, her face instantly pale. "They went into the maintenance corridor behind the gym."

"There you are!" Bree sprinted up to them. "You heard?"

Kitty nodded.

Olivia grabbed Bree's arm. "Are the police coming?"

Bree smiled wickedly and pointed to her anklet. "Oh, they're coming. They'll follow this baby to the ends of the earth."

Olivia heaved a sigh of relief. "Good." She looked from Kitty to Bree and smiled, trying to appear significantly braver than she felt. "Shall we go save Margot?"

Kitty had never been in the gym when it was totally empty. The flashing lights and blaring sirens filled the cavernous space, accentuating the loneliness. It felt like she was alone in the middle of a zombie apocalypse and there was no one left on earth to silence the fire alarm.

No, not alone. Bree and Olivia stood by her side.

None of them said a word, but Kitty reached out and found their hands—Olivia's on one side, Bree's on the other—and grasped them firmly in her own. They'd started this journey together. They'd understood the risks, and they'd carried out their DGM missions faithfully, each for her own reasons. They'd weathered long-kept secrets, betrayals, lies, and jealousy. They'd bent but they hadn't broken, and, together, they were going to face the enemy who'd been so close to them all along, and now held the lives of their friends in his hands.

And this is how it would end.

There was a part of her that was almost relieved. Ed the Head had deceived them all, and though he was a murderer and a sociopath, he was also their peer, not an adult, not a cop like Sergeant Callahan. Somehow, that made it seem easier, more feasible. Like they had a chance this time. Ed didn't know they were coming for him. For once, they had the upper hand.

Kitty took a deep breath, then in one unified motion, they all walked toward the door marked "Access Restricted" that led to the maintenance corridor.

No one was surprised to find the door unlocked.

Once inside the short hallway with the door closed behind them, the pulsating blare of the fire alarm was muted, and Kitty could finally hear herself think. The so-called maintenance corridor was about ten feet long, with two closets and a door at the far end.

"Any idea where that goes?" she asked.

"Basement," Bree said. "I was down there during the prank

on Melissa Barndorfer. It's a mix of pipes and ducts, some storage, electrical, water, gas, air-conditioning. And the boiler room tucked away downstairs in the back."

"How big?" Kitty asked.

Bree scrunched up her face, thinking. "Spans the whole area beneath the gym and locker rooms, I think. But I haven't seen all of it."

"Where it all began," Olivia mused, quoting Ed's last message. "What do you think he means?"

"It all began with Christopher Beeman," Bree said.

Kitty nodded. "And he hung himself in the boiler room at Archway."

Olivia stared at the door to the basement. "Any chance the basement isn't the creepiest place I've ever been?"

"Nope," Bree said.

"Come on." Swallowing her fear, Kitty marched up to the basement door and yanked it open.

The stairwell to the basement was significantly darker than the brightly lit hall above, and Kitty paused at the top of the stairs as her eyes adjusted to the dimness. Bree and Olivia filed in behind and the door slammed shut, blocking out the majority of the light with one jarring thud.

There was another door at the bottom of the stairs, and Kitty could just make out a dim yellow glow beneath it, seeping into the darkened staircase. The basement lights were on, which somehow gave her the courage to reach for the handle and swing the door open.

The dim lighting was the result of yellow bulbs screwed directly into sockets in the low ceiling, and though it was better than the darkness of the staircase, they still didn't provide enough illumination to penetrate the shadowy recesses.

And shadowy it was. The long, open basement was packed with crap. Old chairs and tables from a variety of historical eras were piled haphazardly along with several rows of plush theater seats. An ancient floor polisher, more rust than metal. Dusty file cabinets and long-forgotten book boxes. A basketball scoreboard from the 1950s, the kind a scorekeeper needed to change by hand. Bags of cement, cans of paint, and a variety of brushes, brooms, mops, and tools. Sixty years of Bishop DuMaine castoffs shoved into one space.

Kitty paused, listening for any sign of life. Nothing.

"Where's the boiler room?" Olivia whispered. Her voice sounded small in the seemingly endless expanse of the basement.

"Stairs at the far end," Bree said.

The closeness of the basement combined with limited light and the odd, disconcerting shapes of piled-up junk made Kitty feel like they were being watched. She kept thinking she heard noises—the creaky springs of an old theater chair, the clanging of pipes, and the soft fall of footsteps. Once or twice she could have sworn she saw something move, a quick dash of motion from behind the stacks of garbage. She felt the girls press in close behind her as she crept toward the boiler room stairs, and her speed slowed down as fear overtook her.

That's when she heard it.

"Ooooooh."

Kitty froze.

"What the hell was that?" Olivia's voice was little more than a strangled squeak.

Kitty swallowed. "I . . . I don't—"

"My head."

Bree caught her breath. "John?"

"How can you tell that's John?" Olivia asked.

"Bree?"

"John!" Bree turned, and dashed around a set of old file cabinets. "John, it's me!"

Kitty raced after her, Olivia close behind. As they rounded some giant metal cabinets, they saw Bree crouched on the floor, her arms around John, who was sitting up against the wall next to a pile of old carpet rolls.

"Are you okay?" Bree cried. Her voice shook.

"Okay," John said.

"What happened?" Kitty asked.

"We split up in the basement," John said. He jabbed his thumb behind him. "I was snooping around and found them. Thought I heard someone behind me and then . . ." He shrugged. "Guess I got clobbered."

"What do you mean, 'found them'?" Kitty asked.

John turned, one hand pressed to the back of his head, and swept his arm across the rolls of old carpet behind him. "Them."

Bree scrambled over to the nearest bundle and pulled away

a blanket, uncovering a face. Even in the dim light, Kitty recognized her.

"Tammi Barnes!" Kitty and Olivia dashed to the other bundles, yanking their covering away to reveal Xavier Hathaway, Wendy Marshall, and the Gertler twins.

"Are they dead?" Olivia asked.

Kitty pressed her fingers to Wendy's neck. "No," she said with a sigh of relief. "Drugged I think, but alive."

Bree pulled out her phone. "We have to call the cops."

John shook his head. "No signal down here. I already tried."

"Thank God Ed didn't kill them," Olivia said.

"Ed the Head is the killer?" John looked incredulous. "I don't believe it."

"Believe it," Olivia said.

"I'll explain later," Bree said. "Right now, we need to find him."

"Okay." John pushed himself to his feet, steadied by Bree. "Which way?"

"Nuh-uh," Bree said. "You're getting out of here."

"Without you?" John said with a laugh. "Hell no."

"John," Kitty said. "We need you to find the police. Convince them that their missing persons are down here." Kitty glanced from Bree to Olivia. "We're going to need backup."

John gripped Bree's shoulders. "I don't want to leave you."

"I know," she said.

He took a deep breath, then gave Bree a swift kiss on the lips, and staggered back the way they had come. Kitty prayed that they could stall Ed long enough so that John could return with the authorities. It was their only chance.

They waited until the sound of John's footsteps disappeared into the depths of the basement before they continued. The door at the end was closed, just like in every horror movie Kitty had ever seen. Opening a closed door in a situation like this was never, ever a good thing. But somewhere on the other side, Margot was in trouble, might need her help. And Kitty had to get to her no matter what.

With a sharp intake of breath, she threw the door open and rushed inside.

She stood on a small landing overlooking the boiler room. Four or five metal stairs led down to the concrete floor, where a tangled mass of pipes snaked out of what looked like an enormous furnace. Bound and gagged on the concrete floor in front of the boiler was Margot.

"Margot!" Olivia raced down the steps, Kitty and Bree close behind, and began to pull at the ropes tied around Margot's wrists. "Are you okay?"

"*Mmumff mum,*" Margot cried through her gag.

Olivia pulled down her gag.

"Get out of here," Margot said. Her voice shook. "Hurry."

Kitty loosened the rest of her bonds. "Not without you."

Bree grabbed Margot's hand. "Where's Logan? We've got to get out of here before Ed comes back."

"Ed?" Margot said, obviously confused.

"Yeah," Kitty said, eyeing her. "He's the one who kidnapped you. It was Ed all along."

341

Margot slowly shook her head from side to side as a massive tear rolled down her cheek. "No, it wasn't."

"What?"

"I'm afraid Margot's right," a voice said from behind them.

Kitty spun around. Blocking the only exit at the top of the stairs, gun casually pointed at them, was Logan.

FORTY-SEVEN

IT TOOK KITTY A MOMENT TO PROCESS WHAT SHE WAS SEEING: that it was Logan, not Ed, who held them at gunpoint.

"But . . ." Olivia looked back and forth between Kitty and Bree. "I don't understand."

"I know," Logan said. "That's what makes it so awesome. None of you suspected me. Not even Ed, and he hates me."

Olivia shook her head. "But you . . . I mean, the photo. Ed had you bound and gagged."

"He staged it," Bree said.

"What does Ed have to do with this?" Margot asked.

"He was at the theater that night," Olivia said. "He attacked you. We thought."

"No," Margot said. She was staring at Logan, her face blank, her eyes devoid of emotion. "*He* attacked me."

Logan's smile tightened. "Yes."

Kitty caught a slight flutter of Logan's eyelids, and for a split second, his trigger hand faltered. He may have been a liar and a murderer, but his feelings for Margot were real.

"How could you?" Kitty said, laying into the one weakness she knew Logan possessed. "You love her. How could you hurt her like that?"

"I did it *because* I love her." Logan's eyes softened as he shifted them to Margot. "I hope you understand."

"You tried to kill her because you love her?" Bree exclaimed. "Pretty fucked-up way of showing it."

"What do you know about love?" Logan asked. "You and John and your *Star Wars* quotes and your witty banter. It's the most superficial crap I've ever seen."

Bree jutted out her chin defiantly. "You don't know anything about us."

"Really?" Logan descended two steps down from the platform. "Have you done anything at all to deserve John's love? He pined for you for years while you drooled over that idiot in the band. Then you miraculously discovered feelings for him only after he became a rock star? Sounds like the definition of superficial."

"Maybe," Bree said. "But at least I didn't try to kill him."

"He was afraid of what Ed was going to tell me," Margot said. Her body was utterly still, and her voice was growing stronger by the minute.

Logan nodded. "Yes."

"And he had to make sure I never talked to Ed."

"I knew you'd understand." Logan smiled at her.

Margot stiffened. "Tell me why. You owe me that."

"Christopher was my roommate at Archway," Logan said. "More than that. We were like brothers. That place was a hellhole, and after the first six weeks I was ready to put myself out of my misery. But Christopher talked me down off the ledge, kept me sane." Logan swallowed. "He saved my life."

"But that was before Ronny," Margot said.

Logan nodded. "I saw how much time Christopher was spending with Ronny, and I was worried. I didn't like Ronny from the start, but Christopher said I just had to get to know him. First he gained Christopher's trust, then his love. He manipulated Christopher over the whole Coach Creed thing. He knew Creed made Christopher's life a living nightmare, and he goaded him on during all those late-night chats, until they managed to get Creed fired.

"Christopher thought he was in love, right up until Ronny threatened to blackmail him over some emails and photos Christopher had sent. Romantic stuff. Christopher was devastated. And I . . ." Logan took a slow breath through pursed lips, the emotion overwhelming him. "And I couldn't save him."

"You killed the people you blamed for his death," Margot said.

Logan nodded. "Creed was a monster and a bully. Rex threatened to kill him if he ever breathed a word of what happened between them. And Ronny betrayed him. They all deserved to die."

Kitty couldn't believe what she was hearing. All that time Logan had been stalking them, manipulating them, and killing in their name, he clearly thought it was for justice. Just like DGM.

"But Sergeant Callahan had the watch," Olivia said, still not getting it.

"Because I sent it to him," Logan said. "Pretended it was from a grateful citizen. Greedy idiot bought it, too, which made it really easy for you to think he was the killer."

"So you wanted to get back at Ronny, Coach Creed, even Rex?" Bree said, glaring at Logan. "I get it. For the most part they deserved what they got. Why bring us into this?"

Hatred flashed across Logan's face. "Because you started this! You think you're so righteous, you and your DGM pranks. Christopher told me all about your betrayal. How you mocked him for being gay. And now you think you're absolved of that because of DGM? Not so much. I followed Ronny here, and when I found out that he would be going to school with you in the fall I thought I could kill two birds with one stone: you and Ronny. I grew my hair out, streaked it blond, changed my name, and played this dumb surfer role—Ronny never even recognized me. I got Mika drunk at that party and planted her in Ronny's car. I knew you couldn't resist getting revenge for Kitty's best friend. *I* made sure Margot found the DVD with the video on it. *I* left the note on the door in Ronny's bedroom to lead you on a wild goose chase. *I* recruited your loved ones for a new DGM then framed them for murder so you'd feel the same pain of loss I felt when Christopher died."

"You want to get back at me?" Bree said. "I'll take it." She stepped forward, hands up in surrender.

"Bree, no!" Olivia cried. She grabbed her hand, yanking her back.

"It's the only way," she said. "He's right, I started this with Christopher. You guys haven't done anything wrong. You don't deserve to pay for my crimes."

"Haven't done anything wrong?" Logan laughed. He shifted the gun to Kitty. "You got your friend kicked out of school so you could take her spot as team captain." He switched his focus to Olivia. "And what you did to Margot is unforgiveable."

Olivia dropped her eyes. "I know."

"I'm getting revenge for all the victims. You, your former targets, all of you. They're just as horrible, just as guilty of making people feel small and victimized. This isn't just about Christopher anymore. My mission is to protect the innocent by ridding the world of people like you." He paused, and turned his eyes to Margot. "The only one of you who is truly blameless is Margot."

Margot blinked several times, but other than that, her face was completely blank.

Logan reached his empty hand toward her. "Come with me, Margot. I've got the others tucked away in the basement. All bullies. All horrible people." He nodded at Kitty. "Just like them. We'll shoot them and the rest, lock the door, and leave their bodies here. Make it look like a murder suicide and blame the whole thing on DGM."

Margot stared at him but didn't say a word.

"Don't you see?" Logan continued, his finger twitching against the trigger. "We can expose the hypocrisy and end their reign all at the same time. The world will know what horrible people they really are, and we can be together. I love you and—"

"Leave her alone!"

◆ ◆ ◆

Margot was still processing Logan's words when she saw an arm fly around his neck. Thin and angular, with a knobby elbow, Ed's arm was unmistakable as he hurled himself through the doorway, catching Logan from behind.

"I won't let you hurt her," Ed shouted, trying to wrestle the gun from Logan's hand. "I won't let you hurt anyone else."

Logan threw his body back, slamming Ed into the door frame. Ed grunted, loosening his grip on Logan's neck, his other hand still locked on to the gun. Logan bent forward, flipping Ed's body over his head. There was a moment of confusion, a blur of arms and legs and bodies as the two of them fought over possession of the gun, then with an earsplitting crack that sent convulsions racing through her, the gun went off.

Margot heard someone groan, then she saw Logan heave Ed's body down the stairs. Kitty caught him, and lowered Ed to the ground. As she did, something clattered to the concrete floor at Margot's feet.

The world seemed to slow down. Olivia screamed, then burst into tears, while Bree rushed to Ed's side. She pulled off her sweater and pressed it to the widening red spot on his abdomen. Meanwhile, Margot's mind had gone utterly blank as she grappled with the reality of what was happening. Logan was a killer, and he'd just shot Ed.

"Where's he hit?"

"Stomach, I think."

"What should we do?"

She should have been crying like Olivia, or angry like Bree, but instead it was as if all of her emotion had drained away, leaving just her brain. The chaos and noise sounded distant and far away as Margot bent down and wrapped her fingers around the handle of the gun.

She expected it to feel hot to the touch since it had just been fired, but it was surprisingly cool. And heavy. She'd never held a gun before, but she could see how easily it fit in her hand, how well designed, how simple it would be just to aim and pull the trigger.

Logan stood at the top of the landing and reached down toward Margot. "Give me the gun."

Instead, Margot swung around, aiming it up at him. He looked confused, almost hurt, then his face softened. "Come with me, Margot."

"Margot," Kitty said. "Don't listen to him."

"We can leave together."

"Margot, please," Olivia sobbed.

Margot looked at her friends, huddled on the ground around Ed's body.

"They're not your friends," Logan said, as if he could read every thought that passed through her mind. He stood very still, blocking the exit. "But I am. I love you. And I know you love me."

She did. She truly did. She'd never felt as alive in her entire life as she did when she was with him. His presence was calming, his strength addictive. She'd been able to stand up to Amber, stand up to her parents. For the first time, she felt as if she had the strength to take control of her life.

"Yes, I love you," Margot said.

"Margot," Bree said. "Don't do this."

"He's a killer!" Olivia cried.

Margot merely smiled. "I'm going to make you so happy," she said.

Then she raised the gun and fired.

FORTY-EIGHT

LOGAN DIDN'T MOVE. HIS BODY DIDN'T RECOIL, HIS HANDS didn't fly to the wound. He didn't blink, didn't waver, didn't utter a word. He just stared at Margot, the smile slowly fading from his face. His eyes went glassy, and then he simply collapsed onto the landing. His body shuddered once, and was still.

"I'm sorry," Margot whispered, her throat so constricted she barely made a sound.

She felt Kitty's hand on her shoulder. "Are you okay?"

Margot tore her eyes away from Logan's motionless body. "Yes," she said. And she meant it. She placed the gun in Kitty's hand.

"You scared the shit out of us," Bree said.

Margot smiled out of the side of her mouth. "Sorry." Her eyes strayed to Ed, his head cradled in Olivia's lap. She crouched next to him on the floor, taking his hand gently in her own. His eyes fluttered open and he forced an easy smile, but his skin was unnaturally pale.

"He's losing a lot of blood," Bree said. The sweater she held to Ed's wound glistened, utterly soaked.

"My fault," Ed said. "This is all my fault."

"Don't talk," Margot said.

"John's getting help," Kitty added. "You're going to be fine."

Ed shook his head. "I need to explain." He pushed himself up on his elbow, wincing with the effort. His right hand, fingers streaked with blood, crept toward his jacket pocket. He fumbled blindly, then pulled away. In his hands, he held a corner of paper that looked as if it had been torn from a larger sheet.

Margot lifted the scrap of paper from his hands. Words were printed on one side, and she recognized them right away. "The last scene of *Twelfth Precinct*." She glanced down at Ed. "This is from my prompter's script."

Ed nodded, and motioned for her to turn the page over. As she did, she found another set of words. These were handwritten.

"'Keep your mouth shut,'" she read aloud, "'or next time she dies.'"

A memory stirred. Margot was watching Logan onstage, dancing with Olivia in the finale. He was all smiles, until he saw something in the audience and the smile dropped. He looked scared. "Logan saw you the night of the show. Saw you arrive at the theater."

Ed nodded. "He must have thought I found out that he'd been at Archway too. He managed to sneak backstage. When I got there I found this note beside your . . ." His voice trailed off.

"You're going to be all right," Olivia said. Tears streamed down her face. "Just rest, okay? You're going to be fine."

Ed closed his eyes. "I was trying to protect Margot and I

thought I could deal with the killer on my own. Then the photo . . ." Ed's eyes flew open, his face pinched. "Margot?"

"I'm here," she said, leaning closer to him.

Ed smiled. "He sent me a photo. In the envelope."

Kitty laid her hand on Margot's shoulder. "Logan threatened to destroy what we loved," she explained.

"But he screwed up," Ed continued. "I could see his reflection in the photo. I tried to keep everyone safe. Called 911, but they wouldn't listen."

"I had that problem, too," Bree said.

"So I pulled the fire alarm, then I went looking for Logan. Only—" Ed was interrupted by a violent cough. A trickle of blood appeared at the corner of his mouth. Thundering footsteps pounded overhead. The authorities had arrived.

"Ed?" Margot cried. "Hold on. You hear me? Don't give up."

"But you're safe . . . now. I am considerably . . . out of . . ."

Ed's head lolled to the side as John led the paramedics down the stairs.

FORTY-NINE

IT FELT STRANGE TO BE BACK IN THE COMPUTER LAB.

Kitty looked around the windowless classroom. On the surface, it was just like old times. Margot sat in front of a computer, her fingers flying deftly over the keys. Bree had tilted her chair back and propped up her legs on a desk while she steadfastly chipped away at whatever flecks of polish still remained on her fingernails. And Olivia was late.

One by one they'd slipped away from the melee down at the gym. After Logan, Ed, and the former DGM victims had been rushed away by paramedics, the girls had each been questioned by a very confused and distraught Sergeant Callahan, called in on his day off in the wake of the shootings. And once they had been released, they had made a beeline for their old meeting place.

Footsteps hurried down the hall and Kitty whisked the door open before Olivia could knock.

"Sorry!" Olivia said, her voice breathless. "Sergeant Callahan was asking like a million questions about what we were doing in the boiler room with Logan."

Kitty arched an eyebrow. "And what did you tell him?"

"Same as we discussed. We each got an envelope threatening to hurt someone we cared about if we didn't show up at the gym today."

"Do you think he bought it?"

Olivia scrunched her mouth up to the side. "Not sure. He wanted to believe our story, but I'm not sure he's been able to wrap his head around it yet."

"Should be pretty open and shut," Bree said. "Since Logan confessed to everything before they rushed him to the hospital."

"True," Kitty said. For some inexplicable reason, Logan had insisted on speaking to the police before the EMTs loaded him into the ambulance. He'd then confessed to the murders, attacking Margot, and arson at the warehouse. He claimed to be using the DGM name to commit the crimes and even said he'd threatened Bree into a false confession, which wasn't entirely a lie.

"Why did he take responsibility?" Olivia asked. "Why not expose us instead of protecting our connection to DGM?"

Kitty shook her head. "I have no idea." She eyed Margot, who steadfastly stared at the computer screen. She was hacking into the hospital's admittance database. "Any updates?"

Margot shook her head. "No."

What was she feeling? Of all of them, she'd been through the most. Should she ask how Margot was doing? Offer to talk whenever she felt like it? Or just let her grieve in silence until she was ready to discuss?

Margot's face was a blank slate, no hint of fear or loss. Maybe that was how she coped with her pain: she muscled it aside until it lost its sting.

She closed out of the hospital site and switched to the Menlo Park Police Department's website. "Donté, Mika, Theo, and Peanut have all been released from custody," she said after a few clicks of the mouse.

Olivia laughed. "What I wouldn't give to have seen the look on Peanut's face when they booked her into juvie."

"But juvie's so much fun!" Bree said with sarcastic enthusiasm. She rolled her foot in a circle, wiggling the GPS tracker. "The wardrobe, the company, the culinary delights."

"Thank you," Kitty said to Bree in all seriousness. "For what you did."

Bree shrugged it off. "It was nothing."

"No," Olivia said. "It wasn't."

Bree dropped her eyes to her lap in embarrassment.

Margot abruptly spun around in her seat. "So the question is," she said, in her usual matter-of-fact way, "does DGM stay together or not?"

Kitty blinked, caught off guard by the question. "I . . . I don't know."

"We did what we set out to do," Olivia said.

"Maybe it's time to walk away," Bree added.

Margot arched an eyebrow. "Do you really want that?"

Again, Kitty didn't have a ready answer. It had been bugging her for hours, the decision about what DGM should do next. Everyone at Bishop DuMaine would know that Kitty, Bree, Olivia, and Margot were in the gym when Logan and Ed were shot. Their carefully maintained camouflage of disparate lives would be obliterated.

Then again, with Bree exonerated, she could claim that Logan forced her to confess to being DGM, and no one else knew the rest of them were involved. With the new DGM cleared of any wrongdoing, and Logan unmasked as a killer trying to frame DGM for his crimes, there was an opportunity to carry on.

"No," Kitty said at last. She smiled broadly. "As long as there is high school, there will always be mean girls and bullies who deserve a bitch slap."

"I've got a list," Bree said with a smirk.

"But . . ." Olivia clasped her hands before her. "But if we keep this up, does that mean we have to keep pretending that we're not friends?" She looked around the circle. "Because I don't think I'd like that."

"Me either," Kitty said.

"Me either either," Bree added.

For the first time that day, Margot smiled. "Me either cubed."

"My math is crappy," Kitty said. "But I think that means we at least have some kind of unanimous resolution. Friends?"

The girls nodded. "Friends," they said together.

"How about this," Kitty suggested. "We postpone any decision on the future of DGM until we determine whether or not there's a need for its services."

"A hiatus," Margot said.

Bree smiled at Olivia wickedly. "That means we take a break."

"Duh." Olivia rolled her eyes, then smiled right back at Bree.

Kitty was pretty sure this was the first time the computer lab hadn't witnessed any bickering from the two of them.

"And if DGM is needed," Kitty continued, "we've got backup."

The girls nodded in agreement.

"Then I guess we'll do this for the last time," Kitty said, pushing herself to her feet. "For now, at least." She shot her hand forward.

"I, Kitty Wei, do solemnly swear, no secrets—ever—shall leave this square."

"I, Margot Mejia, do solemnly swear, no secrets—ever—shall leave this square."

"I, Olivia Hayes, do solemnly swear, no secrets—ever—shall leave this square."

"I, Bree Deringer, do solemnly swear, no secrets—ever—shall leave this square."

Kitty gazed at the three smiling faces beaming back at her. She had no idea what the future held for DGM, but she knew one thing for sure—their friendship would last no matter what.

"Don't get mad," Kitty said, fighting back tears.

"Get even!"

EPILOGUE

One week later

OLAF PULLED THE CAR INTO THE BISHOP DUMAINE FACULTY parking lot Sunday morning, and shifted into park, allowing the engine to idle.

"All right, darlings," Mrs. Deringer said in her bell-like voice. "I believe this is your stop?"

Bree leaned forward from the backseat. "You're just going to Sacramento, right? No last-minute itinerary changes to Marseilles?"

"Villefranche-sur-Mer," her mom corrected with a wink. "And besides, if I was going back to France, don't you think I'd have more luggage?"

Bree turned to the back of the SUV, where a dozen bags were piled so high there was no way Olaf could see out the rear window.

"That's no moon," John said, under his breath. "That's a space station."

"Olaf and I will be back in three days," her mom continued. Then, in a rare moment of parental responsibility, she peered around the headrest at John and pointed a perfectly manicured finger at him. "And no sleepovers while we're gone."

"Yes, ma'am," John said with a salute.

She shifted her gaze to Bree. "Or I'll have Brendan Callahan put that thing back on your ankle."

"Mom," Bree said. "What happens then? After you and Dad talk?" She had to know. She'd been trying not to get excited over the last week, hoping rather than believing that her mom would stay in California. But if things went badly during this mini-reunion between her parents, would her mom flee to Europe again?

"Bree," her mom said softly. "Rome wasn't built in a day. But I promise I'll be back Tuesday night and then . . ." She took a deep breath. "And then we'll play it by ear, okay?"

"Okay," Bree said. She felt John's hand creep around her back and give her a tight squeeze. "Do me a favor, though?"

Her mom sighed dramatically. "Another favor? I've already busted your friends out of jail, convinced your dad to lift your house arrest, and found a darling little rent-free guest house for your friend Tina."

"Tammi," Bree corrected.

Bree's mom waved her hand. "Same thing. What else could you possibly need from me?"

Bree smiled. "Tell Dad I miss him."

"Ah," her mom said slowly. "Yes. Now hurry up. You're going to miss your friend's game."

Olivia's mom was still confused. "You have a friend on the volleyball team?" she asked for the billionth time.

"Yep," Olivia said simply. Not worth trying to explain the whole situation. She looped her arm through her mom's as they climbed into the bleachers. "One of my best friends, in fact."

"Oh."

"Mrs. Hayes!" Peanut stood up in her seat a few rows above them, and waved at Olivia and her mom. "I saved seats for you guys."

Olivia led her mom halfway up the bleachers, then slid into the row next to Peanut. As she sat down, she noticed the smiling face of Theo at Peanut's side. His hand lay on the bench next to Peanut's with their pinky fingers pressed up against each other.

Didn't see that one coming.

"Hi, Olivia!" Theo said. She'd never seen him so happy. "Is this your mom?"

"June Hayes," her mom said, stretching out her hand to Theo. "I'm a bartender."

"And a fabulous actress," Olivia added.

"Cool!" Theo said. "To both."

A whistle blared and the players began to trickle out of the locker room onto the court. Theo jumped to his feet. "That's my cue," he said. "I'll catch you after the game?"

"I'll be here," Peanut said. Olivia noticed that Peanut's eyes followed Theo all the way down to the court. She didn't even notice Kyle sitting with Tyler and a few other members of the now-disbanded 'Maine Men on the other side of the gym.

Olivia considered asking Peanut about Theo, but judging by the deep blush that had spread from Peanut's chest to her face, she decided that was a conversation better left for private. Instead, she scanned the bleachers. "It's packed in here today."

"Bishop DuMaine versus Gunn," Peanut said. "Should be an offensive battle."

Olivia looked at her friend sidelong. "Since when have you been interested in girls' volleyball?"

Peanut's blush deepened. "Since, um, last week."

"That's what I thought."

Olivia craned her head and scanned the bleachers behind her. She was looking for Margot or Bree, but didn't see either of them in the crowd. As she was searching, her eyes landed on a familiar face.

Amber Stevens, sitting by herself.

"I'll be right back," Olivia said, excusing herself from the row. Before her mom or Peanut could ask why, Olivia hurried up the stairs.

"Hey," she said, taking a seat next to Amber.

"Hey."

So much had happened between them. Too much. Olivia didn't even know where to begin the healing process of their friendship, wasn't sure she even wanted someone like Amber in her circle. And yet Logan had taken something from Amber as well. Rex may have been an unholy douche, but Amber had loved him. Olivia couldn't ignore the fact that she was hurting.

"You here by yourself?" Olivia asked.

Amber shrugged. "Yeah. I didn't have anything else to do. And I didn't want to be home."

It might have been the most honest moment of their friendship.

"Come on," she said, tugging Amber's arm. "Come sit with us."

She half-expected Amber to protest, put up a front, and act like she didn't need Olivia's charity, but instead, she bit her lip. "I'm not sure I'm welcome."

"Amber," Olivia said with a smile. "You're always welcome."

Kitty stood in the center of her teammates, Mika by her side, and stared at each of them in turn. She stomped her foot once, then clapped her hands, stomped twice and clapped again.

"How do you feel?" she cried at the top of her lungs, continuing the rhythmic stomping and clapping.

The team mimicked her movements and responded in unison. "Fired up!"

"I said, how do you feel?"

"Fired up!" they replied, even louder.

"But how do you *feel*?"

"FIRED UP!"

"I'm ready."

"Set!"

"You're ready."

"Set!"

"She's ready."

"Set!"

"We're ready."

"Set!"

Then Kitty pumped her fist in the air to the beat. "Ready! Ready! Ready! Ready!"

The whole team crouched low, shifting their weight back and forth from left to right, and clapped rapidly together. "Set! Set! Set! Set! Go Dukes!"

The team high-fived one another, fully pumped up for the game, and headed to the bench for their final assignments from Coach Miles. As Kitty left the court, she caught sight of Barbara Ann jogging out of the locker room.

She was suited up and ready to play, her long blond hair was swept up into a tight ponytail with a white headband across her forehead, and her knee pads dangled from one hand.

Barbara Ann paused when she saw Kitty, the look on her face a mix of anger and confusion. She shook her head, casting her emotion aside, then gave Kitty a slow nod.

Kitty smiled and nodded back. It wasn't thanks, it wasn't forgiveness, but at least Kitty knew that Barbara Ann now had a chance at a collegiate future.

As Kitty stood there smiling to herself, she saw Donté waving at her from the sidelines.

She jogged over to him. "Hey!"

He wrapped his arms around her waist and kissed her lightly on the lips. "I never get tired of watching you do that."

"Do what?" Kitty asked.

Donté smiled, his bright eyes twinkling with mischief. "That little booty shake during the warm-up." He spun around and did an exaggerated imitation of Kitty's pregame dance moves.

Kitty snorted. "If I looked like that, I really doubt you'd have asked me out in the first place."

Donté laughed, and pulled her to him for another embrace. "Kitty Wei, I'd have asked you out no matter what."

Margot climbed to the last row of the bleachers at the Bishop DuMaine gym and wrapped her arms around her waist. Had it really only been a week since she'd last been here?

One week. The world had changed in one week.

Margot smiled to herself, mirthlessly. The world had changed in an instant, she'd just taken a week to get used to it.

A whistle blew from the gym floor, and Margot took her seat as the game began. She didn't really care who claimed victory in the match, although her allegiance would always be to Kitty. In the end, both teams had gotten a significant amount of attention from college scouts, which meant that they'd both won.

Margot's eyes strayed to the opposite side of the bleachers, where Olivia sat between her mom and Amber Stevens. Even Amber deserved a second chance, Margot supposed. She could probably forgive Amber for what she'd done, but there was no way she'd ever forget.

Ten rows in front of them sat Bree and John, literally entwined. She snuggled into the crook of his shoulder, her face resting blissfully against his chest while John stroked her back with his free hand.

Margot sighed. She remembered the way she had felt when Logan embraced her. The safety. The protection. She'd wanted to stay in his arms forever.

The pain of Logan's betrayal had dulled, the grief ebbed, and now all Margot felt was an overwhelming sense of loneliness. She'd been stoic about her self-isolation in the past, but Logan had been a taste of forbidden fruit that she wouldn't soon forget. Sure, he was a sociopathic serial killer, but he loved her, and more importantly, he'd made her feel as if she was worth being loved.

Margot took a deep breath and slowly exhaled through her nose. She just had to remind herself that she would be fine on her own. She had friends, she had support, she'd even earned the respect of her parents in a way she'd never believed was possible. She could live without love.

Because she had a goal now. Margot's hand strayed to her bare arm. No longer obscured by an oversize sweatshirt, the scars of Margot's suicide attempt were open to the world. Never again would she hide them. Never again would she live in shame of the pain and hopelessness she'd felt that day. She'd go forward displaying them proudly. Because she'd overcome that day, and lived to be a stronger person. And if her story of struggle could prevent just one person from taking the same drastic steps, it had all been worth it.

"Hey, bacon, what's shakin'?"

Ed the Head plopped down on the bench next to her. Margot had been so wrapped up in her own thoughts, she hadn't even noticed him sidling across the row toward her.

"Edward," she said with a nod of her head.

Ed winced as he pulled a small notebook from his back

pocket. A near-fatal bullet wound to his stomach hadn't been enough to keep him from the biggest school sporting event of the season. "So I've got six-to-one odds on Kitty and Bishop DuMaine." He inclined his head. "Care to place a wager?"

"That's illogical," Margot said. "Should be fifteen to one."

Ed whistled. "You think?"

"The Lady Dukes have a renewed sense of school spirit," Margot began, laying out the reasoning behind her statistics. "The murderer has been caught, the police presence was removed from campus, Father Uberti officially dissolved the 'Maine Men, and students have returned to normal high school life. Haven't you noticed the rah-rah attitude around here this week?"

"The little lady has a point." He let his notebook fall to his lap and leaned closer to her, dropping his glibness for a moment. "And how are you doing?"

Margot glanced at him sidelong. It was a loaded question and he knew it. "Logan's facing life in prison," she said coolly, "and the police decided my actions in the boiler room were in self-defense. I suppose that's a win-win."

"I see." Ed leaned back, propping his elbows up on the bench behind them. "So I know your boyfriend tried to kill me and all," he said with his trademark smirk. "But do you think you could find it in your heart to be my business partner? Clearly, surgery has muddled my brain."

Margot shook her head. She had to give it to Ed—despite all he'd been through, he still maintained his sense of humor.

"You have to answer me one question first," she said.

"Just one?"

Margot nodded.

"Hit me."

Margot cleared her throat. "I get that you found out that Sergeant Callahan was Christopher's cousin."

"Don't you want to know how?" Ed asked eagerly. "It was a pretty awesome prank I pulled at the Beemans' house and—"

"I get," Margot said, interrupting him, "that you withheld that information from DGM because you thought you were protecting me."

Ed's gaze faltered but he didn't say a word.

"And I even get that you doctored the carbon copy of the speeding ticket from October first to the seventh to give yourself an alibi."

"If you hadn't been in a coma," he said, smiling wickedly, "you'd have seen through that ruse right away."

"But what I don't get," Margot continued, "is how after months of investigation, you never found out about Amber Stevens's summer at Camp Shred."

Ed cringed and grabbed his stomach. "Ouch. That hurt worse than getting shot."

Margot smiled. "So in light of your questionable skills, if we work together, I want sixty percent."

A look of horror passed over Ed's face. "Forty."

Margot arched an eyebrow. "Surely you can do better than that," she said playfully.

Ed rubbed his chin vigorously as if waging an internal debate. "Fine," he said at last. "Fifty-fifty split. But this is going to require long hours working together. Do you think you can handle it?"

Margot turned to Ed. His face was all smiles, but his eyes held a sadness that she alone understood. "Yeah," she said. "I can handle that just fine."

DGM

ACKNOWLEDGMENTS

This book is dedicated to my friend and fellow writer Laurel Hoctor Jones. She's has been my trusted reader and story doctor since *Ten*, and I could not have gotten through this sequel without her. I am truly a fortunate writer to have her in my corner.

As usual, it takes a village to make a book, and I have one hell of a team in mine.

My editor, Kristin Daly Rens, went above and beyond with this book and our tight editorial schedule. She worked at least as hard as I did, and her dedication to and love for these characters kept me inspired.

My agent, Ginger Clark, has also worked tirelessly behind the scenes on behalf of this series. Equal parts cheerleader and reality check, she knows when to hold my hand and, more importantly, when to tell me to pull on my big girl panties and deal. And I wouldn't have it any other way.

Huge thanks to Alessandra Balzer and Donna Bray for believing in me. Again. And again. The B+B and HarperCollins team is absolutely amazing, and I'm so lucky to be able to work with them: Kelsey Murphy, Kathryn Silsand, Michelle Taormina, Alison Donalty, Caroline Sun, Olivia Russo, Nellie Kurtzman, and Jenna Lisanti. All rock stars.

Speaking of rock stars, Curtis Brown has their own lineup, and I'm eternally grateful for the work these folks have done throughout my publishing career: Sarah Perillo, Jonathan Lyons, Holly Frederick, and Kerry D'Agostino.

Amber Sweeney, you are my marketing guru, my design go-to, and the motor that powers my online machine. I literally cannot thank you enough for all you've done, but I'll try—thank you.

On the front lines, I have to thank my amazing husband, John Griffin. I absolutely could not have written this book without his continued support—everything from listening to me whine about deadlines and plot points, to shouldering the majority of the household chores so that I could have more time to whine about deadlines and plot points. I love you desperately.

Then there are you guys, the readers. I'm not sure I've ever thanked you before in the acknowledgments, so I'm rectifying that now. The only reason I get to do what I do is because of you. So thank you for making this dream of mine possible, and I hope you love the conclusion to this series as much as I do.

And lastly, as always, for my mom.

DON'T GET MAD . . .

Find out how the mystery began.

More spine-tingling reads from
GRETCHEN McNEIL

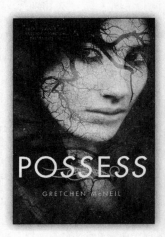

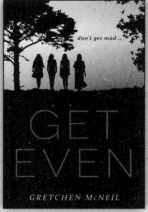

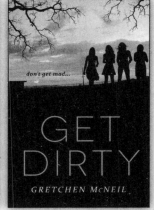

BALZER + BRAY

An Imprint of HarperCollinsPublishers

www.epicreads.com